Psycho

A.M. McCoy

CONTENTS

You know those over the top alpha, possessive, morally grey men that say things like *"Mine"* and *"Good girl"*?

Well I'd like to introduce you to Maddox Renner, the gummy bear of a man who says those things, but he also says things like *"As far as I'm concerned, that's my baby"* and *"Forever, because even in death, I'm yours."*

Hope you're ready for him.

CHAPTER 1 - OLIVIA

THE LINE WALKERS

My blood ran cold when I took the first punch. By the fourth one, that coldness turned into agonizing pins and needles as each punch or kick landed against my body.

I curled into a ball, forcing myself to protect my vital organs and precious bits from the attack. I didn't know if it would work, but I had to try.

I had to fucking try.

"Stupid cunt!" Damon's demonic sneer made my skin crawl as he screamed at me from above. "You just couldn't do as you were told, could you!"

"I'm sorry!" With my face down and covered, I cried and hiccupped through the pain. I wasn't dumb enough to think he was done beating me for fucking up.

He never quit that fast.

"No, you're not!" He barked, grabbing me by the hair and picking me up until I dangled with my toes barely touching the floor. "But you will be when I'm done with you."

I finally opened my eyes, staring at the man I thought I loved through my blurry vision. He was unrecognizable to me.

I guess that happened when drugs took hold of your soul like they had his. A few months ago, I'd been smitten with his bad boy vibes and dark lifestyle.

As I took it all in today, I realized it was probably going to be what killed me. *He* was going to be what killed me.

If it wasn't from his physical violence, it'd be from dehydration or starvation. Because two days ago he locked me in the windowless room in the basement of his club, and I hadn't had a drop of water or a bit of food since. The only way I knew how many days I had been alone in the darkness was because of the bouts of vomiting that hit me each morning without fail.

Those had been reliable like clockwork for weeks now, knocking the wind out of me every morning at six o'clock.

Which meant I was running out of time. And I had to make a move, or I was going to disappear into nothingness like all the others before me. I couldn't do that. I couldn't just give up.

So, as he slammed my back into the wall to scream at me some more about what a useless piece of shit I was, I fought back. Not because I thought I could actually win against his massive body, but because with each hit he returned, he didn't pay attention to me picking his pockets for his cell phone.

When I finally got it free, I pushed it behind the shelf on the wall stocked with toilet paper and then cowered away from him. I had absolutely no strength left in my body to fight him off and he tired of me quickly. He only enjoyed himself when I fought back.

I fell to a heap on the ground at his feet as he delivered one last kick to my side and spit on me. "Next time, maybe you'll fucking listen to me." He cursed.

And then he walked out of the room and locked the door behind him, trapping me in the darkness once again.

I weakly reached over to the shelf from my curled-up ball on the floor, feeling around for the brick of technology, and cried out silently when I found it. There wasn't much time before he realized he was missing his phone, and even less time before he traced it back to me.

If he came back in the room and found me with it, I was dead.

But if I didn't manage to pull off my escape, I was dead anyway.

So, through the blood dripping down my face, I painstakingly typed in the only phone number I had memorized and prayed to God she answered.

A wave of dizziness washed over me, spinning my vision as I listened to the relentless ringing.

When her angelic voice finally answered, I sobbed in relief. It was the first time I really cried since Damon first hit me two months ago. I wasn't sure I'd ever be able to get them to stop once the tears started, either.

"Peyton." I cried, slurring my words through the pain and fatigue. "Help."

Her voice echoed through the phone in panic. "Olivia? Livy!" She screamed when I didn't reply. I suddenly felt like I was lying under a blanket of water as my eyelids drooped closed. "Livy!"

"He's going to kill me." I whispered, hoping she could understand me through the gurgles of spit and blood pooling around my lips. "Help."

"Who? Who's going to kill you? Where are you?" She cried as air blew through the phone line before she screamed in the background, "Dane! Olivia's hurt. Help her!" There was shuffling on the line and then my sister's husband took the phone.

"Olivia. Tell me what you can."

He was so calm and in charge, my split lip curled up in a faint smile. Dane would find me. If anyone could, he would. "Hell Eater's Lounge." I whispered, curling my arm over my stomach as each breath hurt more than the last. "Basement storeroom."

"Who hurt you?" He demanded with that same calmness, but I knew there was darkness deep inside of Dane that would show its ugly head for this.

"Dam—" I coughed as more blood filled my mouth from my split lips. "Damon Kirst."

"Stay with me, Liv." Dane commanded, and then I heard him talking to someone else in the background. "Maddox. I need your help, it's Peyton's sister."

I tried to focus as Dane literally assembled the troops for me, but I was so tired, sleep weighed down on me like a warm blanket. Dane's voice sounded so far away as he came back to me. "Liv. Talk to me. Stay with me, brave girl. I've got someone coming to you. He's the best of the best and he's close. But you must stay with me. C'mon, Olivia."

Peyton's fearful sobs echoed behind his voice, and I felt bad that she was so sad. I never wanted to add to her burden like this. Our whole lives she took care of me, and now it seemed she'd do the same at my end.

"Tell P I love her." I slurred, "And I'm sorry."

"No!" My sister cried and Dane barked out loudly over her, finally raising his voice as he lost control of himself.

"Olivia, focus! Stay with us!"

The phone slipped from my fingers, and I couldn't gather the strength to pick it up again as I hugged my stomach. "I'm so sorry, little baby. I tried."

CHAPTER 2 - OLIVIA

THE LINE WALKERS

I didn't know where I was or what I was lying on, but I never wanted to move again. It was the softest thing in the world, and I was claiming it as mine. If I had a flag, I'd stick it in, so everyone knew this cloud was mine.

Unfortunately, the last couple of months taught me never to let my guard down, so I had to at least open my eyes and check where I was. Slowly, I pried my stuck eyelashes apart and peeked at my surroundings, hoping I wouldn't attract attention to myself as I got my bearings.

The room was dark except for one lamp that was on in the far corner of the room, casting a warm glow down on an empty leather chair. As my eyes adjusted, I blinked a few times and moved my hand over the soft pillowy thing I was lying on and realized it was a bed. One look at each side of my body let me gather it was a giant, freaking bed. Like double the size of a normal queen.

I turned onto my side and tried to look around the rest of the room, but the agonizing pain in my ribs took my breath away and I gasped.

"Try to stay still." From somewhere in the inky blackness, a voice, gravelly and low, called out, making me flinch and pull the blankets higher as I searched the room, my eyes darting around in fear. I saw nothing in the shadows. "Your ribs are broken."

"Who are you?" I whispered, flicking my gaze around the room as best as I could from my position. "Where are you?"

From one corner of the room, the shadows morphed, and then a bear stepped out into the light. I watched, paralyzed by fear, as he neared the bed, my eyes feeling like saucers in their sockets. In the rational part of my brain, I knew he wasn't an actual bear, but damn, did he look like one.

A big damn grizzly bear standing at the end of the bed, staring down at me.

"I'm a friend of Dane's." He crossed his arms over his massive chest and just stared at me. And I stared back, not sure what else to do. He had black hair, and a thick black beard covered his tanned face from cheek to neck. I wasn't sure, but it felt like he used it as camouflage to blend in with the shadows.

Especially given that his clothes were all black, too.

"You saved me?" I whispered in confusion, trying to remember everything that happened when I was on the phone with Peyton right before I blacked out.

"I got you out." He stayed still, "I didn't save you."

I dropped my eyes from his gaze and brushed my fingers over my stomach briefly. "Thank you anyway."

His eyes fell to my hand, and I carefully dropped it back to my side, hoping he didn't know what I had been doing at first. "You saved yourself," He scowled, almost as if he didn't like my gratitude. "All I did was get you out of there."

I opened my mouth, but a buzzing came from across the room, and he looked over his shoulder.

"I'm sure that's your sister." He glanced back at me again and let his eyes fall to my abdomen once more before turning and walking away without another word.

Even though it hurt like a bitch, I pushed my hips to the edge of the bed and forced my feet off until I sat up with them dangling over the floor. The damn thing was so tall, they were still a foot above the ground.

"Oh, my god!" Peyton cried, and I looked up as she shoved her way around the bear and ran to me. "Livy, what the hell happened?" She crouched down in front of me and pushed my hair out of my face, but I hissed when she caught a tender spot on my forehead.

The bear crossed the room again without a sound and barked at her, "Be careful, Peyton. She's covered in wounds. Go easy."

My sister's eyes welled up with tears as she looked me up and down. "I think I've died a thousand deaths since answering your call."

"I'm okay." Smiling at her, but it felt more like grimacing. "I'm just tired."

"What happened?" Dane asked, standing next to the bear and crossing his arms as he stared at me. It didn't feel like he was asking me, so I just looked away as the big guy stepped in.

"Made my way in through the kitchen entrance. Didn't take long to find her." He paused, and I looked back over at him, catching some sort of silent communication between the two men before he went on. "Slipped back out with no one spotting us."

"So, he doesn't know she's gone." Dane clenched his teeth. "Perfect."

"What does that mean?" I interrupted, brushing Peyton off as she kept fussing over me. "Damon must know I'm gone by now; I stole his phone to call for help."

"Either way, he'll never find you again." Dane stated plainly, and I tried to let his dominance reassure me. I liked the man, even if he was obviously a few crayons short of a full box. Compared to the bear standing next to him, still staring back at me in that unnerving dark way he had since he stepped out of the shadows, I was sure Dane was the more level-headed one out of the duo.

"So now what?" I asked, letting my body slide off the mattress, hoping like hell Peyton would catch me if my knees buckled. Sure enough, as soon as my weight hit my ankles, they gave out, and I fell into her waiting arms. My big sister was always there to clean up my messes.

"You can't go home." Dane stated plainly. "So, you'll come to Hartington and when you're ready, you can tell us what the hell you were doing with the Hell Eaters."

"Dane." Peyton sighed, deflecting his tone and glaring at him before tilting her head to the side with a sad smile. "I've been begging you to visit for months now, anyway. Looks like now you're stuck indulging me."

I grimaced again as she wrapped her arm around my back and helped me take a few steps. "Guess so." Slowly making our way towards the front door, I leaned my head on her shoulder, breathing in her familiar scent. I tried to take in as much of the room as possible, like there'd be some clues to who the bear was. I could tell it was his place, but I didn't think many people saw the personal space of the man very often.

Dane and the man chatted in hushed tones until we got to the door, and I turned to look back at them before Peyton could usher me out.

"Thank you. Again." I said, and the burly man's dark eyes left Dane and looked at me. I couldn't read the expression behind them at all.

He didn't speak, but nodded his head once and then just stared as I turned away and let Peyton get me out into the hall.

Why was his silence so loud?

And why was I so freaking intrigued by it?

CHAPTER 3 - MADDOX

THE LINE WALKERS

"What really happened?" Dane asked me in hushed tones as Peyton led her sister from my apartment.

Why the fuck did watching her leave make me anxious?

"It was a shit show in that place. Looks like Kirst is running a brothel, of sorts." I sighed, rubbing my hand over my beard as I fought the urge to look back at the door. "I almost wish I had met more resistance on my way in or out, it doesn't seem right to leave so many hearts still beating after looking at her."

He took a deep breath and looked at the door, giving me all the freedom I needed to look again myself. "She's a hacker. I've tried keeping tabs on her but—" He faded off.

"But you're busy with your perfect wife and too busy to take care of her sister." I finished for him. It wasn't like he was in the wrong for not watching over Olivia, but it also burned something inside of me to know she essentially fell through the cracks.

Too many innocent people fall through the cracks.

"That makes me feel—" He tightened his lips, and his shoulders deflated, "guilty."

"Not used to that, are you?" I rolled my eyes and walked over to the kitchen, taking a bottle of water out of the fridge and drinking it all down.

"No, to be honest. I've never fucking cared about anyone but P, ever before. And for the most part, Olivia makes it easy on us by only dealing in small time shit, even if she is really fucking good at it."

"Until now, though. We both know the Hell Eaters are bad news."

"Which makes me wonder what the hell she was doing for them that they suddenly believed she was disposable."

I flashed back to finding Olivia curled up in a ball on the floor of that dark storeroom, huddled around herself and how she curled around herself again in my bed when she came to. "I don't think they did. If Kirst wanted her dead, he would have just done it."

"You think he was keeping her alive for some reason?" Dane's eyes squinted in speculation.

"I think there's more to it than what we know so far."

"Hmm." He hummed and then started walking toward the door. "Thanks for getting to her so quickly."

"Yeah." I replied, because there wasn't anything else for me to do. He effectively dismissed me. There was no reason for me to be involved further.

Except—.

He left, and I walked over to the window, looking over the private parking lot behind my building, and caught Peyton leading Olivia to their waiting car.

The two sisters looked so alike except for Olivia's hair being a darker auburn color. Peyton never attracted me, but, damn, I found her sister beautiful.

Right before Olivia climbed into the car, it was almost like she could feel my eyes on her and she looked up at the tall building, finding me in the darkness.

Her green eyes glowed through the dark night and my body reacted the same way it did when they first fluttered open as she laid in my bed. Warmth spread through my limbs followed by some sort of tingling to other parts, and then she looked away, getting into the car, severing the connection.

I silently watched as Dane got in the front seat and drove away, taking his wife and sister-in-law to the secluded Hartington Estate where they'd be safe.

Leaving me with nothing but silence and time. So, I did what I did best.

I went to work.

Hunting.

I was going to figure out exactly what happened between Damon Kirst and Olivia Everett. I was going to avenge every single scar that now marred her perfect skin.

CHAPTER 4 - OLIVIA

THE LINE WALKERS

"You can't go." Peyton huffed, sitting down on the end of the bed in the guest house, and pulling my things back out of my bag. "It's not safe."

I snorted and kept adding more things to the bag even as she kept pulling them out, "It's not safe for me to stay here any longer. Lincoln has gone feral and only Dane remains." My clothes and toiletries had randomly appeared inside of the guest house the morning after my rescue, but conveniently none of my computers or electronics came with them. Though Peyton assured me that someone had emptied my apartment and *secured* my things. They didn't let me have them.

She waved me off, "He's fine."

"He's hiding." I deadpanned. "You deserve to enjoy your new married bliss without your little sister lurking in the guest house."

"He's fine." She repeated. "He's busy working, that's all."

"That's what I should be doing! *I'm* not fine." Forcing her to look at me, I stopped. "I hate being cooped up here. I have to go back to the city. Believe it or not, P, the fresh air makes my head throb. I need the pollution and the chaos, and I need my life back."

"You can't have your life back, you know that!" She ripped my toiletries bag from my hands and set it back on the bed. "It's not safe. Not yet."

"What does that mean?" I put my hands on my hips, careful to avoid the sore ribs on my right side that I tried to pretend didn't still hurt like a bitch every single morning, and stared back at her. Dane and my sister were keeping things from me about the Hell Eaters, and I hated feeling like the little kid being told, *we'll tell you when you're older.*

It was my mess, not theirs, and I needed to see it cleaned up.

Even if the idea of coming face to face with Damon again made my heart seize up and nausea roll through my stomach.

"It just means that you have to stay here a little while longer." She sighed, pleading with her eyes for me to just follow her directions.

"I can't P." I grabbed my bag and put it back in my luggage. "I refuse to be kept in the dark about my own mess."

"Is that why you're fighting me on this?" She huffed, "Because I'm trying to protect you?"

"I don't need your protection!" I cried out in frustration. "I'm almost thirty years old, P. I'm not a little kid anymore."

"I know that!" She stood up and put her hands on my shoulders, "But you have no idea what it did to me to hear you like that on the phone." Her voice cut out, and she looked down at my chin instead of my eyes, "I thought I was going to lose you, and I can't get that feeling out of my head."

I closed my eyes as the same familiar feeling of grief washed over me. "I'm sorry."

"No, don't you dare apologize for calling me, that's not what I'm saying." She dropped her hands off my shoulders and pushed her hair behind her ear. "I just need you to understand why I'm neurotic about your safety right now."

"I don't know how to just sit here." To reason with her, I tried explaining myself. "I'm not an idle person, P. I have a job and responsibilities and stuff I need to see to. And sitting here in the dark is *killing* me!"

She chewed on her lip and looked off toward the house. "What if I made Dane update you?" She asked, and I scrunched my eyebrows at her in speculation. My sister's desperation to get me to stay was evident, but I wouldn't be fooled. "I mean it, what if we went upstairs right now, and he told you what he knew? Maddox is here and they're working on it, and if he tells you what he knows, will you stay?"

My brain misfired on the name I only heard once that night I was rescued, and I fought to keep my face devoid of anything as I mulled her offer over. Did I want to know exactly what Dane knew about my royal fuck up with the Hell Eaters? Yes. Did I want to know when I could go back to my old life, if ever? Also, yes.

But was the main reason I wanted to go up to his office simply to see the bear that rescued me that night in the daylight? Definitely.

"It's a start." I feigned indifference, but as she rolled her eyes and then left toward the main house, I followed her in a trance.

I couldn't tell if I was more nervous to hear what they found out about me and what I did, or to see the bear again.

Fucking hormones.

I slid my hands in my hoodie pocket and followed Peyton up the stairs and to the ominous door into Dane's office. My sister looked over at me and gave me a reassuring smile before putting her finger over the scanner and opening it up.

"Women present." She called out like the men were going to be caught doing something indecent as we walked in.

At his desk, Dane sat and talked with the bear that stood behind him, its weight on his shoulder as they looked at the screen to discuss something shown there.

Maddox.

The enigma.

My gaze drifted across his immense physique as he leaned down towards Dane, and I struggled to remember even a fragment of his heroic rescue from the basement. But it was all blank.

For days, the same repetitive questions had played out, continuing relentlessly in a monotonous cycle.

Did he carry me?

Did he fight his way in? Or our way out?

Why did he get involved at all?

And why was he still involved?

"Puppet, how's Liv?" Dane asked as he stared at his wall of screens. A part of me was massively jealous of the spread he had. The amount of work I could get done with that layout—whew.

"I'm fine, thank you." I replied, and both of their heads snapped up from the video they were watching and looked over at me.

"Hi." Dane said, pushing his chair back, but not before locking his screens with a kill button. "How are you?"

I shrugged and leaned against the wall to avoid staring at the burly man to my right. "I'm going home."

Dane surprised me, he just leaned back in his chair and smirked. "You don't have a home anymore."

I squinted at him, "What does that mean exactly?"

"It means," He stood up and leaned on the edge of his desk to face me head on, "That I ended your lease. So, you *technically* don't have a home."

I didn't particularly like my apartment, but it had been mine. Gritting my teeth, I looked over at my sister where she sat on the couch, "You're actually into this domineering stuff?"

She pursed her lips and cocked her head at me. "It's for your own good."

"I can't stay here." I huffed. "Don't get me wrong, I appreciate all of your help, but I'm suffocating here."

Dane's eyebrows dropped over his dark eyes and the bear crossed his arms behind him, finally tempting me to look up at him and the reaction was the same as the first time I saw him while I laid in his bed.

A bit of fear. A bit of wonder. And a whole lot of something else I wasn't ready to admit to.

"What would you have us do, Olivia?" Dane asked, drawing my attention back to him. "If you go back to Boston, you'll be in danger. Period."

"So I'm supposed to do what?" I asked, weaker because I knew he was right. "Hide here for the rest of my life in a guest house I'm not even wanted in?"

"You're wanted—," Peyton cut in, but I held my hand up and silenced her.

I stared right at Dane and dared him to lie to me. "You hate me being here." I settled, and I thought for one second a flash of regret moved across his face, but it was gone so quickly I couldn't know for sure. "Almost as much as I hate being here."

"It doesn't matter what either of us wants, Liv." Dane sighed, "The facts remain the same." He got up and walked back around his desk, unlocking his screens and bringing up a page, motioning for me to come next to him to read it. "You're *wanted* by the enemy. Enough for a hit to be put on your head."

I knew it would happen, considering the accusations against me. But seeing the price printed in black ink still gave me whole-body shivers.

Fifty thousand dollars.

I didn't know if I should be glad or upset that my life was valued so highly. Either way, seeing it in person made my stomach churn, and I placed my palm over my stomach in my hoodie pocket.

"See why you can't go back?" Dane reasoned gently.

"I can handle it." I stared at the screen to avoid the painful sympathy in his eyes. "They've already charged, tried, and sentenced me. I'll clean up my own mess."

"What did you do, exactly?" The bear finally spoke, my eyes flicking over to him. "Because we can't find any trace of you inside of the Hell Eaters' operations." His brows furrowed deeper into his black eyes. "And believe me, we've dug deep."

I tried but failed to hide the smug smile that pulled at my lips as I looked back at Dane. "I didn't know it was possible to freeze out *The Ghost*."

"Damnit, this isn't funny, Livy!" Peyton snapped from the couch, and I looked over at her as embarrassment burned in my chest. "This is serious! So serious that Dane and Maddox have been working around the clock for a week straight, trying to find out a way to stop this whole thing from claiming your life!"

"I never said it was funny." I replied with a calm venom I perfected during my time with the Hell Eaters' inner circle. "Excuse me for smiling for the first time in months." I swallowed down the emotion that burned in my gut as my sister blushed with guilt. "It won't happen again."

"Liv—" Peyton sighed, and I hated how that sound made me feel like an insolent child. Again.

"I have to go." Once more, I tried to make it clear to anyone who might fucking listen. "I can't stay here, or it'll destroy my already shit relationship with my sister. You'll have to physically restrain me if you want to stop me." I shrugged dejectedly. "But I can't stay here."

I walked out of the office, ignoring Peyton's call for me as Dane told her to let me go. It wasn't as if I had a plan exactly, but I had to keep moving. If I stopped, I'd crumble.

It was the same thing I repeated nonstop for the last few months when I realized I was in so deep with a crew worse than death itself, with no way out.

I guess when you stare death in the face long enough, it doesn't hold the same power over you anymore. Or at least it shouldn't have until the life growing inside of me was a factor.

CHAPTER 5 - MADDOX

THE LINE WALKERS

I t wasn't easy, but I finally convinced Dane what we both already knew.

Olivia needed to leave Hartington. If we didn't help her do that, she'd get herself killed trying to prove she could do it on her own.

I leaned against the side of my truck and stared at her closed front door, waiting for her to show her bravery, even if everyone else thought it was stupidity. I knew better.

When the solid oak door swung open a few minutes later, I held my breath and watched as she towed two suitcases behind her, struggling to get through the doorway. "Need a hand?"

She gasped and snapped her head up to look at me, and then froze.

Fuck, those eyes. Why'd they have to look like one of those perfect princess's eyes, all wide and full of wonder? And clouded with uncertainty.

Olivia looked around the driveway like she was expecting someone else, and I tried not to let that rile me up as I let her process it.

"I have a car coming." She fought with one suitcase as it got stuck and I couldn't stand by anymore. I closed the distance between us and reached around her short frame and grabbed the handle, lifting the bag over her head and set it down in the driveway behind me. "You can't stop me from leaving."

"Does it look like I'm stopping you?" I raised a brow at her and took the other bag, pulling it around her, and then carried them both to the bed of my truck and put them in.

"What *are* you doing, then?" She crossed her arms over her chest but stayed put.

"Taking you to your new apartment." I walked to the passenger door and opened it for her, waiting for her to take me up on my offer. "I agree that you need to leave Hartington. Dane is—" I shrugged, "Difficult. So this is the only way to ensure your safety while giving you the space you both need."

"Where is this apartment?" She took a tentative step away from the house.

"In the city." I tilted my head, joking. "Where the smoke and chaos can settle your mind."

"Why are you helping me?" She squinted her eyes pensively. "What do you get out of it?"

I shrugged, "I have nothing else to do right now." I nodded to the open door, "Either get in or don't. It's up to you. But we both know Dane won't let you off this property with anyone else but me, so you pick."

She chewed on her bottom lip and then sighed, admitting to herself the truth. "Thank you." Her breathy voice washed over me as she gently climbed up in my truck, and I barely refrained from touching her to help. Something told me she'd cringe from my touch, and not just because I was a beast.

I got in the driver's seat and turned the truck around, watching her out of the corner of my eye as she stared up at the windows where Dane's office sat overlooking the property. Was she regretting leaving? Or was it just how she left things with her sister?

"Give it a day." I stated, drawing her attention back to me as I drove down the long winding drive, "And then call her."

She stared at me, so I looked over at her, but she stayed silent and turned back to the windshield. Olivia Everett was used to holding everything tight to her chest, something I could understand.

"Thank you." She said again, but I didn't reply. "You don't like those words, do you?"

"I don't see a point in them."

"You don't see a point in appreciation, or voicing it?"

I drove down the road, contemplating my answer. "Voicing it, I guess. People shouldn't do things simply to have them acknowledged. Just do the nice things and expect nothing in return."

"Hmm." She hummed and then yawned behind the sleeve of her sweater.

The oversized frumpy thing hid every inch of her from shoulders to mid-thigh. But that was her point, I was sure. When I found her that night, she had on a ripped-up T-shirt and shorts, almost as though someone had snatched her from her bed and thrown her into that basement.

Today, though, she hid. And I couldn't help but wonder if that was her normal style, or a product of her ordeal.

"Feel free to take a nap." I glanced over at her. "You've got time."

"No," She shook her head but toed her shoes off and brought her feet up onto the seat and crossed them. "I'm okay."

"Suit yourself." I shrugged. Part of me wanted her to sleep simply so I could watch her. The other part of me wanted to pry deep into her mind and life through conversation, but I didn't know where to even start. I couldn't remember the last time I held a conversation with a woman for the fun of it.

She yawned again and propped her head up on her hand, leaning her elbow on the center console. I could smell the faint, almost imperceptible, citrus notes in her shampoo as her head was close; my grip on the steering wheel involuntarily tightened.

Maybe inviting her into my space was a mistake. Maybe it was too dangerous for her to be so close to me after all.

I couldn't think of a time before that I had ever lusted after a woman the way I did Olivia, her every movement seemed to captivate me.

And if the nagging little piece of my brain that told me she was hiding a secret bigger than her involvement with the Hell Eaters under that baggy sweater was right, she was off limits.

So, fucking far off limits.

THE LINE WALKERS

Olivia's head was using my forearm for a pillow on the center console between us, and her fingertips were peeking out of the sleeve of her sweater, laid against my wrist like she was cuddling into her pillow.

And I was bricked up so hard, I could hardly push the brake without moaning.

As I parked the truck, I silently thanked the powers that be for the reprieve I was going to get when she stopped touching me finally, and also cursed those same powers for ending my torment too soon.

I wanted to bask in that torment for just a while longer.

Watching her sleep, I noticed the subtle rise and fall of her chest, a light snore escaping her lips now and then, accompanied by the occasional drip of drool. Completely unaware that I would be coming home later that day with a captivating woman, I left my house that morning without taking the time to clean up, a decision I would later regret.

But there was no going back now, and I wouldn't change anything about it either. There was only one way to get to the bottom of her secrets; to completely immerse myself in her life, leaving her no alternative but to tell me the truth.

Or dig them out myself.

The how didn't matter to me.

So, I gently brushed my fingers over the softness of her dark red hair, trying to memorize the texture of it, before I shook my arm under her head, waking her.

She turned and stretched like a napping cat and ended up on her back, facing up at me and as her eyelids fluttered open, while I stared down at her. My appearance must have been unsettling, a creepy, lingering lurker; but the sight of her, ethereal and beautiful, was impossible to ignore.

"Jesus Christ." She gasped, sitting up and throwing herself toward the door to create space between us.

"Good morning," I smirked, and then looked away as she tried to get her bearings. "You sleep like the dead."

Olivia wiped her sleeve over the trail of drool still lingering at her lip and looked around outside the truck. "Where are we?" She asked.

"The apartment." I answered. The dark private parking garage under the building gave little away and I kind of liked the way she hesitated to jump out.

"I'm so fucking lost." She chirped as I lifted her bags out of the truck and motioned for her to follow me.

I explained some things as we walked up to the door. "We monitor the building around the clock with top-notch security, and we restrict parking garage access to tenants only." She looked over her shoulder, noting that only my truck sat in the empty lot and then followed in after me. "Doors are all coded, as well as the stairwells and other exits."

"Jesus." She sighed as I typed in the third code since walking in to gain access to the elevator. "Wait a second." She hesitated as I ushered her into the elevator. I knew she'd probably recognize the place eventually. "This is—"

"My building." I responded, clicking the top floor where the apartments were. Mine and now hers.

"Yours—" She pressed her back into the wall as the car climbed up to the sixth floor.

I leaned against the other wall and stared at her, "Mine."

"Does anyone else live in *your* building?"

"Just you." I ushered her out into the hallway she recognized from leaving last week and led the way down the long corridor. "I bought it a few years ago and I'm renovating it from the top down."

She silently watched me as I walked past my door and went further down to the only other door across the hall from mine. Waiting for her to speak was painful, but I recognized her keeping those same damn thoughts and feelings locked down tight inside of herself, so I just kept leading her the only way I knew how.

By taking care of her.

Opening the door to her new apartment, I stepped aside and let her go first. It was far bigger than the one I lived in across the hall, but that was because mine was a studio and I didn't need extra space; yet she would. Silently, I watched her, my breath held, as she slowly took in the space, her eyes darting from a plush velvet sofa to an intricately carved desk; I tried to gauge her reaction from the subtle twitch of her lips. Liv was essentially a stranger, but it didn't stop me from studying her. I wanted to crack that hard exterior she hid behind, though I didn't know why I cared.

"What do you think?" I walked past her, leading her to the primary bedroom—the scent of fresh linen filling the air—setting her bags down on the end of her bed. "Will this work?"

She finally looked up at me, and those big doe eyes staring up at me struck me again. She whispered, "It's too much," Glancing at the enormous bed again almost longingly. "I can't stay here."

"It's here or Hartington." I reminded her, crossing my arms across my chest, daring her to challenge me, because we both knew I was right.

A nervous swallow escaped her lips, her eyebrows jumping as she turned away, trying to mask the secret behind her eyes. I walked up behind her, brushing my fingers lightly against her shoulder before I turned her to face me. But then I wish I hadn't.

Tears, thick and hot, streamed down her plump cheeks, escaping the pressure of her tightly squeezed eyelids. The urge to make them stop was foreign, but no different from the urge to remove my hand from a burning fire. I acted without thought, brushing my thumb over the swell of one cheek and then the other. Instead of removing my hands, I cradled her head in them, noting how she was so small that they dwarfed her. And then those bright green eyes opened, and the emotion in them overwhelmed me.

Fear.

Remorse.

And something that looked a lot like anger.

"Talk to me." I urged quietly, "Tell me what's happening inside of this brilliant mind of yours."

Her shoulders shook, and she closed her eyes, tilting her head down to look away from me. To hide herself from me.

I fucking hated how that made me feel. Sure, I was used to women shying away from me whenever I came around, but with Olivia, it didn't feel like she was hiding from me but hiding herself.

"I can't help you if you don't tell me the truth." I tried again.

"No one can help me." She whispered finally and dared to peek back up at me, "I messed up. I can't take it back."

"The Hell Eaters aren't the biggest and baddest monsters out there, Olivia." I ran my thumb over her cheek again in a weird, intimate way I'd never used on a woman before. "You've found yourself in the company of one of the worst." Her eyes rounded even more, and her full lips parted, "I'll protect you from whatever haunts you, Little Storm. Let go of some of those secrets and let me help."

"I—," She stopped and reluctantly took a step back, dropping my gaze as my hands fell from her cheeks. There would be no point in making her stay in my embrace, so I let go. "I can't."

"Fine." I sighed and took a deep breath. "This entire apartment is yours to do with as you please. And I'm across the hall if you need me." I moved toward the door, intending to leave her be in the solitude she created for herself.

"And the codes?" She called out as I got to the door. "For the elevator and the doors."

And now she was going to make it difficult for me. "You won't be needing them. If you leave, I'll be with you."

Her eyes squinted with anger, "So I'm a prisoner."

"You're protected." I challenged, "There's a difference."

"Excuse me if I don't see that difference right now." She dropped her hands off her hips and turned away from me.

"When you're ready to share what you know about the Hell Eaters, so Dane and I can eliminate the threat to you, let me know."

I knew she wouldn't fold right away; Olivia's backbone was too strong to let someone help her that easily.

It was just anyone's guess how long she'd carry the weight on her shoulders alone.

CHAPTER 6 – OLIVIA

THE LINE WALKERS

E ight days.

Eight fucking days inside the perfectly perfect apartment that Maddox sequestered me to with a full stocked fridge and pantry somehow stuffed with every single food I could ever dream of. Plus, a streaming service overflowing with movies and shows I'd been planning to watch, and a bed—an exact replica of the unbelievably comfortable one I'd left two weeks prior, its plush comfort still vivid in my memory.

What more could a girl ask for, really?

Oh yeah, independence and autonomy.

Those were nowhere to be found.

Sure, Maddox hadn't actually shown his face once since he left me in the loft that very first day, but I knew he was around.

He left me *things*.

On my doorstep.

Only because there was a kitchen chair and umbrella jammed under the doorknob to block the entrance, creating a makeshift barricade;

the pressure of the wood against metal felt as stubborn as my resolve against his potential entry, even if he had the code.

Without it, I wasn't sure he'd respect my space.

But every single morning, when I dared to take a peek through the peephole in the door, there was always something waiting for me.

The first day was food.

Sweets to be exact. Cakes, brownies, eclairs, cookies and even a still perfectly frozen tub of ice cream. As if he somehow knew when I would grab them off the welcome mat.

The next day there was a stack of DVDs. They weren't new block-buster movies, but they were oldies. 90s Rom Coms.

My guilty fucking pleasure.

The day after that, salty snacks. Pretzels, chips, popcorn and pick-les. Which was trippy and weird, because the night before I'd been up for hours craving pickles.

And then there they were.

Like he was in my head somehow.

That morning, I sat in the center of the massive recliner, wearing just an oversized band tee, eating directly out of the jar of pickles as I watched *You've Got Mail*. It was that day that I realized what he was doing.

Maddox was taking care of me, just like he said he would. Even though I'd essentially told him to shove the offer up his ass that first day.

The day after that a cell phone was laying there waiting for me. I half hoped it would be a regular phone, like those used by regular people, but two seconds after powering it on, I realized someone had changed it for a prisoner.

I could only call out three phone numbers. Peyton, Dane, and Maddox.

As if I'd ever use the last one.

But it was nice to talk to my sister whenever she wanted to. Which was every day.

The days after that were even more spoiling. And every single day when Peyton would either come over to visit for a few hours in my solitary confinement or call and video chat with me for the entire afternoon, she'd giggle and excitedly ask what the gift of the day was, like it was the cutest thing in the world.

Because it was.

I just couldn't figure out why he was doing it. One, it wasn't like he was the most romantic guy in the world; I was sure. I mean, the man looked far more wild than housebroken, for one.

And two, I was pretty sure he had more than a few screws loose, thanks to my extensive history with insane men in the last few years.

Yet every day, more and more gifts came, like clockwork.

Blankets in the softest fabric I'd ever felt before.

Neon lights to decorate the space with, that suspiciously matched the ones I had around my apartment before it was taken away from me.

But the gift waiting for me this morning had set every alarm bell off in my head and my anxiety through the roof.

A pamper basket.

And it wasn't just the basket itself that was alarming. The luxury bubble bath and soaking salts were incredible and when I first saw them, I almost ran straight to the huge soaker tub in the primary ensuite to jump right into a hot bubble bath with them. Hell, even the moisturizing face masks made my girly side tingle a little as I took them out of the basket.

But the item at the very bottom of the basket made my skin feel like it was on fire as I stared at it.

Cocoa butter lotion.

For stretch marks.

He knew.

Jesus fuck, how did he know? How *could* he know when I never uttered the words out loud one time since finding out myself?

Maddox knew I was pregnant.

And I was totally fucked.

A loud knock on the apartment door scared me and I stood frozen in the middle of the living room, staring at it.

I hadn't put my homemade lock back when I grabbed my gift, which meant if someone knew the lock code, they could—.

"I'm coming in, Olivia."

A second later the door opened, and Maddox walked in, eyes scanning the space until he found me in the dimly lit room. Why did he have to look so feral and so sexy, all wrapped in one?

His massive body was always in black. Black pants, black shirts, and black boots, without fail. They hugged his muscles like a second skin, and I found myself more than a few times wondering if his skin was soft and bare under the clothes, or if his manliness trailed under the fabric with a thick coating of hair. Was his chest hairy in a forty-year-old virgin way, or dusted in a rugged highlander kind of way?

"Are you okay?" His concerned voice cut through the mental daydream I was having about his body hair, and I blinked it away and tried to get my sex crazed hormones to stop controlling my brain.

"Fine."

He shut the door behind him, eyeing up the makeshift lock set to the side, and grinned as he came deeper into the space. "I see you've gotten the things I've left you." He mused as he put his hand on the blanket laid over the back of the chair I was obsessed with while he held my stare.

"I did." I replied and then remembered what the fuck I was holding and dropped the lotion like a hot potato back into the basket. And then my brain finally caught up to the rest of the world around me and I remembered what I was wearing.

Or not wearing, I should say.

Booty shorts under an oversized shirt, and a pair of thick wool socks pulled up to my knees. Of course, I didn't have a bra on, those were torturous lately, and I was far from being dressed for visitors.

I crossed my arms over my chest and tried to act tough as I faced him. "What do you want?"

The problem was, by crossing my arms, my tits bunched together and created even more for him to see through the thin white fabric, and his eyes flicked down with my movement, like they transfixed him.

I locked that tidbit of knowledge away for a later time as Maddox finally looked away from them and back to my face. He sat down on the arm of the couch and spread his feet wide, somehow seeming to take up even more room in the space now that he was shorter, and my brain went back to imagining his muscled thighs and what they'd look like naked and–.

"I think it's time we talk." Maddox cut through my daydream again, and I tried to focus, even as my face heated in a blush. Sometimes I hated being a redhead.

"I already told you; I'll handle my mess." I repeated for the umpteenth time since he, Peyton, and Dane had all tried to get information out of me about what I did with the Hell Eaters before they tried to kill me.

"Is that what you're calling your unborn child?" He cut in and my heart seized in my chest. I had somehow forgotten his little clues to knowing while his muscles distracted me, but there was no denying it now that the words hung in the air between us. "A mess?"

I stared him down, unwilling to wilt under his intense stare as he dared to accuse me of that. "How did you know?"

"Does it matter?" He tilted his head to the side and then nodded to the couch behind him, "Sit down, and talk to me."

"No." I shook my head, blinking away even though I wanted to do exactly what he said. "I can't."

"Liv." He replied and the gravel in his voice when he said it made my knees want to buckle under pressure from it. "I told you; I can't protect you if you won't let me in."

"I didn't ask you—"

"Enough." He commanded in a loud voice, and I instantly shut my mouth and stared at him with wide eyes. Not once had he moved quickly or spoken loudly in our previously brief interactions. Truth be told, he frightened me with it. "Please," He almost pleaded and held his hand out toward the couch again. "If you won't talk to me, at least sit down and cover your body up before I lose my fucking mind."

"My—" I stammered and once again his eyes fell to my tits that were essentially bare now that I had dropped my arms. "Oh."

I moved over to the chair and grabbed the blanket he bought me off the back, covering my legs and holding it to my chest as he rubbed his hand over his face and turned to sit down on the couch, facing me. "Better." He leaned forward and rested his elbows on his knees. "Now, if you don't want to talk, then listen." I scowled at him, but he kept going on, "Tell me about the Velvet Cage."

All the blood in my face dropped and my stomach clenched tight as my brain processed his words. "The—what?" He couldn't know. No.

"The prostitution ring you ran with the Hell Eaters."

Fuck, he *did* know.

Was it stupid that the disappointment in his eyes as he said those words hurt more than any physical blow I took over the last few months?

"I didn't run it."

"Then tell me what you did do." He implored, waiting and staring at me as I tried to figure out what to say.

Telling him the truth would be a death sentence.

But it seemed I was already toeing the line as it was, given the bounty out on my head.

Either way, I was going to die for what I did.

I took a deep breath and said it out loud for the first time. "They blackmailed me into scamming the Johns out of more money than agreed upon."

His eyes tightened around the corners, and faint lines showed in his skin. "The Hell Eaters blackmailed you?"

"Damon did." I clarified.

"What does he have over you?" Maddox questioned, but I waved him off.

"It doesn't matter. Either way, I gave into it."

"The prostitutes that work in The Velvet Cage aren't cheap, are they?"

"No, they're not."

"Making the Johns, influential men." He surmised. It was kind of nice not having to explain it all to him, one detail at a time.

"Yes, they are."

"And you stole from them, essentially." He sat upright.

"That's how Damon spun it when he got caught." I admitted, "And I suddenly found myself on the shit list of about thirty different powerful men that I couldn't pay back."

"Because you never saw the money, did you?"

"Never." I sighed, "I just worked on the computers to move it from them to him."

"How'd they find out?"

I shrugged, "The same way the bad guys do when every shitty plan falls apart. Greed. He took too much, too many times, and they connected the dots."

"Why did he kidnap you, then?" He ran his hand over his beard, "Why not just hand you off to them?"

I scoffed and smiled for the first time in a while, "Because I'm really fucking good at what I do. If he gave them his *tool*, they'd use it against him. And he'd be the one left out in the end."

Maddox sat up and I watched that missing piece fall into place for him. Dane and he had found out about the Velvet Cage but couldn't figure out why Damon held me prisoner instead of just killing me. "He was going to sell you to the highest bidder." With a curse, he ran his hand up and down his thighs. "He was going to use you."

"Bingo." I whispered, "And now he lost the only thing that was going to keep his own head on his shoulders."

His stare darkened, and he leaned forward again, staring right back at me, "He doesn't win this, Olivia. He doesn't get to hurt you anymore."

"You don't get it though," I stared back at him, "It's not just Damon Kirst that's after me anymore. There are dozens of men; *powerful* men, hunting me down. They all either want to kill me or use me. If I could, I'd sever Damon's head myself and throw it in a fucking shoe box and deliver it to the next most powerful man on the list and work my way up, but I can't!" I shook my head as that same overwhelming sense of dismay washed over me. "I'm toast."

He slowly rose to his feet and towered over me, so I had to lean all the way back in the chair to stare up at him, "No, *you* don't get it,

Storm." His phrase sounded like a pet name, and my stomach fluttered at the idea of being important enough to someone to have one of those, even if I didn't understand it. "I told you the very first day right here in this living room that I'm the worst monster out there. And now you're going to write me a list of every man that is after you."

I shivered under the intensity of his stare and the power I felt in his words. I'd spent years around dark and depraved men thanks to my stupid desire to play with fire, but Maddox had a different aura around him than any man I'd ever met before.

Maddox didn't fight or pretend to be powerful and dangerous.

He just fucking was.

"And then what are you going to do?" I asked, licking my lips as I fought through the fear and the arousal fighting for control over my good senses.

His obsidian black eyes fell to my lips, and he licked his own, like he could taste them that way.

"And then I'm going to let my psycho loose to save you." His eyes fell to my stomach under the blanket, "And your baby."

CHAPTER 7 - MADDOX

THE LINE WALKERS

"Tell me again why we're not starting with Damon?" Dane asked as we walked through the dark yard of a man on my list.

Thirty-two men, including Damon Kirst, leader of the Hell Eaters crew, were on my list. And my mouth watered, imagining how much blood would pour in Olivia's name.

My little Storm with her dark and cloudy eyes that had seen too much.

Done too much.

I was going to renew some of that darkness in violence for her, because *of* violence done to her. Yesterday, she finally let me into her pretty little head, releasing some fears she had inside of there and how they got there to begin with. Today, I was already making my first move.

Terrance Gaves.

Hit number one.

An entrepreneur that built a shipping logistics company up to a fortune five hundred business in just a few years. And then sold it for a crap ton of cash. He was married with three kids and a hefty addiction to cocaine and sex.

Perfect family man.

By tomorrow morning, his wife would be a widower.

Lucky gal.

"Because I want Damon to know we're coming for him." I replied, mapping out the interior layout of the massive house in front of us based on the blueprints I had got this morning. "I want him to fucking fear me before he ever even knows who I am."

Dane chuckled and pulled a leather glove on. "Well, when's the wedding?"

I ignored him, "Stay to the two side, and wait for my signal."

"Yes, sir." He mockingly saluted and disappeared around the front of the house.

"Fucking go time." I hissed and cracked my neck, letting my true self take the lead to have a little fun.

THE LINE WALKERS

"Do you have any fucking idea who I am!" Terrance screamed as I pitched him forward, while stepping on his wrist. His shoulder dislocated with such ease; it was pitiful actually.

Just like the puddle of piss he was now sitting in, on the marble floor of his foyer. I didn't intend to leave the mess for his wife and kids when they got back from vacation, but I was enjoying watching him make the mess.

I wasn't a complete dirtbag, just a psychopath.

"Do you have any fucking idea who *I* am?" I replied, throwing him down onto the floor face down with his now doubly useless arms still cuffed behind his back.

"What do you want?" He gasped, turning his cheek to the side to look up at me as he huffed and puffed.

For a forty something year old man, he was in terrible shape. Even with no arms at all, he should have been able to roll over or something to make himself seem less pathetic.

"I don't want anything from you." I replied as Dane sat on the foyer table, swinging his legs back and forth like a child. He was really embracing his inner weirdo, and it was freaking Terrance out even more. Which was the point, but Dane wouldn't be touching the man. Even if Olivia was his sister-in-law, this one was personal to me.

Maybe I'd let him have one or two of the other thirty men on the list. Maybe.

"You're the messenger." Dane sang like a wacko and Terrance scurried across the floor like a slug to get further away from him. "Aww, I don't think he likes me."

"What kind of message?" Terrance demanded, "To who?"

"Does it matter?" Dane cocked his head to the side and jumped onto his feet a few inches away from Terrance's face with a resounding thud. "You'll be dead."

"No, please!" The man begged, "I can send the message without dying, please! I'll help you. Please, just don't kill me! I have kids!"

"Do you tell the prostitutes you sleep with from the Velvet Cage about your kids?" I questioned, drawing his attention back to me as Dane circled around him. "Or do you tell your kids about all the blow you're wasting their inheritance on?"

The man's eyes rounded, and he finally mustered up the courage to roll onto his back to look up at me like a man. "I don't know what you're talking about."

"Yeah, okay." Dane sneered and looked over at me, "So, how we doing this? Bullets? Knife? Fire?"

Terrance's face paled as he realized he really wasn't walking away after all.

"Knife." I stared down into our captives' eyes as I replied, "But cut all of his fingers off before he's dead."

"Really?" Dane paused. "Going to keep them as a souvenir?"

"No." I looked up at my friend and he tipped his head back as he started to understand. "I've got someone who wants body parts in shoe boxes."

"Ah," Dane nodded with a sinister grin, "It all makes so much more sense now."

He pulled one of Terrance's arms out and stood on his hand as I did the same, and then we both went to work, slicing through his bone and taking each of his fingers until I had a bag full of ten digits as a keepsake.

When it was done, Dane slit Terrance's neck as I took the cocktail napkin from my pocket with the Hell Eaters Lounge logo in the center. I laid it on the dead man's chest and stabbed one of the knives into it, making sure the message was clear to all.

The Hell Eaters were to blame.

One way or another.

It wouldn't take long for the bodies to start piling up and the message to get even louder. I was coming for them. Each and every one.

CHAPTER 8 - OLIVIA

THE LINE WALKERS

I leaned against the door and checked the peephole, and sure enough, there was a box sitting on the mat. I fought the urge to smile, but failed.

Was Maddox *flirting* with me?

Was that how feral bears flirted? Foraging and bringing their crushes gifts like cozy blankets and food?

I mean, if I thought about it long enough, that did kind of sound like something a bear would do to flirt with a girl, but what did I know? I was a pregnant almost thirty-year-old with no baby daddy in sight, *thank god*, being held hostage in a luxury tower of sorts by my feral gate keeper.

My life was a weird fucking fairy tale, I didn't have time to contemplate animal rituals.

I opened the door and picked up the box, before staring down the hallway to Maddox's closed door like one day, maybe he'd be waiting out there for me to get his gift. But he wasn't, so I went back inside.

My phone rang, and I rolled my eyes as I set the box down and went into the bedroom to get it.

"Yes, there was a gift. No, I have not opened it yet. And good morning to you, too." I stated in place of a greeting.

Every morning, Peyton called to see what Maddox gave me. Even though she planned to visit me in my opulent prison later that day, she still called first thing to find out what had been delivered.

Yesterday, I ignored her call while Maddox was visiting and when I called her back later, I avoided telling her about the cocoa butter lotion. I just couldn't stomach the idea of telling her I'd fucked up again, and ended up pregnant on top of the whole mess I was already in.

"Well, open it up!" She prodded, eager to see what today's gift was. It was kind of nice finding commonality in something so mundane and normal with Peyton for the first time in forever.

I seriously doubted it was a pair of shoes, considering I hadn't put shoes on in weeks thanks to my confinement, but anything was possible. "Okay," I grinned, flipping the top up, "It's a—" I screamed bloody murder and slammed the lid down back on top of it.

"What?" Peyton screeched through the phone. "Liv! What is it?"

"Uh," I stammered and tried to form a sentence to describe what was in the box waiting for me. "It's uh—" I swallowed and instantly regretted it as nausea bubbled up in my throat. "Fuck."

"LIV!" Peyton's scream through the phone followed me as I ran to the toilet and threw up my orange juice. "Are you puking?"

Dane's voice came through the speaker as I retched again, "What are you screaming about Puppet?"

"Liv screamed! She opened a box from Maddox and then screamed and now she's puking."

"Oh!" His sick voice cheered through the line as I rested my forehead on my arm. "She got the fingers."

"The what?" Peyton gasped.

"Stop talking." I groaned, "Or I'm going to puke again."

Dane chuckled, "I told him not to actually hand deliver you the proof." His sick laugh sounded again, "Hand deliver—get it?"

"He gave her *body parts*?" Peyton cried and then gagged, "I think I'm going to puke."

"Hang up!" I yelled and retched again. The last thing we needed was an audible puking war to keep us both going.

"Olivia!" Maddox bellowed from the front door, and I groaned, as a cold sweat broke out over my skin.

"Go away!" I yelled and then retched again.

"Damnit." He appeared at the doorway and moved behind me, kneeling at my back and pulling my hair out of the spray as I heaved again. "I'm sorry, Storm."

"Fingers!" I gasped, "You gave me fingers!"

"Would you have preferred the entire skull?"

Gag. At least this time, there was nothing left to join it.

"Shh," He ran his hand over my back as I pathetically laid my head back down. "I'm sorry."

I flushed the toilet, desperate not to let him see the mess, and then slowly lifted my head. "It's okay." I sighed, "I did say I wanted the head. I just didn't think you would actually do it."

He chuckled softly and then grabbed a washcloth from the stand next to the sink and ran cold water over it. "Here."

I wiped my mouth and then flipped it over and cooled my face with it before finally looking over my shoulder at the man. "Morning sickness is a bitch."

He put his hands under my arms and helped me stand up before leading us out of the bathroom. "Couch or bed?"

"Pickles." I replied, and he scoffed.

"Excuse me?"

"Pickles are the only thing I want right now. But I'm all out."

"I gave you a giant jar of them a few days ago." He led me to the couch, and I curled up under my favorite blanket. At least this time, I had been prepared for guests and was fully clothed. Though the way he had looked at me last time in my thin nightshirt made me feel warm and fuzzy all over.

"I ate all of them that day. And it's not as if I can just go to the store."

"Why can't you?" He shook his head.

"Because I'm a prisoner!"

"Jesus, woman." He rubbed his hand over his beard and sighed, "You have to vocalize your needs to me if you want me to figure them out. I'm way out of my pay grade right now. But you have to tell me if you want or need something so I can make it happen."

"I'm sorry." I pouted, feeling stupid for needing something I should be able to provide for myself.

"Stay put. I'll be right back."

"Wait," I called when he walked to the front door, afraid he was about to go to the store all for a jar of pickles. "You don't have to—"

The door shut in response, and I sagged into the couch. *Crap.* My eyes scanned the room and landed on the red shoe box still on my counter and I covered my nose with my blanket and sank further into it. The fingers were still on my kitchen counter.

"Here." Maddox came back in, with two giant jars of pickles in his hands, and he paused when he saw me hiding. "What?"

I pointed with just my nose at the counter. "Fingers."

"Oh, yeah." He set the jars down and then carried the box out to the hallway and set it on the floor before coming back in. "Sorry."

He picked up one jar and a fork from the drawer and came back to the living room. He sat down on the couch next to me and I hated how fucking normal it felt to share a piece of furniture with the man after everything else that happened. Yet there we were, chilling like he hadn't killed a man for me and gave me his fingers.

"Wait." I stammered as he popped open the jar and stabbed a fork into a pickle and then held it out to me.

"Are you going to puke again?" He recoiled comically, and I glared at him.

"No. The body the digits were once affixed to—" I droned on, trying not to say any words that might trigger the nausea again.

"Uh huh—" He tilted his head, waiting for more.

"Is it still warm?"

He sat back up fully and grinned and his perfect white teeth momentarily blinded me before he sarcastically replied, "Stone cold."

"You killed him?"

"Deader than a doornail."

"Which one was it? Or who, I mean?" I took the offered pickle and took a bite of it, no longer able to resist the snack so easily presented to me.

"Terrance Gaves." He watched me closely as I chewed, mulling that over in my head.

Terrance Gaves was sick and demented in the head, every time he visited a woman from the Velvet Cage, she left with some sort of wound, visible or not it didn't matter.

"Good." I chewed and looked back up at him. "He was a sick fuck."

His eyebrows rose slightly, and he grinned again, "So you're saying I should have played with him longer—"

"Shut up." I barked, pausing to see if the nausea would come or not from his flippant words, but there was none, so I took another bite. "No descriptive words. Or I'll puke in your lap."

"Yes, ma'am." He took the fork and speared another pickle and handed it to me. "So, pickles, huh?"

"I fucking hate them, actually." I deadpanned even as I groaned from my next bite. "But I can't stop."

"Whatever the baby wants, right?" He asked, and his words felt like a physical shift into a conversation I didn't want to have.

"You didn't tell Dane or P, did you?"

"No." He watched me closely, "But can you tell me why you didn't?"

I picked at a stray string on the blanket as I contemplated how to answer that correctly. Then I decided just to speak it into existence. "Because I'm not sure I'm going to keep it. So, there doesn't seem to be a reason to tell them if I don't."

He watched me silently for a long time, like he didn't know what to say exactly. Then he asked a question I had hoped he'd spare me. "Who's the father?"

I took a deep breath and instinctively placed my hand on my still non-existent bump and whispered the answer. "Damon."

"Did you—," He paused and turned to face me on the couch with one leg bent between us. "Did he—?"

"Rape me?" I filled in the missing words for him, and he nodded. "No." I sighed again, "But it wasn't consensual either. Sex was part of the blackmail." I shrugged like it didn't kill me to expose myself so openly, "But my birth control didn't work and now I'm here."

"And you're thinking of abortion? Or adoption?"

"I can't carry a baby to term and give it away." I admitted. "I'm not that brave."

"I think carrying a baby to term period is brave, Olivia."

"I don't think I can do that either." A tear fell over my lashes, landing on the blanket covering my growing little baby, as I whispered.

He slid his hand under the blanket and into the pocket of my hoodie where mine rested against my stomach, lacing our fingers together. I blinked away the tears and looked up at him, and damn if it didn't feel like my entire world hung on whatever he was about to say.

I needed someone to have something to say that would help me.

"Whatever you decide, I'll help you through every step of the way. You're not alone in this, Storm. You don't have to hide it from everyone."

My voice broke, "I feel like such a fool."

"I know." He tilted his head and squeezed my fingers, "But imagine how strong you could feel if you owned the entire thing and made it all turn out however you wanted it to."

"Strong." I chuckled humorlessly. "I can't remember the last time I felt strong."

"Give it time." He gave me a one-sided grin again, "Just wait and see how strong you come out of all of this in the end."

CHAPTER 9 - MADDOX

THE LINE WALKERS

My little Storm was asleep on my shoulder, and I couldn't find the gumption to move. The building could be on fire around us, and I'd be hesitant to move away from her touch. The cute little snores escaping her made me chuckle, and the way she burrowed deeper into my sleeve anytime I dared to move even the slightest bit made me... burn.

It felt like every inch of my skin was being electrified by her desire to be closer to me. Even if she was asleep while she was doing it, I couldn't help how it made me feel.

We were still on her couch, having spent the entire day watching movies, and I even cooked her dinner. Turns out she'd been living off the junk food and avoiding the healthy stuff without my supervision.

Which was going to end now.

If I wasn't around to cook her dinner, I'd have it delivered. Liv was growing a human, for fuck's sake; she needed to eat some protein.

My phone buzzed in my pocket, and I pulled it out, already knowing what it was and dreading it.

I'm here. Go time.

Dane once again insisted on joining me for night two of my hunting and I would have told him to never mind and that I wasn't leaving the couch until Olivia woke up and kicked me out, but I had scheduled three separate hits for the evening. And I didn't want to fall that far behind schedule by skipping it.

Be down in a few.

I tucked my phone away and as gently as I could, I slid out from under Olivia's body, slowly lowering her down onto the couch and on a pillow. Squatting down in front of the couch, I pulled her blanket up over her shoulders and her eyelids fluttered open and she looked around.

"Did I fall asleep? Again?" She blushed a little and tried to sit up.

"Shh," I pushed her back down and adjusted her blanket again, "It's okay. I was just going. Go back to sleep."

"Going." She repeated and then bit her bottom lip as she brought her hands up under her face. "Hunting?"

"Yes." I pushed a lock of hair back over her ear, unable to resist touching her, and she stared up at me with her turbulent eyes.

"You don't have to do that for me."

"Yes, I do." I countered, resting my elbows on my knees so I wouldn't keep touching her. "But don't think it's something I don't want to do. Because I do. I want to rid this earth of those men. It will be a better place without them. It's who I am."

"You say that like I should cower from you because of it." She challenged and sat up, propping her head on her hand. "I don't, by the way." Her eyes roamed over my face as she paused, "I'm not scared of you. You're too kind to me to let your darkness toward others affect me."

I smiled, and I watched her reaction to it as she nibbled on her bottom lip and stared at mine. "You should be scared of me, Storm." I reached forward and used my thumb to pull her lip free of her teeth, tracing my fingertip over it. "Because my kindness to you is so fucking foreign to me, I don't know if it can last."

She snapped her teeth together, nipping the end of my thumb, and grinned at me. "I'm not the kind of girl to run from fear."

"Maybe so." I growled, pulling my hand from her face and standing up, towering over her. She leaned back against the back of the couch so she could look up at me. "But you should be, because I'm darker than anyone you've ever met before. I just hide it from you."

"Not very well," She huffed, "You delivered me fingers."

"Careful," I warned, "Or it will be eyeballs in the morning."

She fake gagged and then snuggled back into her pillow. "Who's on the list tonight?"

"Ramsey Tuft, Quintin West, and Isaac Renfield."

Her eyebrows rose, "Three in one night?"

I shrugged, "It could be five or six if Dane didn't slow me down with his theatrics."

She snorted and smiled as I turned and walked toward her door. "Hey, Maddox." Something about hearing my name in her sweet honey voice made me burn for her. I looked back at her, and she rolled over onto her stomach, resting her chin on her hands as she went on, "Be careful, okay?"

"Yeah, okay." I replied, overwhelmed by what her concern made me feel.

"I mean it." She stared at me as I clicked off the lights and opened her door. "I'd be pretty bummed if you didn't make it back in the morning."

I grinned and shook my head, leaving her apartment completely.

Yeah, Storm, I'd be pretty bummed if I didn't get back to you, too.

THE LINE WALKERS

"So," Dane huffed as he threw the body on the floor next to the other two. "What souvenirs are you keeping for Livy this time?"

I rolled my eyes as I finished carving my knife through the chest wall of Isaac Renfield. Gurgles escaped through his mouth as I punctured his lung, "Damnit, you made me miss."

Dane chuckled and kicked the head of Ramsey Tuft, where he lay lifeless already. "Not me, I was fucking perfection tonight."

I rolled my eyes and worked through the rib cage and got what I came for. As I pulled it free, I grinned.

"Hearts." Dane shrugged, "A little over kill if you ask me, but whatever she's into."

I put the heart into a plastic bag and added it with the other one I already pulled from Quintin's chest before Dane joined me. "She threw up from fingers, what makes you think I'd give her bloody hearts?"

"Well, if they're not for her, who are they for?" He crossed his arms, "Are you a vampire all of a sudden?"

"They're for Damon." I wiped Isaac's blood off my knife and put it away.

"Ooh, I like it." He grinned, kneeling down to carve the heart out of his kill. "Did you get any info out of Liv today about that?"

"Yeah," I replied, gathering my supplies up. "Cliff-note version, Damon used blackmail to get her involved with the scheme. Stealing money from these fucks got him in hot water and he blamed Liv. He then tried to trade her to the highest bidder to get himself out of it. That's why he kidnapped her and kept her alive instead of just taking her out like we thought he would."

"And then we took his get out of jail free card." Dane surmised as he pulled the heart free of the chest. "Effectively screwing her."

"Hence this list."

"Remove the threats, ensure her safety." He shrugged, dropping it into a bag. "I like it."

"I don't." I mused, "However, it's her only chance at a real life again."

"Well, not her only chance." He said, wiping his knife off and pocketing it. "She has you, after all. And me."

"Hmm." I hummed, trying to avoid whatever he was getting at, but he wasn't having it.

"She does have you, doesn't she?" He stood up and walked around the bodies, "Or are you going to pretend you're not obsessively interested in her?"

"I'd kill you if she asked me to." I shrugged, "If that says anything."

He tipped his head back and chuckled, "Says just about everything I need to know."

"Good, then shut up and help me drag these bodies out onto the front porch."

He paused mid-laugh as he looked toward the front door. "The street is five feet from the front door."

"Exactly."

"Ooh, Maddox The Whisper Renner isn't fucking around tonight, ladies and gentlemen. He's showboating."

THE LINE WALKERS

I got out of the shower and scrubbed a towel over my hair and beard as I groaned. I was so fucking tired.

It was almost four and pulling off another three hit night with Dane as company was proving to be exhausting. I'd been at it for almost two weeks already and the list was getting shorter. But so were the opportunities to find the targets.

The plan had worked well enough that the remaining seven hits were in hiding. Which was exactly what I wanted.

Because it meant I had some down time coming up. Time to spend with my Storm. Fuck, I missed her. Every day I spent a few hours with her before working on the list, but it was never long enough.

I had never been friends with a woman before. Aside from a couple that I casually fucked; I didn't want women around me. They couldn't handle the whole me, just the parts I could lessen to fit their agenda when my hand wasn't enough to suffice anymore.

But Liv. God, fucking Olivia Everett drove me wild. I wanted to engross myself in every single part of her. The friend part that shared her snacks when she made me watch her stupid movies. Or the weird part that talked about things like morning sickness, trimesters and cravings. My favorite part, though, was the vulnerable one; the one that laid her head on my shoulder on the couch and relaxed into me like it was the only time she could actually loosen the tense muscles in her shoulders. Like it was the only time the clouds cleared from her green eyes, and she was just calm.

Those were my favorite moments.

My cock hardened again for the hundredth time today and I palmed it through my towel, trying to figure out if I had the energy to jack off again before I passed out. I had done it as soon as I walked back into my apartment after spending the entire afternoon with Liv pressed against my side on the couch before I went to work. I'd been so worked up I came in less than thirty strokes.

My cell phone vibrated across the counter as I stood in the middle of my studio apartment contemplating it and I looked at the screen.

Liv.

Fuck.

"Storm, what's wrong?" I snapped as I answered. She had never called me before, which meant something was wrong.

"Nothing's wrong." Her sleepy voice sighed, "I guess I just wanted to know if you were sleeping through the noise."

"What noise?" I asked, and then an enormous crack of thunder vibrated outside, shaking the entire building. "Oh."

She chuckled quietly, "I guess you were, I'm sorry for waking you."

"You didn't." I paced as I talked. "I just got home."

"Oh." She whispered and I could almost see her lying in her bed holding her phone in the dark talking to me from across the hall. "I shouldn't have called."

"My bed or yours?" I asked in reply, already knowing she was going to back pedal and take back every bit of courage it took her to call me in the first place.

"Your—what?"

"Where are we sleeping for the next few hours?" I explained, "Because you're alone and scared, and I can sleep through a hurricane, so where do you want me?"

"I—" She hesitated and then cleared her throat. "Yours."

"Come on over." I replied and then opened my front door before stepping into a pair of athletic shorts.

I heard the click of her door open through the hallway and hung up as she peeked around the doorway into mine. And even as tired as I was, I tipped my head back and laughed.

The only thing I could see was her toes and above her nose. The rest of her was tightly wrapped up in a blanket burrito so big that I imagined it hid a jar of pickles somewhere. "Do you think I don't have any blankets?"

She grinned and pulled her mouth out from behind the layers, "I wasn't willing to risk it."

"Hmm." I shut the door behind her and then clicked off the two lights that were on as I followed her over to the bed. At the end, she hesitated and looked over at me.

"What side?"

I raised a brow at her and crawled in on one side, holding the blankets out for her on the other. "I'll be honest, I usually sleep in the center, so I might end up fighting you for space."

She snorted and dropped her blankets as she walked around the bed, but I couldn't form a coherent sentence as I watched her lush body move. She wore a black shirt-style nightgown that, in the grand scheme of things, was pretty modest. But what wasn't modest was the way it stressed every single curve of her body, making them visible to my depraved eyes.

She wasn't wearing a bra, and her nipples were hard and proudly present as she skipped around the bed, making them shake and sway and as she crawled up onto the tall mattress. I could tell by the lack of lines showing through the fabric pulled tight over her ass that she was panty-less.

Damnit, I was throbbing hard again, in no time at all.

"Mmh," She curled into the blankets, pulling them up to her chin again, thankfully hiding her sinful body and my now very hard cock as I turned on my side to face her. If I stayed on my back, the blankets would tent from how hard I was. "This blanket is the same as the one you bought me, isn't it?"

"Yes." I replied and cleared my throat as it came out like a puberty-stricken boy, and she giggled lightly. "It is."

I clicked off the lamp next to the bed and suddenly we were in complete darkness, aside from the occasional strikes of lightning outside.

Silence hung in the air between us until my eyes adjusted to see her face clearly and then she spoke up. "Thank you for letting me crash your night."

Our faces were only a few inches apart, and I boldly reached forward, finding her bare knee under the blankets, curled up toward her chest and ran my fingers over it reassuringly. "I'm kind of getting addicted to your presence, I think."

Her eyes rounded slightly and then she bit her lip, "Same." She whispered. "It seems weird when you're gone."

"You're safe here, Storm. You don't need to be afraid when I'm gone."

"I didn't say I was afraid." She clarified, swallowing quickly and then gently laid her hand on top of mine where I left it on her leg. "Lonely is more accurate. I think I have Stockholm Syndrome."

My heart was racing a million miles a minute from just the touch of her hand on mine, and I tried not to ruin it by doing something stupid. Like blowing all over her knee with my aching dick. That would be epically stupid.

"And when I'm not gone?" I probed further, "What are you then?"

"Scared." She uttered and went on, "Scared that I'm fabricating something inside of my head between us because of your friendliness toward me."

Suppressing the desire to grip her upper knee tightly, I felt an instant surge of arousal from her words. "I'm not friendly, Storm." I acknowledged and then ran my thumb back and forth over the soft flesh of her inner knee, enjoying the way her eyelids fluttered briefly before she stared back at me through the dark.

Liv argued, "You're nice to me. You're kind and attentive and gentle with me, like no one I've ever met before."

"You make it sound like a bad thing."

"It is." She nuzzled her face closer only a fraction of an inch, but my eyes fell directly to her lips. "Maybe if you were rougher and crass, I'd know if you wanted me. But when you're just nice and gentle, I'm afraid all of my hormones are fooling me."

"You're pregnant, Storm." My hand slid up to her thigh. "I *have* to be gentle with you."

"I'm not breakable, Maddox. Even to a man as big as you are." She closed her eyes. "But I guess that's the answer I needed to hear after all."

"What is?" I probed, knowing exactly where she was going.

"You don't want me, because I'm pregnant with someone else's kid. I get it, it's fine." Her cheeks were red, and even in the darkness, I could feel her embarrassment. But she was wrong.

So. Fucking. Wrong.

I pushed my hand further up her thigh and then pushed them apart as I rolled us until she was on her back, looking up at me with her legs spread and me leaning over her. "I'm gentle with you because you're pregnant, Storm. I'm kind to you because I actually like you. But don't think that doesn't mean I haven't wanted to throw you down and spread your thighs just like this and rut into your body every single second since I first had you here in my bed." I dragged my hand down to her hip and brushed my thumb over the smooth mound above her pussy. "But I'm a man who knows nothing about pregnancy and what is safe. Therefore, I haven't made my wants known."

"You want me?" She whispered, digging her sharp fingernails into my forearm as I leaned over her.

"Fucking hell Storm, yes, I want you."

She closed her eyes, and her chest rose and fell with large breaths, straining the confines of her shirt against her massive tits. "I thought I was crazy." She whimpered. "I'm crazy with need, Maddox."

"Tell me what you need, Storm. I told you to tell me and I'll see to it, but you need to use your words."

"I need you." She panted, "Fuck, I need you to touch me or something." Her panic was rising as she kicked at the blankets over her. "I feel like I'm going to combust if I don't come while you touch me. Or watch at least."

I grinned and crawled over her leg so I was hovering over her between her thighs and as she kicked the blankets the rest of the way off, I could smell her arousal. "This is safe. For the baby?"

"Yes!" She cried, "It's safe!"

I leaned down, keeping my body from touching hers at all as I hovered over her lips, "Tell me to kiss you."

"Kiss me, please." She pleaded and buried her fingers in my hair, pulling me down until our lips finally fucking touched. Liv's moan made goosebumps burn across my skin as she eagerly sucked my tongue into her mouth. She was desperate for relief, and I felt bad that she had been keeping it a secret from me. There were a million ways for a man to make a woman come without having sex with her, and I would have eagerly done any of those for her the whole time had I known. "Don't stop." She whined when I pulled back to stare at her.

"Shh, Storm." I kissed my way down her neck and bit her ear as she rocked her spread thighs up and down under me, like she was desperate for contact. "Let me take care of you."

I sat on my knees and lifted her nightgown up over her body, revealing her lush, full figure to my eyes for the very first time, and I was addicted.

"I'm going crazy here, Madd." She dragged her nails down my arms as I lifted her nightgown up over her tits and then leaned down against her body, keeping my weight off her. "I need you."

"I'm right here." I blew on one of her puckered nipples and she cried for me, arching her back and burying her fingers in my hair. "You want me to suck on your nipples, pretty girl?"

"I'll die if you don't." She gasped, "I'll literally combust into flames and burn in them if you don't actually touch me!"

I grinned and watched her face as I flicked my tongue across one of them, making her entire body shiver. "Are you always this needy? Or is it the hormones?"

"I don't know, just make me come!"

I chuckled and then sucked her nipple deep into my mouth while playing with the other one. She was crying out, clawing at me, and grinding her wet little pussy against my abs as I feasted, and I couldn't stop. I didn't want to. There was nothing on earth I wanted more than to make her orgasm.

And within a minute of playing with her breasts alone, she did just that.

"Good girl," I praised, flicking her nipple and watching her shatter underneath me. "That's my good girl, Storm. Come for me."

"Oh, my god." She went limp beneath me and gasped for her breath as I watched from my position. "I didn't know it could feel that good."

I grinned, sucking her nipple again, and she moaned deep in her chest. "Wait until I do it to your clit."

"Fuck yes." She rocked her hips against my abs, but as I watched her face, her eyes sank further with each blink and I stayed silent and still as they closed one time, and didn't open back up. Twenty seconds later, she started snoring.

My cock was as hard as stone, and my balls screamed to be emptied, but my chest; that felt weirdly satisfied as I climbed up the bed and covered her naked body up with my blanket and laid down beside her.

If I never felt the inside of her pussy wrapped around my dick, I'd still be a lucky man if she let me make her come with my mouth like I just did. Because even if I was a psycho, Olivia Everett showed me exactly how much she wanted me, just as I was.

And now I was obsessed with her.

She was mine.

And so was her baby.

CHAPTER 10 - OLIVIA

THE LINE WALKERS

"Mmh," I groaned, rolling over and stretching my arms above my head as my body protested against the movement. I was so comfortable I didn't want to even wake up. My morning sickness had let up a bit in the last few days, which meant I didn't get the abrupt wake up every morning and I was going to enjoy every single slow wake up I could get.

The delicious scent of food tickled against my nose though and my always hungry stomach growled, forcing me to open my eyes and figure out what the delicious scent was. But as soon as they opened, I let out a startled shriek and hastily sat up in bed.

Maddox's bed.

He was standing in his kitchen, wearing only those same black shorts, as he looked over his massive shoulder at me. "Good morning, Storm."

I pulled the blankets up to my chin as hot sexy flashbacks from sometime before dawn assaulted my brain and lady bits. Hissing out,

"I fell asleep." Wishing the bed would swallow me up and drop me out somewhere far, far away, I cringed. "I can't believe I fell asleep."

He put something on a plate and set it down on the counter on his way over to the bed. My eyes instantly roamed over his hulking dad bod in the light since last night it was so dark when I butted my way into his apartment and bed. I finally had the answer to the mental conundrum of whether or not his body was hairless as I stared at the light dusting of black hair over his chest and abs. God, it fucking suited him.

I wanted to drag my fingernails over it. And the ink that covered his chest and stomach too, fuck.

"You were tired." He knelt on the bed and leaned over me, "We both were."

"You promised to do something to my clit, and I fell asleep." I stared at him with wide eyes. "I'll never get over the regret."

He chuckled, showcasing those perfect teeth under his dark beard, and then he cut the distance between us and kissed me. Maybe he meant it to be a soft, slow peck, but when he hesitated to pull away, I ran my tongue over his lip, and he responded with his own lick. "Careful, Storm. Or your food will get cold."

"Something else is getting hot." I smiled against his lips, mentally begging him to get back into bed with me.

He growled and deepened the kiss, burying one hand in the hair at the back of my neck and holding me there for his attention. Had a man ever kissed me so thoroughly before? I didn't think so. "Be my good girl, eat your breakfast, and then you can come on my face again."

I sighed dreamily and looked up at him, I'd do just about whatever he asked of me with that kind of reward. "Fine." He backed up, and I slid out of bed, pleasantly surprised by the warmth emanating through the flooring. "Ooh, this is nice." I wiggled my feet on the hardwood floor.

"Yours has it too, didn't you see the control for it?" He went back to the kitchen, plating food.

"I didn't know what all of those controls were for." I shrugged, wrapping my arms around myself and following after him. "You'll have to show me sometime."

"Is that why your place is always so cold? And you use blankets like clothing?"

I shrugged again, "How was I supposed to know the heat came out of the floors?"

"Woman." He groaned and caged me in against the counter, bringing his face right in front of mine. "You. Have. To. Tell. Me. What. You. Need."

"I. Don't. Know. How." I contested, and he pursed his lips.

"You did last night." He cocked his head to the side, "You needed me to keep you safe from the storm and you called me. And I rewarded you for it."

"Hmm." I uttered. "Technically, I only called to see if you were sleeping through the thunder." I shrugged. "Then you got all bossy and made me come sleep with you."

"Made you?" He sat back on his heels and crossed his arms, "Did I make you beg to come too?"

Now it was my turn to cross my arms, "Technically, yes."

He grunted and ushered me out of the kitchen. "Go sit down to eat so I can do it again."

"Mmh." I moaned with extra flare and glanced over my shoulder as he followed my path with his eyes glued to my ass.

"How's the nausea?" He asked after a minute, "Anything not sound appealing?"

"I feel good, still." At his small table, I sat down and tucked my feet under me. "I don't want to jinx myself, but I think I'm over the worst of it."

"Does that mean I can throw out the four jars of pickles I bought yesterday?" He asked, carrying over the plates.

I aimed my fork at him and tried to give him my best intimidating stare, "Not if you want to live."

"Thought so." He sat down across from me and picked up a cup of coffee and watched me as I started cutting into the pancakes and eggs he made.

"What?" I paused, with a bite halfway to my mouth.

"Eat, and then we'll talk." But he didn't make any move to eat his own food.

"Why do I feel like I'm not going to like the conversation you choose?" I quickly took the bite off the fork, because if I was right, I wanted to enjoy my meal before he ruined it.

He shrugged and forked a bite of eggs to eat.

"Because you won't, but I think it's necessary."

"Well then," I stabbed a giant piece of pancake and shoved it into my mouth. "Talk about something else for now. Talk about what the souvenir was last night."

He sat back in his chair with a grin. "There were three souvenirs last night."

My eyebrows rose as I took another bite. "Busy man."

"They're in the fridge."

I swallowed the bite of eggs that now tasted like fingernails and washed it down with some water. "What is in the fridge, exactly?"

"Their hearts." He stared at me, and I tried to keep any emotion off my face. "Have you ever seen a human heart in person before?"

"Can't say as I have."

Maddox cocked his head to the side, "Do you want to?"

I opened my mouth to decline forcefully, expecting the nausea from the finger episode to return, but there was none. Every day he would tell me what gift he got me from someone on the list of people that wanted me dead, and I would forcefully ignore any mental imagery of the items that tried to assault my brain.

But today, no disgust came. I doubted it was because it was hearts, those seemed as grotesque as the fingers, ears, eyeballs and other organs that he had collected, yet I was mildly intrigued.

"I don't know." I paused, "Quintin's sounds appealing, but only if I can take a meat tenderizer to it for the fun of it."

He raised one brow at me, "That sounds personal."

I shrugged, not wanting to turn my calm and relaxed psycho into a raging and vengeful one before I finished my breakfast. "He was an evil man."

"Explain that further."

I took another bite of my pancakes and brought my knees to my chest, trying to word my next sentences carefully. "He had a thing for thick girls, but not in a fantasy way. He liked the big girls so he could degrade them and break their spirits because of their looks before he fucked them." I watched him closely, trying to read his expression as I recalled the memory. "One time, Damon made me meet him at his club during selection hour," I explained, remembering the way that bastard's words and hands had felt when they hit me, I gritted my teeth. "I almost didn't make it out of there without him—" I closed my eyes and shook my head, "You know."

"Raping you." Maddox leaned forward, resting his elbows on the table. "You almost didn't make it out of there without the man raping you."

"Yeah," I whispered, and cleared my throat, trying to brush it off. "But he didn't. Damon doesn't like to share his toys."

Maddox's massive chest rose and fell as he filled his lungs, watching me like a hawk. "Come here."

I scowled, "What?"

"Come here." He pushed his chair back and challenged me with his dominant eyes, "Now, Storm."

"Why?"

"Because I'm struggling to stay calm hearing about how they treated you. I'm struggling not to go back and mutilate the fucker's body even more than I did last night for what he did. I'm pissed that I didn't know that before I went for him. And I need to calm down, so you don't see that side of me."

"You don't scare me." I whispered, not really believing it.

"Yes, I do." He closed his eyes, "And I hate that. Now, get your ass over here so I can calm down before I hulk out and scare you with my darkness."

Not really sure why I was getting to my feet and walking closer to the man who just admitted to being triggered, I rounded the table and as soon as I was within reach, he lifted me onto his lap, straddling him. He was so fucking tall we were face to face even though I was sitting on him, and I instantly ran my hands up his shoulders to the back of his neck, feeling the tension there.

He leaned forward and buried his face in my neck, taking a deep breath as he wrapped his massive arms around my body, pressing me to him tight. "I don't recognize this feeling inside of me, Storm."

"Describe it." As I ran my nails up the back of his head, he let out a noise similar to a purr and his chest rumbled against my breasts, which were firmly pressed against him. So, I did it again.

"Like I want to hurt anyone who's hurt you." He replied, his voice strained, "It's overwhelming, a tidal wave of emotion consuming me like never before, leaving me breathless. The urge to protect and avenge you is more powerful now. I feel like I'll snap under the need to act on it."

"Act on something else, then." I pulled his head back by a handful of his hair and rocked in his lap. "Because I'm safe and sound, right here. Because of *you*."

"Maybe I'll do just that." He reached behind me and the plates and glasses rattled as he shoved them aside.

"What are you doing?" I asked and then shrieked when he put me on the table and pushed my thighs wide. I was naked under my nightgown and on display for him in the bright morning light of his kitchen but when I tried to close my knees, he pushed them wider apart, staring at my exposed center and licked his lips with a feral look in his eyes.

"You ate your food like my good girl, and now you get your reward." He pulled my hips forward, making me reach behind me to support myself as only my tailbone touched the table. Leaning forward, Maddox licked me from ass to clit and sucked it into his mouth, pulling a startled scream from my lips that ended on a moan. He growled, twisting his face back and forth against my pussy and letting his whiskers stimulate me everywhere. "I want my beard covered in your cream, baby girl. Let me use this sweet pussy to calm my psycho down."

"Fuck!" I moaned when he dived back in, pushing his tongue into me and sucking. "Just like that." Giving into the pleasure he was intent on giving, I held myself up with one hand behind me and scraped my nails through the hair on the back of his head, pulling him against me harder as I arched my back and rode his face like a good little slut.

Who was I to tell the man who was risking his life for me that he couldn't pleasure me sexually to calm his inner demons?

Duh.

He pushed a finger into me and curled it as he looked up at my body. "Take this nightgown off. I want to see your sexy tits."

I hesitated, knowing my curled over position was going to leave my stomach all sorts of rolled over and unappealing, but then he bit my clit to challenge me, and I gave in. If he wanted to see me, I'd let him.

I'd do just about anything for him with his perfect mouth, pushing me even closer to an orgasm with each flick of his tongue.

I took my nightgown off and threw it on the floor, leaning back and arching into his mouth more when he hit my G-spot just right with his thick finger. "Yes, Maddox. I'm so close."

He hummed against my clit, staring at me, and reached up to play with my nipples, pushing me over the edge and into bliss. "Good girl," He growled as I tipped my head back and lost it for him. "My good little Storm, let it all go for me."

Maddox slid his hands around my back and pulled me off the table and back into his lap, where I laid my head on his shoulder in total relaxation. The man was a walking psychotic grizzly bear who killed men for me and delivered their body parts to my doorstep in between other sweet gifts like blankets and jars of pickles. Yet I didn't hesitate for even a second before falling into his embrace to relax.

At least I was relaxed until I felt the rock-hard proof of his own need under me with only a thin piece of fabric separating our bodies.

I wiggled my hips, rubbing him with my ass and pulled back to look at him as his eyelids lowered and his nostrils flared. "Careful, or I'll take you to bed and not let you up for days."

I leaned back into his neck, shook by how comfortable I was in his embrace, and nibbled against his neck. "That's kind of what I was hoping for."

He growled and pulled my head back to kiss me. I had never kissed someone with a full beard before, but I loved kissing Maddox. There was something so erotically masculine about it. "Well, unfortunately, we don't have time." He sighed, "We have an appointment to go to this morning."

I calmed in his arms and leaned back to look at him. His words from before breakfast came back to the front of my mind, where he told me I wouldn't like the conversation he wanted to have. "What did you do?"

He tightened his arms around my waist and held me as I tried to create more space between us. "I made you an appointment with the best OB in Boston."

Glaring at him with rising indignation in my chest, "You had no business doing that."

"I know." He replied instantly, taking some of the wind out of my angry sails, "But I think you should at least get a checkup. You can't just kill time hiding away eating pickles and watching your silly movies for the rest of forever, Storm."

I tried to stand up to get away from his warm and soothing body and put some space between us so I could be mad at him. "I know that. But I don't know what I'm going to do yet."

"You haven't seen a doctor yet, have you?" He asked, holding me tight until I stopped fighting him. "Don't you want to at least know everything is okay before you make any other decisions?"

"No." I admitted, staring at him straight in the eye. "I don't want to know anything."

"Why?"

My nose burned as tears pooled in my eyes, and I hated how I was breaking apart for him to watch. "Because it will just hurt more." I whispered.

"It doesn't have to hurt, Liv." He ran his thumb over my cheek, wiping away the tears that dared to fall over my bottom lashes. "It doesn't have to be a bad thing."

"How can it not be?" I cried, "I got knocked up by a man who I hate. Who did terrible, horrific things to me. I literally wish death upon him every day. How am I supposed to have his baby? What if it's a boy, and he's just like his father? I'm all alone!"

"It's not his baby." He said firmly. "It's yours, Liv." Maddox lowered one hand to my still naked belly and the warmth from his rough palm made me cry harder. "This baby is yours. All yours. And Damon Kirst will never have a hand in its life, because I'm going to eradicate him for you. I'm going to protect you from him." He slid his other hand from my cheek to the back of my neck, pulling me forward to rest his forehead against mine. "I'll protect your baby and neither of you will ever be alone again."

I cried harder, as he wrapped both arms around my naked body and held me to him, right there in his kitchen. After a while I whispered my biggest fear, "You don't even know me, Maddox. What happens to us when you change your mind? The decision to keep this baby is for life, literally."

He growled, tightening his arms around me. "I can't describe the way taking care of you makes me feel, Storm. But I'm not a quitting man, and I won't quit on you. I don't have all the answers for the rest of forever, I'm just asking you to go see the doctor and get some answers about this baby first. And then we can go from there."

"How are you so confident?" I took a calming breath but kept my face buried in his neck.

"It's probably the lack of raging pregnancy hormones rushing through my body."

I bit his neck and snickered at his joke. I didn't want to laugh, but I didn't want to cry anymore either. "You're probably pretty right."

"Let's just take it one step at a time. And step one is getting showered and dressed for your first appointment."

"Will you go with me?" I finally leaned back to look at him. "I don't know if I can go in there alone."

His earth-shaking smile lit up his face, and he nodded, "You weren't going to keep me out of there even if you didn't want me there."

CHAPTER 11 - MADDOX

THE LINE WALKERS

Olivia's leg bounced obsessively as she sat on the tall exam table, waiting for the doctor to come in. "Easy Storm, you'll bounce yourself right off that table."

She glared at me, adjusting the sheet covering her naked bottom and chewed her lip. "Why do you call me Storm?"

I raised my brows at her, surprised by the question. "Because your eyes are always so full of emotion when you look at me. They look like you've got storm clouds circling in there, waiting to let loose."

She pursed her lips, and I was pretty sure she didn't like that answer, but a soft knock at the door stopped her from telling me exactly what she was thinking and the doctor walked in.

"Hello, Olivia." The woman said, walking over to the sink and washing her hands. She was probably in her sixties, with gray hair and glasses on her nose. There was something about her that just screamed, experienced. And I liked that. "My name is Dr. Pompano, I'm the head of the OB department here."

"Hi." Olivia smiled at her, though I could tell it was brittle, and took the older woman's hand when she held it out to shake.

"Your chart was kind of empty, so why don't you start at the beginning, and we can chat about what brings you in." Dr. Pompano said as she took a seat.

"Um," Olivia opened her mouth and closed it twice before her eyelids closed and she blurted. "I'm pregnant. But I've been in denial, and I haven't started any prenatal care or vitamins." She swallowed, "I'm sorry."

My hands curled in my lap at the blame she was putting on herself, but before I could reassure her, Dr. Pompano stepped in gently.

"That happens more often than you'd think," she smiled knowingly, "The only thing that matters is that you're here now, and we're going to get things on the right track." The doctor flipped through the papers Olivia filled out when we arrived. "It says here you don't know when your last period was, but your guess is three or four months ago, and you were irregular long before that. Do you know how far along you are?"

Olivia shook her head gently, "I only took a pregnancy test when the morning sickness got really bad."

"Okay." The doctor stood up, "No worries. Why don't we start with an ultrasound, and we can at least figure out a due date and then we can fill in the rest as we go. Lay back for me and we'll take a peek."

I stood up, no longer able to just be a spectator, as I slid my hand into Olivia's and she squeezed it tight as she lay back on the table as the doctor pulled the leg rest out. "Breathe, Storm." I whispered, and Olivia took a deep breath and smiled at me.

"Thanks."

The doctor smiled at me and then looked back at Olivia. "We'll start with a tummy ultrasound, and if you're not far along enough, we can take a peek with the internal wand." I eyed the long dildo looking thing on the ultrasound cart and almost snarled at the idea of that thing going inside Olivia before I ever did but refrained. The last thing I needed was to be kicked out for being jealous of a medical device. "Ready?" Dr. Pompano asked and Olivia nodded, pulling her shirt up to expose her abdomen.

I obviously didn't know Olivia before she was pregnant, but I could tell by looking at her lying down that her baby bump was already showing. There was just a slight roundness down low that wasn't natural when lying flat on your back.

Her baby was right there.

She squeezed my hand again as the doctor poured on the goop and ran the wand over it. There was a large TV at the end of the exam table on the wall for us to look at while the doctor looked at the screen on the cart. Before I could even mentally prepare myself, it suddenly appeared.

Olivia's baby. Clear as day. Wiggling around like a perfect little angel.

"Oh, my god." Liv whispered as we watched the very clearly defined features as the doctor scrolled over different parts of it, clicking away and taking different still shots.

"I'm just taking some measurements here," The doctor explained, "The femur and the skull can tell us a lot about a baby's gestational age." She worked and the longer I stared at the screen, the more in awe I became.

"Sit down." Olivia hissed at me, drawing my attention back to her, "You look like you're going to pass out."

"I'm fine." I scowled at her, but the doctor pulled the wand from her stomach and pointed at the chair.

"Sit down, Dad. We have a strict no passing out rule here."

Ah, fuck. I collapsed into the chair and leaned my elbows on the bed, clinging to Olivia's hand in both of mine as that word rattled around in my brain.

Liv didn't correct the doctor, and neither did I, but I stared at her and there were tears in her eyes as she silently stared back. We were in such uncharted territory, neither of us were prepared for that to happen. But I didn't hate it.

I didn't even dislike it a tiny bit.

"Okay," The doctor went on, taking a few last measurements as we watched silently. "So, according to these measurements, you're about eighteen weeks along."

"Eighteen—" Olivia gasped and looked from the doctor to me with wide eyes.

"You're okay." I reassured her, kissing her knuckles squeezed in my hands.

Dr. Pompano went on, "That makes your due date March twenty-ninth. But that could change a little as we watch this little one grow over the next few weeks." She smiled brightly, "A spring baby is the best, in my opinion." She hit a button on the machine and a printer started printing out a dozen or more photos. "Would you like to hear the heartbeat?"

Liv swallowed and flicked her gaze to me like she couldn't decide. I decided for her. "Yes." I replied. She needed to feel the realness of her situation for her to embrace it. That meant hearing the heartbeat and letting me be a part of it.

A few seconds later, the steady fast thump of the heartbeat echoed through the speakers and Liv dissolved into tears, covering her face as she heard her baby for the first time.

Dr. Pompano went on, explaining that Liv needed to take vitamins, and watch what she ate and get as much sleep as possible. I listened to every single instruction, intent to make sure Liv followed through with it, and when we left, we had a long strip of black and white photos and an appointment to go back in two weeks for another scan to find out the gender and get a full head to toe picture of the baby.

We were both silent as we rode back to my place, but her hand was in mine and I knew we were both just absorbing it all. She was almost halfway through her pregnancy already, so we didn't necessarily have a lot of time to dwell.

When we went upstairs to the loft, she walked ahead into her apartment almost on autopilot, and I followed her.

"I have to tell Peyton." She finally said as she threw herself down on the couch, pulling the blanket that matched the one on my bed around her.

I went to the wall unit and turned the heat on before taking a seat on the coffee table in front of her. "She'll be ecstatic."

Focusing on my face, she blinked and said, "I'm keeping this baby." She whispered like she actually doubted herself before. "I need to know if you're sure you want to go along for the ride with me though as more than just a friend—"

I kneeled on the ground in front of her and slid my hands up her thighs over her leggings, so she had no choice but to focus on me and my words. "If you'll let me, I want to be a part of this."

"I don't understand why you want to be, to be honest. I don't understand what you get out of it."

"I get you." replying plainly, "I get this baby." Sliding my hand over her stomach, she covered my hand with hers. "I know you don't remember the night I rescued you from the lounge, but when I got that call from Dane in the middle of another meaningless night, I felt like I finally had some sort of purpose. And then I saw you, laying there on that cold concrete floor, curled up around yourself, and I knew there was a reason I was the one to find you."

"Maddox." She sighed dreamily, "I felt the same way when I woke up here. It was strange and overwhelming, but it just felt—"

"Right." As I finished for her, she smiled brightly.

"I can't believe I'm going to have a baby."

"I can't believe you're letting me be a part of it."

She scoffed and ran her nails around the back of my neck, scooting to the edge of the couch. "Even if you are a psycho that brings me body parts of the men you kill for me, I know without a doubt that you're the safest place for me." She tilted her head, "For us."

I closed the distance between us and kissed her. I had no words to do any justice for what I was feeling because it was all new and foreign to me, so I just wanted to thank her with my affection.

But my needy little minx had other plans as she slid off the couch into my lap, deepening the kiss.

"You keep saying that I need to tell you what I need from you." She uttered, kissing her way down my neck to my ear and sucking on the lobe. I nearly came in my pants as she rocked in my lap, sucking on my ear in rhythm, like a fuck boy.

"I do." In response, I tried to maintain my focus.

"Well, I have a very pressing need right now, that I'm afraid if you don't see to it, I'll go insane."

I growled, putting my hands on her waist and rocking her harder and faster in my lap as she moaned at how it felt. "Tell me." I said and cut her off when she started to, "In explicit detail, Storm."

"Take your shirt off," She panted, "I want to feel your skin."

I reached behind my head and tore at my shirt, throwing it on the ground behind me somewhere. "Like this?"

"Mmh," She hummed, running her hands over my shoulders and down my arms. "I fantasized about what you'd look like with your shirt off from the very beginning." She looked in my eyes, "It's far better than I could have dreamed of."

I chuckled and rolled my eyes. "Details. Needs."

"Oh yeah," She grinned and then dragged her nails down my back and up my spine to my neck. I couldn't hold off the groan that escaped at how good it felt, and her smile widened as she watched me. "I want to see you naked."

"Oh, yeah?"

"Mmh-hmm." She hummed, chewing on her bottom lip. "It's only fair, you've gotten me naked a couple of times now. Yet you've always stayed hidden from me."

"What part of me do you want to see most?" I challenged.

But it didn't take much prodding because my little Storm was needy. "Your dick." She licked her lips seductively. "I can feel it, but I want to see it."

"Your wish is my command." I stood with her in my arms and laid her back on the couch as I stood between her knees. Her eyes were locked on mine as I undid my belt and then my jeans, but as I pulled my zipper down her stormy green eyes finally fell to my waist and I watched them as I pushed my jeans and briefs down, giving her what she wanted.

"Holy mother of anacondas." She whispered and seductively looked up at me from under her lashes. "Can I touch it?"

I gritted my teeth, trying desperately to keep my cool, knowing she was going to end up taking my cock soon for the first time, so I was willing to let her play for a bit.

But just for a bit, because I was a hair trigger away from folding her knees back to her shoulders and slamming in deep.

The doctor reassured us that sex was safe for her and the baby both right up until labor, and I'd be making sure to follow the doctor's word to a T.

"If you want to."

"Oh god, do I want to. I want to do far more than just touch it. But we can start there." She put her palms flat on my thighs, right above my knees and slowly moved them upward and in toward my hard dick where it hung for her, dripping with need. The second her cool fingers slid around the base to lift the weight of it up, I growled. She grinned seductively, "Do you like my hands on your cock, Psycho?"

I ached to show her just how much of a psycho I could be for her. Anyone else would have lost their teeth for calling me that, but her, God, it made my cock weep for her more. She liked my insanity, just as much as I liked hers.

"I think I'd like your pretty red lips on it more."

She twisted her hands, fisting my cock up the length as she stared at me. "Like this?" She tentatively ran her tongue up the underside of the head, collecting my pre-cum and then rubbing it against her lush lips like a colored stain she couldn't wait to wear.

"Just like that, Storm, play with it nice and slow, baby."

She opened her mouth and wrapped her lips around the thickness of me, while twirling her tongue across the underside. And the whole fucking time, her eyes were on me. Locked on me. Focused on me.

"Do you like my lips on your cock, Psycho?" She repeated in challenge before running her tongue up the length of me. "Does it feel as good as you'd hoped?"

"Mmh, better." I moaned, sliding my hand through her hair and bunching it behind her head so I could see her better as she started taking me as deep as she could. She'd have to dislocate her jaw to deep throat me, but damn, she was making my toes curl just how she was.

"Fuck, Storm." I growled when she dropped her lips to the base of my cock and then twirled her tongue around my heavy sack.

"I want to ride your cock." She purred, using her hand to cup my balls and massage them. "I want to slowly take you deep while you play with my tits and touch my skin with your big, rough hands. I want to feel so fucking full with you inside of me. I *need* to ride your cock, now."

"Then be a good girl and come on my face again, because my cock's going to rip you apart if you're not dripping for me first."

"Mmh," she leaned back, stared up at me, and opened her mouth to say something, but before she could speak, the front door banged open into the wall, interrupting her.

I whipped my head to the door, ready to throw Liv's body down behind the couch and fight the intruder, when a familiar face came into view instead.

"Oops," Peyton chuckled theatrically, looking over a pile of takeout boxes as she finally saw us in the living room. And then she screamed, and covered her face with her hands, completely forgetting about the tower of boxes as they fell onto the ground, spilling food everywhere.

I grabbed my pants and started pulling them up as Dane ran into the apartment, following Peyton's scream, "What's wrong?" He yelled and then froze when he saw me tucking myself away as Olivia buried herself behind a blanket in horror. "Oh."

"Out!" I barked, nodding to the door behind them, and Dane raised his brow at me comically. "Now!"

"No fun." Dane joked, grabbing Peyton, who still had her hands over her face and pulling her from the apartment. "We'll be across the hall."

When the door shut behind them, Liv peeked out of her blanket burrito with wide eyes. "My sister just saw me sucking your dick."

I snorted, picking my shirt up off the floor and putting it back on. "She saw you stroking my dick, not sucking it."

She scoffed, "You have to make them leave. I can never face her again."

I rolled my eyes and pulled her up by her shoulders, sliding my hands under the blankets. "You have to. Because you have to tell them to go, so I can get back to making good on seeing to all of your needs." I grinned when she moaned and leaned into me. The scents from the spilled food were apparently too much to resist because her stomach growled between us and I chuckled. "Hmm, it may have to wait until after we reorder all that food and gorge, though."

"Promise me we'll get back to it, though?" She looked up hopefully at me.

"I'm making you come on my cock tonight, Storm." I reassured her, "Nothing's going to stop me."

CHAPTER 12 - OLIVIA

"I can't believe he didn't—" I pursed my lips, barely refraining from complaining about not getting dicked down before Maddox left on a hunt with Dane.

"Didn't what, exactly?" Peyton raised her brows from behind her hard cider on the other end of the couch. "Please, finish that sentence."

"Fuck me!" I cried dramatically, throwing my head back against the couch. "He was supposed to fuck me, but your husband stole him."

She giggled and rolled her eyes. "You act like you can't wait a few hours."

"I can't." Sticking my bottom lip out, I whined. I didn't tell her how my wild hormones were making my unfilled kitty literally throb as she spoke, but I was running out of excuses to avoid the conversation. And I was a little excited to share the news, too. Terrified, but a little excited. "We haven't—you know. We were finally going to break the tension building and then BAM! interrupted."

My future didn't look so bleak and uncertain now that Maddox vowed to stay by my side and help me through it. Maybe telling my sister she was going to be an aunt would help build that excitement a little more, too. Or it could go totally upside down wrong and I would feel worse about myself after.

"Well, Dane needed help with something so," She shrugged. "Guess you're stuck with me for a while longer."

"Rude." I deadpanned and then giggled when she poked her toe into my leg.

"I kind of like having you around and accessible again." She said, looking down at the blanket between us. "I've missed you."

I didn't tell her what I had been up to the last year or so, but I didn't need to. It was pretty evident that Dane filled her in on the story. Even though she was busy with her new husband, and I was busy with my mess, I still felt guilty. "I'm sorry."

She waved me off, "I know you were in over your head. I just wish you would have come to me before it got to this point."

There was nothing else to say to that, so I didn't bother. Not really sure why, but her disappointment in me chapped my ass more than it should have. Instead, I kept my mouth shut about my news and turned my attention back to the movie we were watching.

There was nothing a little Coyote Ugly couldn't fix.

THE LINE WALKERS

I fell asleep sometime after one, giving up on Maddox coming back as I crawled into bed.

His bed, not mine.

Was there any protocol for a midnight booty call with the man who vowed to be a pseudo dad to your fatherless, unborn baby, whom you hadn't actually ever fucked and only barely got to ride his face and lick his cock? If there was, I was too horny to care what it was.

Was I desperate? Yes.

Was I needy? Yes.

Was I pathetic and naked in his bed, literally dripping for his cock without knowing when he'd finally show up? Bingo.

Peyton had left a little before eleven, driving Dane's car back to Hartington after he called her and told her they were going to be busy longer than expected. But my eyes were too heavy to stay open any longer, so I went to bed.

In my dreams, I could feel his warm, rugged body pressed against mine as I whimpered and cried out with pleasure while he satisfied me. Only after the second fantom orgasm did I wake up and realize they weren't dreams or fantom orgasms at all.

As I finally forced my blurry eyes to open, I pulled the blankets up off my chest and found the man laying between my legs, feasting on my body like it was his last meal. "Madd." I moaned, arching my back and stretching.

"There you are." He chuckled, "I wondered how many times I could make you come in your sleep."

"Cock." I mumbled sleepily. "Now."

He kissed his way up my body until he laid between my legs, sliding the thick length of his cock through my wetness, coating it.

"My pretty little Storm wants my cock?" He teased, sucking on my nipples and working me up further. "I thought I was going to steal a quick shower and then come over and sneak into your bed, but instead I came home and found your sexy naked body sprawled out in my bed, just begging for my cock."

"Yes. You promised to fuck me." I fought through the haze of desire and delirium as he kept playing with me. "So, fuck me, already."

"Beg me."

"Please, Maddox. Please."

"Try again, Storm." He growled, pinching my nipple as I came spontaneously, coating his cock with my cream and finally opening my eyes enough to see him clearly as I crashed over the other side of it. "I don't want your pretty trivial words; I want the ones that prove to me you know exactly who you're about to be fucked by. Prove to me you understand who I really am." He looked wild with his hair blown in different directions and grime on his skin, and it all kind of clicked. My perfect fucking psycho.

"Fuck me, Psycho." I purred. "Push that big thick cock deep into my pussy and claim it. We both know once you're there, I'll never take another one again. You'll ruin me for anyone else."

"That's fucking right," He hissed, pulling one leg over in front of him so I was lying on one hip with my shoulders still flat on the bed. "My girl."

"Mmh," I closed my eyes and tipped my head back as he pushed the head of his cock through my pussy lips and into me. He only gave me the head as he held my knee back before pulling out and then doing it again. "Fuck, you're so thick."

"Open your eyes, Storm." He demanded, and I looked up at him again as he leaned forward and kissed me. "Look at me as I claim you."

"Is that blood?" I finally saw that the grime on his skin wasn't dirt, but dried crimson stains splattered across his neck and chest like he'd used a chainsaw on a body or something.

"Things got a little out of hand."

"You let your psycho free, didn't you?" I asked as he pushed halfway inside of me, making me moan for him.

"For you." He growled, pulling out and then slowly, inch by inch, fed me his entire cock as he stared at me through the dim lighting. "I let him free there, so I'd be gentle with you."

"I don't want your softness, Madd. I want your true self." As I shifted my hips and arched my back, I opened myself up to him for the next thrust, resulting in a shared moan when he reached the deepest point. "Just like this." I dragged my nails down his chest, over the splatters as he leaned down to suck on my nipple. "That's it, baby." I cried as he reached between my thighs and pinched my clit.

"Come on my cock, Storm. Milk me. Take my come and feel my claim on this tight fucking cunt."

I rolled my hips, riding his cock from beneath as he fucked me in long, painstakingly perfect thrusts while he sucked on my breasts and rolled my clit. He was working my body over in a way that no one ever had, giving me everything I could dream of and making me come yet again.

"Fill me up." I cried, digging my nails into his pecks as I came. I felt the skin break under them as I pierced his flesh and he roared, slamming deep over and over again. Watching Maddox Renner come, feeling him fill my body with his claim and hearing the words of affirmation he gave me at the height of his pleasure, was hands down the most humbling thing I'd ever experienced before. "That's it. Show me how psycho you really are." I purred for him, smoothing my hands down his chest as he hung his head, slowing his thrusts but still giving me every inch of his cock from root to tip as we both came off the high.

When he couldn't take it anymore, he pulled out, and I thought he'd fall down in bed beside me, but instead he pulled my legs apart and opened me to his hungry eyes. Even in the dim light, I could see where he was looking as he stared down at my entrance. My entire body tingled with the intensity of what had just passed between us in the darkness and as his black eyes slowly slid up to mine, he growled one word that encompassed everything that happened.

"Mine."

CHAPTER 13 - MADDOX

THE LINE WALKERS

I lay on my side, watching Liv sleep with her naked body snuggled in against mine. When I got home last night, my plan to shower off the evidence of my job gone awry with Dane before going to her fell flat. My pretty perfect little Storm was already waiting for me.

I took her twice over night, once when I first got home, still covered in dried brain matter and blood. And then again after a quick shower, when she wrapped her sexy curvy body around mine, as I crawled back into bed.

Just like she was right now, breathing her soft little pants against my chest.

I thought she was asleep, but without even signaling that she was awake, she parted her lips and spoke. "So, who's brain was on your skin when you fucked me last night?"

I snorted at the absurdity of her question and tightened my arms around her waist as she snuggled deeper. "Good morning, Storm."

"Morning, Psycho."

I pinched her ass, and she wiggled and finally opened up those striking green eyes and looked up at me. "My psycho should scare you. Which means you shouldn't toy with it."

She shrugged and ran her hand over my chest, gently dragging her nails down over my chest hair. "It kind of makes me wet, actually." She chuckled, and I grunted before she moved on. "Do you want me to be afraid of you?"

"No." I replied instantly, "But I think you're the only person in the world that isn't."

"Will you ever hurt me?" She stared up at me, and I ran my thumb over the plump swell of her cheek.

"I'd die before I ever did anything to hurt you, Storm." Running my thumb down over her bottom lip, "And I'd rip anyone to shreds that tried before they even got near you."

"And this baby?" She whispered, "Will you love and protect it as if it was yours?"

I rolled us over, so I was on top of her, resting my weight on my elbow even as she wrapped her legs around my waist and hooked her ankles together, pulling me in further. "It *is* mine." I took both of her hands and pinned them next to her head, threading my fingers through hers. "You are mine."

"Doubt keeps trying to break into my happiness." She whispered, revealing her vulnerability to me. "I'm afraid that you'll change your mind."

I pulled my hips back and my morning wood nestled against her wet opening, still coated with my come from both times last night, and I pushed my head into her. "Did you not tell me last night that once you took me, you'd never have another?"

"Yes." She moaned when I pushed further into her. "But it's not me I'm worried about."

"I'm yours." After pulling out, I slowly gave her all of me until her eyelids fluttered and she tightened her fingers in mine. "I give you my word, Olivia."

"Show me." She rocked underneath me.

"I've made promises to many people over the years. I've given my word, and I've earned my reputation by it. But I've never promised *myself* to anyone. Never." I thrust into her and watched as she smiled in pleasure from it. "You are mine, and I am yours."

"Yes." She tightened her ankles around my back and rolled her clit against my groin each time I bottomed out. My girl was so responsive to my touch, and I didn't know if it was the hormones or if she was just that turned on, but I was feral for it. I loved watching her lose her mind for me. "Madd." She moaned, "I'm so close."

"I know, Storm." While keeping my hips pressed down, I moved them back and forth until she clawed at my hands and opened her mouth in silent ecstasy. "I can feel you tightening around my cock, desperately trying to milk my come from it."

"Please, baby. Please, I want you to come with me."

I pulled out and slammed back in, drawing a delicious cry from her lips. It wasn't like I had to work hard to come, two more pumps into her tight body and I was right there with her. "You want my come, do you?"

"Yes!" She cried, "Now, Madd. Please, now."

"Take it." I growled, pumping into her as her body tightened even more as she came on my cock. "Take every bit that I give to you, Storm." When I was done pumping, I rolled until she laid sprawled out on my chest, still impaled on me and the little flutters her tightness gave with her aftershocks kept me hard and eager for another round.

She softly giggled after a few minutes and tipped her head up to look at me. "Does it ever get soft?"

Pushing her hair back from her face, I winked at her, "Not when it's still buried deep inside of you. No chance."

"Hmm." She wiggled and then sat up, putting her hands flat on my pecks to straddle me before slowly lifting herself up and then lowering back down onto my cock. Unable to resist, I palmed both of her big breasts and played with her nipples while she slowly rode me. "A girl could get used to this."

"A girl better. Because I'm obsessed with filling your pussy up with my cock and my come. And I don't plan to stop anytime soon."

"Good boy." She winked and then quickened her pace, keeping her eyes locked on mine as she rode me like a pro. "That's my good, fucking boy."

THE LINE WALKERS

"You avoided my question earlier, by the way." Liv said, looking over the tops of her knees as she painted her fingernails on her couch. I sat at the kitchen table, working on my laptop, so I didn't have to be away from her. I was obsessed, and I didn't feel any shame or hesitation about it.

"Did I?" I looked back at my screen, trying to focus on the map of targets left and their most frequented whereabouts.

"You did." She said, lifting her hand in the air and looking at her nails, "But that's okay, you can answer it now."

I grinned behind my hand and leaned back in my chair to give her my full attention. "You'll have to remind me."

She pursed her lips and then gently blew on her nails as she stared back at me. "Who's brain matter were you wearing?"

"Ah," I nodded, remembering that question right before she rode me like a bronc in a rodeo. "It was a paid hit, unrelated to the Velvet Cage."

"But you won't tell me who?"

"Why do you want to know?"

"Because I want to know everything there is to know about you." Raising one brow at me, "Including what you do when you go full Psycho, and come home wearing brains."

I couldn't help but roll my eyes at her, but the seriousness in her demeanor made me pause. "You really want to know?"

Shrugging her shoulders, she put her nail polish down and slid her feet to the floor. "I want to know you, Maddox." I watched as she slid her dry hand over her lower stomach and silently waited for me to go on.

"Her name was Carleen." I answered and, as expected, her eyes widened with the information. "She was part of the Cartel decades ago."

"And were you paid to kill her?" she asked calmly.

"Dane was." I replied, "But he needed some help to get to her. So he called in backup."

"Do you kill women often?"

I licked my lips and closed my laptop, leaning forward on my elbows to stare at her. "Not as often as men, but often enough."

She swallowed, mulling that over. "Do you do it differently than a man?" She waved her hand. "The actual killing, I mean."

"Sometimes." I replied, understanding what she was asking. "But when the woman is responsible for the deaths of dozens of families full of women and children, then we treat her no better than any other monster we eliminate."

"Hence the brain." She whispered.

"It wasn't the first part of her to get splattered, but it was the last thing she felt."

Liv licked her lips, and I was afraid she would get emotional or nauseous even at the conversation, but she didn't. "What did she do to those families?"

"Do you really want to know?" I asked, "The woman was a monster."

"I want to know."

I rose from the table and went to her, dragging her feet onto the couch as I sat and rubbed them, recounting Carleen Delgado's horrors inflicted on innocents. "She was the mother of a leader. And I guess you can say that it takes a certain kind of monster to raise one." I rubbed my thumb into Liv's arch as I recounted the tale. "She would find impoverished families in Mexico, which wasn't hard where they were. And she'd offer them help, under the guise of being some sweet older lady. She'd befriend the women at the market or church and offer them meals and help with their obvious needs."

Liv deadpanned, "So kind of her."

"And when the women got hooked on her friendship, she would begin offering things to the rest of their family. Jobs, places to stay, money, food, you name it, she gave it."

"I'm sure it came with a catch." Liv said ominously.

"A big one." I affirmed, "She'd pull the rug out from under the women after a while, making up some tale about needing the money back or needing something in return for her generosity. She'd weave a story about how she was in trouble and needed it, or she'd be in trouble. Obviously, those women couldn't repay her, if they could, Carleen wouldn't have gotten her claws in them to begin with. And when push came to shove, Carleen's son would step in. He'd demand repayment with interest, and if they couldn't pay, then he'd have them on the hook for labor. In some cases, they would take husbands or older sons from their homes and ship them off into the drug game. Other times, men from the cartel would show up at their homes in the middle of the night and take payment out of the women and their daughters right in the middle of the street."

"Jesus." Liv sighed, "Rape, you mean?"

"Yeah, most of the time, the young girls never got back up off the ground when the cartel was done with them. That woman decimated entire families in the dark of night.

She stared down at the foot that I was rubbing, chewed on her bottom lip while keeping her hands covering that bump under her t-shirt. "And you made it hurt when you killed her?" She asked, looking back up at me with glassy eyes.

"She fucking screamed for mercy. But she found none from me."

"Do you believe a person is good or bad based on their DNA?" She whispered and my chest ached for her, knowing what she was really asking.

"No, I don't." I slid under her legs, pressed myself against her, and then, wrapping an arm around her, pulled her onto my lap. "I believe that a baby is born innocent and good to their core. Behaviors are taught and evil is grown and festered inside of someone based on someone they're around." I tipped her head back, so she'd look up at me again when she stared off at the wall behind me. "Your baby is good, Liv. You are good."

"But Damon isn't. What if some of his evil is engrained so deeply in his DNA that he transferred it onto my baby?" Swallowing, she went on, "That's my biggest fear. And I think the part of me that keeps me held back from fully embracing this as a gift and not a punishment. What if my baby is just like him?"

"It won't be." I reassured her, resting my forehead against hers. "This baby will be just like you. And just like me. Because we're the ones that are going to raise it and teach it right from wrong and good from bad."

She hiccupped and laughed at the same time, but there wasn't much humor behind it. "You're a psycho and I'm a criminal. What the fuck do we know about being good?"

"You're so fucking good, Storm." I countered, "And my darkness will never touch this baby. I won't allow it, on my fucking life."

She took a deep breath and contemplated everything before wrapping her arms around my abdomen and snuggling in deeper. "Sometimes, I think a little darkness in a person's soul can be a good thing." I leaned us back a bit and got comfortable as she continued her thought, "Because only the pure and innocent get hurt. That darkness within us, that which we harbor while striving to do good, protects us from the manipulation suffered by those in Carleen's story. I would have killed that fucking bitch myself if she even tried."

I tightened my arms around her, moved by the way she thought of people like us. "You're damn fucking right about that, Storm. Damn fucking right."

CHAPTER 14 - OLIVIA

THE LINE WALKERS

"Are you going to tell me where we're going?" I asked, shifting in the front seat of Maddox's truck as he drove through the dark night. "I'm getting *'take her to the train statio*n' vibes over here."

He looked over at me where he sat driving with one arm stretched out straight on the steering wheel, leaning over onto the center console, looking like a sexy grizzly bear. It didn't help that he had on a black and white flannel that was giving off hot lumberjack snack vibes.

Lumber snack, if you will.

"Why would I take you to a train station?" He asked, and I chuckled, shaking my head.

"It's a Yellowstone reference." I said, but no recognition lit up in his eyes, "You know, the Kevin Costner cowboy show out in Montana?" Still nothing, and outrage was growing the longer he acted like he hadn't seen the show. "Cowboys, bunkhouse poker nights, barrel racing girls up to no good, and Beth Dutton. Are you fucking serious right now? You've never seen it?"

He shook his head with a small smirk, "Can't say as I have."

"Oh, we are so watching it when we get home." I felt responsible for broadening his horizons into the crazy twists and turns of the drama.

"Whatever you say, Storm." He adjusted himself in his seat as we rounded a dark curve in the back country road. "But let's enjoy our night here first."

I watched as a warm glow lit up the night sky as we neared a remote place that looked like a random empty field in the middle of nowhere. "This is most definitely a train station moment."

"It's a carnival." He scoffed, still not understanding the reference. "A haunted carnival, actually. But now I'm wondering if I should have asked if you liked spooky stuff first."

My heart swelled in my chest as he followed the flaggers and parked in the dark field outside of the event. "I love spooky stuff." I whispered as I looked at the unique attractions on the other side of the gate. When I finally looked away from the sparkly lights and back over at him across the dark truck cab, he was watching me with a strange look on his face. "What?"

"It's kind of our first date." He smiled softly, "But I've never actually taken a woman out on a first date before."

I felt a wave of affection wash over me as the burly man showed his tender side, his smile gentle, a warmth emanating from him that felt uniquely directed at me. "To be honest, I haven't been on an official first date before either. It's a first for both of us."

"And a last." He leaned over the console and ran his fingers over my cheek, drawing my face toward his. "Because you're mine for good now, Storm."

"I like the sound of that." I whispered against his lips before he kissed me tenderly and gently, letting me take more and deepen it as I wanted. When he allowed me to have full control over our touches like that, it felt as if I was in charge of the giant man, although we were both aware of his ability to dominate me at any time. And I'd honestly fold for him in any way he asked me to. The fact that he never made me, did something to my feminine side.

Something warm and tingly.

"Let's go in before I end up driving us back home instead." He growled against my lips. "This skirt you wore is already tempting me to lift it and see what you have on under it." He dragged his fingers up my thigh over the decorative lace fishnets I was wearing under my tan and black flannel wrap skirt.

I dragged my nails down his cheek through his beard, drawing a deep groan from his chest like a satisfied kitten. "Mmh, play your cards right, big guy, and I might let you find out in a dark corner before the night is over."

"I'll hold you to that." He grinned in the darkness before opening his door and getting out. I learned the first time we rode together that he got offended if I opened the door, so I watched him walk around the front of his truck, admiring the power and grace in his walk as he got to my side.

"You're incredibly sexy." I blurted when he opened my door, and he raised his brow in surprise. "Like it should be illegal to look so damn good."

He rolled his eyes, holding his hand out for me and helping me down. When my feet were on the ground, he caged me in against the side of his truck and pressed his body against mine. "Says the woman giving me innocent schoolgirl fantasies mixed with dirty stripper vibes." He dropped his eyes to the cleavage showing above my white sweater and licked his lips. "I can't wait to act them out on you before the night is through."

"Mmh," I moaned, running my hands over his broad chest and rounding my eyes to look young and innocent. "Mr. Renner, I'll be your good girl."

He growled, pulling me off the truck and put his arm over my shoulders, in his signature move, nestling me into his side as we walked toward the loud noises and lights. "That's a shame, because I was thinking that thick ass would look good with my handprint on it."

"Fuck." I moaned, and he tipped his head back and chuckled as we joined the crowd, leaving me unable to act on the need to feel his hand spank my ass in some sexy role play scene.

I'd behave while we were surrounded by other people, but when I got him alone, all the bets were off.

Just like my panties already were.

THE LINE WALKERS

I knew what I was doing, Maddox was easy to read as I tipped my head back, dangling yet another piece of fried dough into my mouth and licking the powdered sugar off my lips. Maddox stared at me as I closed my eyes, moaned, and savored the taste.

The man loved feeding me.

And as a big girl, I should have been worried he was some chubby chaser for it, but he was such a big man himself that I didn't worry one second about the calories as he saw to every craving and temptation as we walked through the carnival.

In his eyes, I saw a complete absence of the judgment I'd come to expect, a look that melted away the doubts planted by men of the past.

Maddox fucking loved my body. I knew that much.

And I deserved to love it too, for once in my life. Even my outfit was revealing in terms of a lot of thick thighs and tits were on display, while fitting in with the New England fall fashion.

I didn't have to worry about hiding my growing belly like I had been doing either. My wrap skirt was A-line, and it camouflaged it enough that random strangers wouldn't care if they could tell I was pregnant or not.

Even though we were only about twenty minutes away from Hartington, I didn't worry about running into Dane and Peyton while we were out; they had some weird hate for all things to do with fall festivals. One time I asked Peyton to go check out a corn maze in the town next to theirs, and I thought she'd have a stroke as she sputtered her way through a hard refusal.

They were such kill joys.

"You're evil." Maddox growled, running his thumb over my bottom lip, gathering up some of the sugar and sucking it off in his own mouth.

"I know." With a smile, I offered him a piece, and he took it with a nibble on my fingers as an extra touch. "I'm happy," shrugging and taking another bite, "I have you all to myself, spooky season fun all around, and yummy carnival food to enjoy. What more could a girl like me want?"

"What are we doing next?" He asked, looking around the carnival. We walked through the haunted house, checked out the pumpkin smashing, I tried but failed to convince him to get his face painted like a zombie, and now we were stuffing our faces. The carnival was closing in a bit, and most of the other guests had started leaving, but I wasn't ready to end our first date.

"How about a haunted carousel ride?" I nodded to the alluring modified kids' ride in the carnival's corner.

My pregnancy limited my amusement park options, but the gentle rocking of the carousel was safe and enjoyable. Despite its spooky and dark theme, instead of a cheery and happy one, it was still safe. Instead of normal horses or carriages, there were zombie horses with pieces of flesh missing from their bodies and headless horsemen holding the reins of the carriages. There were no bright pastel colors to be found, instead everything was dark, and a fog machine covered most of the ride, leaving the riders to disappear into it with each revolution.

It was fucking beautiful. I lived for a tragic beauty over a traditional one.

Maddox didn't respond immediately, but he watched the ride go around a few times and then looked back over at me. I knew instantly he was thinking something sexual, but I didn't know what, as a mischievous glint glowed in his eye. "I think that sounds perfect."

He tossed the empty container from our snack into the trash and leaned forward to kiss me, but lowered his lips to a spot next to them, sucking some of the remaining sugar from my skin seductively, and I melted into him.

Other people be damned, they could watch. I didn't care.

Without another word, he took my hand and pulled me toward the carousel. When we got to the gate, the ride was just starting, so we waited along the fence as it spun around with its eerie piano playing loudly.

There was no one else waiting and the teenager running the ride had his nose buried in his phone as the ride went around, not looking up one time.

Maddox caged me into the metal fence, pressing his body against my back and his fingers pulled my hair over my shoulder so his lips had access to the skin of my neck. "Tell me something, Storm." He murmured against my flesh as I leaned back into him. "Have you ever been fucked on a carousel before?"

My blood warmed instantly, pooling in my belly as his hand anchored into my hip, holding me still as he pressed his hard dick against my back. Words failed me as I imagined taking him in public on a ride decorated with flesh-eating zombies, so I shook my head.

"Well, you're going to." He bit my ear and then his fingers skimmed up the back of my thigh to the hem of my skirt. "I've thought of nothing else all night but how to get up this skirt. And I can't wait any longer."

"Mmh," I turned and spoke against his lips, "It's about damn time."

His answering growl faded as the ride danced around in front of us while his fingers slid up and met the swell of my ass cheek. The fishnet stockings I wore had large gaps in the fabric over the thickness of my ass and his fingers easily pushed through them and directly between my cheeks. "Storm." He hissed when his fingers found my wetness without panties in the way. "You were planning on being dirty tonight, weren't you?"

"Make note right now," I bit his bottom lip. "I'm always planning to be dirty around you. I'm kind of addicted."

The ride came to a stop, the teenager barely glanced up from his phone as a few stragglers got off and when it was our turn to get on, there was no one else in line. "Hey," Maddox called to the teen as he held his hand out to him. I could just make out the faint corner of a folded-up bill between his fingers as the kid eagerly shook it. "Give us a few extra turns?"

"Yeah," The kid opened the hundred-dollar bill and then shoved it in his pocket. "I gotta take a piss anyway, man."

I hid my laugh behind my hand as Maddox ushered me onto the ride as the kid closed the gate behind us, flipping the closed sign over. He hit a button on the ride and it slowly started turning as we walked toward a zombie horse drawn carriage. The carriage was a deep cut out kind of thing that would be perfect for hiding away from any chance of prying eyes.

"Nope." Maddox wrapped his hands around my waist and pulled me with him to the horses in front of the carriage. "You're going riding, Storm. Side saddle."

"What—?" I stammered and then yelped when he lifted me up onto the inside horse. I was in a weird position with both of my legs over the outside of the horse and my ass hanging precariously over the edge of the seat. "What are you smoking, Psycho?"

The horse went up and down like a normal carousel horse but as Maddox pressed his chest to my back as I went up and down; I started putting the pieces together.

"Back that ass up." He pulled my skirt free, and his fingers instantly found my wetness as I scooted back onto them. "Good girl."

"Fuck." I moaned, watching over my shoulder as I clung to the pole for support as he pulled his cock free from his jeans. "There's no way."

"Be my good little Storm and take my cock. Let the ride move you up and down on it. Just stay still and take it."

He was so tall that he had to do almost no adjusting as he lined up under me and with the next down glide of the horse, his cock slid up into me like it was meant to be used for the act all along. "Jesus, Maddox." I moaned, leaning into him further.

The motion of his cock sliding in and out of me wasn't new, but the helplessness of it, literally being suspended and pushed and pulled onto it, was foreign and exciting and incredibly erotic.

"You take me so well, Storm." He growled, sliding both hands down to my ass and spreading my cheeks, opening me up for him even more. "Fuck, yes."

The smoke from the fog machine obscured everything around us as we rode the ride in circles. Faint cheers and laughs echoed from the dying carnival, and it heightened the fun of it all. We were so close to people as we had sex, yet no one could really see us. Even if there was a crowd of people around us, I'd still be Madd's good girl and do exactly what I was already doing. There was no way I could stop myself from taking the pleasure he was giving.

"Your pussy is so wet for me, Storm." He bit my neck on one down glide, and I gasped as tingles started building in my body. "You want to come for me, I can feel it."

"I don't think I have a choice." My breath hitched. "I'm at your mercy."

He chuckled and one palm landed directly on my ass cheek with a sharp crack through the air. "Jokes on you, because I have no mercy."

"Yes!"

"That's it, baby. Come all over my cock before we're found. Tighten down on it and make me come."

"Jesus." I tightened around him and with the next thrust, I shot off on an orgasm bigger than any other I could remember as he growled and came at the same time.

As we caught our breath, he backed up, giving me a break even as the ride continued and then helped me down onto my feet. Almost as if he planned it all along, as we righted our clothing with mischievous glints in our eyes, the ride slowed down and then came to a stop.

"Sorry man," the teen called from his booth, "Carnival is closing, I couldn't keep it going any longer."

"It's all good." Maddox slung his arm over my shoulders and helped me off the platform. "Have a great night."

I buried my face in his side to hide my blush and smirk as we walked away, but as we neared the exit, I looked back and got one last glance at the dark and spooky ride. I'd never look at a carousel again and not remember the way Maddox filled me up with each revolution. And that was fine by me.

The way Maddox held onto his darkness, letting me taste just the edge while protecting me from the full force of it, fed the wild child in me. I always craved bad boys, and the troubled projects I couldn't fix, simply because I wasn't supposed to. However, they never fulfilled me, and I was always left feeling empty and alone. With Maddox, though, his psycho gave me the wild and wrong I hungered for, like getting fucked on a carousel without a care in the world. His protectiveness over me, though, kept me from meeting the hard other side of that wild that I usually did.

He cared for me.

He protected me.

He cherished me.

And I was so unbearably unworthy of his efforts, but I'd be lying if I wasn't planning on eating up every single crumb he was willing to give to me for however long he did.

I was obsessed with a psycho.

He treated me better than any man ever had before.

"Thanks for an incredible first date." I smiled up at him as we neared his truck.

He grinned back and kissed my lips gently, "The first of many, Storm."

CHAPTER 15 - OLIVIA

THE LINE WALKERS

L iving in Maddox Renner's presence every single day was like something out of one of my favorite rom com movies. Sure, there were fewer flower deliveries and boom box serenades, and more blood-stained fucks, and dark stories like that of the woman he killed a while ago.

But it was perfect for us.

Even if the start to our relationship was weird and unconventional, we had fallen into a rhythm and normalcy I never wanted to give up. There were times I missed my old life before the Velvet Cage, where I lived one hundred percent on my own terms, coming and going and doing whatever I wanted whenever I wanted to. I made my own rules and interacted with who I wanted, whereas with Maddox, I sometimes felt a little like a priceless bird in the gilded cage, but I recognized his care and affection for what it was.

He felt in control of my safety when we were in his building, and I couldn't fault him for wanting to keep me safe and happy. Especially because the baby in my belly was growing rapidly. I was an easy target for someone looking to enact revenge, and I refused to just lie down and give myself up.

I followed his rules and stayed secluded in his massive and very comfortable living spaces, both his and mine, as we moved back and forth, like a kept mistress. Really, it wasn't such a bad gig.

Leaving the hospital where I had my twenty-week anatomy scan to check the baby over, head to toe, was a weird, otherworldly experience. We came home with another long strip of black and white sonogram photos I planned to hang on the fridge with the others as soon as I broke the news to Peyton.

Among the second strip of photos, there was an envelope. And in that envelope was a picture with the baby's gender revealed and labeled, yet neither of us had seen it yet.

We both wanted to find out that news together, not in front of a stranger where we could process it all in our own time. I also felt like I couldn't open it until I completely embraced the fact that in less than twenty weeks, I'd be a mom.

And Maddox would be a dad.

God, his steadiness in the entire thing was mind blowing. How could a man be so sure about something so foreign to him? I couldn't wrap my head around it.

But in a way, I didn't have to, because it wasn't just words, he used to assure me he was in it for the long haul. His actions covered any doubt I had left. Every single day, the man woke up and took care of me. Every single day, the man saw to my every need. Every single day, the man showed me his devotion without a single fault.

And I was fucking shaken by it.

And loving it.

I really fucking loved it. And I was falling in love with Maddox too, as wild as that was on its own. I had never been in love before, in my early twenties, I rebelled against what my parents had always imposed on me in an attempt to finally have control over my own destiny. Which meant I slept around, taking advantage of commitment free sex with men who turned me on, and I never regretted that.

But I never loved.

I never cared about the men I used for fun. The same way they never cared about me.

Subsequently, meeting Maddox, even in a messed-up situation like we did, felt so weird to begin with. Now, however, we were in a rhythm and a sense of normalcy day in and day out, and I never wanted to lose it.

Which was why I was standing in my kitchen, watching some YouTube episode of Martha Stewart's, pausing it every five seconds to copy whatever she was doing, in an attempt to make Maddox dinner.

The man cooked for me every day, and he was so good at it. I wanted to repay him for his time and efforts, even if I didn't have a clue what I was doing. If I was going to be a mom, I needed to figure it out.

Martha's voice guided me as I flipped the pork chop over in the pan, sprinkling a little salt and pepper onto it as it seared, before moving over to the next pan, where some rice risotto was trying to burn itself into a hockey puck.

But not on my watch.

Not this time.

I was going to make everything perfect, simply because Maddox deserved it.

He would be coming over any minute now, after some work session with Dane over at his apartment, which meant I was running out of time. I turned the burners off, confident that everything was ready and covered the pans before ripping the apron off and running into my bedroom to get dressed. I didn't trust myself to get dressed before cooking his dinner, because that was a surefire way to ruin my outfit before he saw it.

And the outfit I had planned deserved to be seen before it was ripped off.

I pulled on the champagne sweater dress and buttoned it up, stopping right below my breasts so they were seductively on display. It stopped right above my knee, and I pulled up the white thigh-high stockings that had little lace ruffles on the tops to match the lace bralette I wore under it, peaking out around the deep cleavage showing.

Although far from sexy, the outfit worked perfectly since I was pregnant and we were staying in the apartment's warmth and safety.

It was girly, sweet, but also sexy, and I couldn't wait to see Maddox when he came in.

"Storm." His deep voice called out and my body tingled as I rubbed my perfume into my neck and then put my necklace on.

"Coming." I sang seductively before scurrying out so he wouldn't come to find me in the bedroom. If he found me before I got out of the bedroom, we'd never make it back to the kitchen, thanks to the man's insatiable appetite for me.

Well, to be fair, it was usually me that initiated sex, but that was always after he got me off with his mouth or hands first. Maddox Renner was obsessed with making me orgasm, even if there was no plan or time for him to find pleasure.

And it was mind-boggling.

But tonight was all about him.

"Hi," I breathed as I cleared the hallway and found him lifting lids off of the pans on the stove. He froze with one raised halfway up when he saw me. I could feel his eyes roaming down my body, from the deep view of my breasts to the couple of inches of skin showing above my thigh highs and back up.

"Damn." He growled, dropping the lid, which made a loud clanging as he walked around the massive island in the kitchen toward me. "Dinner smells delicious," He wrapped his hands around my waist and pulled me flush to him, "But you smell better, baby."

I smiled up at him as he lowered his lips to my neck and inhaled and then purred for me when I dragged my nails up the back of his freshly showered scalp.

He wore a pair of blue jeans and a flannel, unbuttoned with nothing on under it, and I could feel his body harden against my stomach as he kissed me.

"We need to eat dinner, or it will burn." I argued, though I didn't work hard to get him to back up. "And I worked damn hard on it."

Begrudgingly, he backed up, "You're right." He kissed my lips once and then put a space between our bodies, "You're going to need your strength for what I'm going to do to your body tonight looking this good."

I swatted him away and led him to the table, pushing him down in the chair as I plated our meals and carried them over. Smirking to myself, I could almost feel the urge inside of him to stand up and force me to sit while he served me, but he stayed put like a good boy.

When we were both settled, I watched him expertly slice into his pork, the rich aroma filling the air, before lifting a generous piece to his mouth and meeting my gaze.

"How is it?"

He chewed and set his silverware down, "This is the best damn pork I've ever had, Storm."

"You're lying." I argued, but he shook his head and leveled me with an intimidating dark stare.

"I don't lie. Not to you. It's really good, babe. It's not dried out at all or anything."

"Really?" I cut into the pork and took a bite, surprised by how juicy it was and then relaxed, "Damn. Martha knows how to cook a pork chop."

Maddox chuckled and shook his head, taking a bite of the other sides and eating them. "What made you want to go to all of this trouble tonight?"

I licked my lips, taking a sip of sparkling water and clearing my throat before answering him. "Do you really want the answer to that?" I questioned, "It might make it harder to finish your meal."

He squinted slightly and put his fork down, steepling his fingers together and resting his chin on them. "Now you have to tell me."

I grinned and mimicked his posture, resting my chin on my fingers. "I have been edging myself all damn day long, thinking about all the ways I'm going to worship your body tonight. The things you do to me every single time we're together have inspired me to be a giver tonight, instead of just taking all the pleasure you always give me. So, eat up," I raised an eyebrow at him and sat up to my full height as I picked my fork back up. "Because you're the one that's going to need the strength tonight, baby."

He growled and his nostrils flared, but he silently picked his fork up and finished eating, staring right at me the entire time like a man possessed.

When I finally finished all that I could eat, thanks to the nerves fluttering in my stomach, I slowly rose from the table, picking up both of our plates and carried them to the sink. As I turned around to go back for more, I found Maddox crowding me in with a starving look in his eyes. "Madd."

"Extremely." He growled. "Psycho, in some ways."

I grinned, not shying away from the darkness growing in his gaze. "Let's get started then." I slid my hands over his bare stomach, loving the way the coarse hair felt against my fingers as I dragged them up over his massive pecks and then to his shoulders, pushing his unbuttoned red flannel wide and over his arms. "You won't be needing this for what I have planned."

"What exactly is the plan here, Storm?" He tried, but I shushed him with my finger of his lips as I took his hand and led him down the hall to my bedroom, turning off lights as I went. When we got to the open doorway of my room, I watched his face when he saw what I had planned for him, laid out.

"Is that a—?"

"Massage table." I purred and pulled him further into the room. "Complete with aromatherapy lotion, a warming pad, and if you're a good boy and let me do this without grumping, there will be a happy ending to rival all happy endings."

"Storm." He growled, eyeing me up and I could see the hesitation in his eyes, but knew it wasn't because he didn't want me to give him what I was offering. He didn't know how to accept it.

"Lay down baby," I pressed my body against his, "Let me take care of you tonight."

"I don't know how." He replied, weaving his fingers through the fabric of my skirt, just below my ass.

"I know." I kissed his chin, since he refused to lean down so I could get his lips as he fought with his self-deprecating vices. "Let's start with just taking these off." Slipping my fingers in the waistband of his jeans, I popped the button free, taking the decision making away from him. I gazed up at him as I dragged his zipper down and then pushed everything down to his knees. "You're doing great so far." As I kissed my way down his chest and sank to my knees, I trailed my lips down his body, helped him kick off his pants, and found myself face to face with my favorite toy in the world.

"Get off your knees, Storm." Maddox interrupted me before I could even touch his throbbing cock, pulling me to my feet with his strong hands. I pouted pathetically, and he rolled his eyes like I was a handful, but then sighed and ran his hand over his face. "Tell me why you want to do this for me."

"To make you feel special." I replied instantly. "To take care of you, even if it doesn't come close to repaying you for all you've done for me."

"You don't need to repay me." He groaned, "That's not why I do it, I'm not looking for anything in return."

"I know." I patted his rumbling chest to calm him down and get off his tirade. "You're the most loyal, selfless and dedicated man I've ever met, Maddox. And it makes all the rough and independent feminist parts inside of me cry tears of agony every single time I let you take care of me." He shook his head and rolled his eyes at my flare for dramatics, but stayed quiet as I went on. "It also warms something inside of me I didn't realize had grown so cold over the years. Your dedication to me and this baby and my entire fucking predicament has changed the physical shaping of my brain matter, allowing me to relax and soften to your protection and domineering, smothering cave dweller affection." I giggled before I finished the sentence, and he pursed his lips. "So let me turn the tables tonight and give back just a little something to you." I saw he remained unconvinced, so I used exaggerated gestures, pouting and batting my eyelashes at him. "Please let me rub your delicious body down and then suck on your cock until you come down my throat, Psycho. I need it."

He growled, the sound rising across the quiet room as he clenched his teeth. Without another word, he turned away and walked over to the massage table and pulled back one of the fancy, lush blankets. "How do I lay on this thing?" He eyed the hole in the headpiece, and I could physically feel how out of sorts the entire situation was making him.

I quickly joined him at the table, folding the blanket down and rubbing my hand over the heated surface below, "Face down baby. I'll do the rest."

He said nothing else but climbed up on the table, glaring at me as he tucked his even harder cock down so he could lie flat and then dutifully, and a bit begrudgingly, laid his face down in the rest and waited.

I quickly covered up his lower half, moving to get the rest of my supplies before stripping out of my dress, leaving me in only the high-tech girlie socks. When I returned to his side, I clicked the playlist on my phone, bathing the room in soft spa music that had a tempo to it that just made my blood flow a little faster to certain parts of my body.

"Thank you for playing along with me, Psycho." I tutted, coating my hands in the pre-warmed lotion, and lowered them to the center of his back.

He grunted in response but said nothing else as I started sliding my hands up and down the length of his back, turning my knuckles over into his muscles, drawing other noises from his lips that sounded a bit like he was enjoying it.

Smiling to myself, I kept working his body over, no longer paying attention to how my body was warming with each stroke of my hands over his body but focused on his pleasure only. Even if I wanted to climb on top of him and ride him like a bull already, I'd wait until he got a full massage out of the process.

I worked my way over each of his shoulders, enjoying the way his noises were slurring together in what I hoped was still bliss. I didn't realize I craved the feel of his body until the lotion covered me to the elbows and arousal soaked me between my thighs—it was an aphrodisiac. God, I knew the man was built and sturdy, but having free rein to touch him was something else.

He was always the one touching me, pleasuring me, seeing to my needs and the switch in roles was empowering.

After seeing to his arms and his neck, I turned and gently pulled the blanket down and off the end of the bed. He didn't say anything, but I could feel the tension building between us as I stood next to the table and started slowly rubbing my hands up and down the length of his massive thighs.

Every single inch of the man was dominant and manly. And his thighs were no exception to the rule as I pushed my knuckles through the grooves of his muscles, pulling my first official moan from his lips since I started my endeavor.

In the darkness, I grinned triumphantly and repeated the motion, feeling the tension in his muscles give way under my touch as I massaged from the base of his tight ass to the bend behind his knee, working him into putty one leg at a time.

On the next upward glide of my hands, I rubbed the inside of his thigh right below his sack that was slightly visible and he moaned again, tightening his hands into fists where they lay at his side.

He was fighting the urge to touch me, I could tell, and after a few more strokes, getting closer and closer to his groin, he gave in, cupping the back of my thigh in his large hand and squeezing. "Storm." My name sounded like a plea and a demand, all wrapped into one.

"Are you enjoying yourself?" I hummed, sliding my slick hands between his thighs and brushing against his taint.

"Be careful, woman." He hissed in an unrecognizable voice as his hand tightened around my thigh.

"Are you enjoying it?" I brushed up against it again, but this time I didn't immediately remove my fingers, instead I gently circled them and his hips flexed and he squeezed every muscle in his body. "Madd."

"Yes!" He snapped, "But stop." I pulled my hand from his body and he rolled over onto his back in a huff, revealing his rock-hard cock standing to attention with an angry purple head. His black eyes found mine and in the dim candlelight they reminded me of scenes from that witch show with three sisters I watched as a kid when men turned into their demon form. "If you touch me there again, I'm going to come." He put one arm behind his head and with the other, he wrapped his enormous fist around his hard shaft and stroked it. "And you promised me I could come down your pretty little throat."

I purred in excitement as his eyes fell to my breasts as he stroked his cock and I eagerly wrapped my hands around this thickness, taking over for him. "You're so right, Sir, I'm sorry."

As I bent over to lick the tip of his cock, his hand instantly nestled between my thighs and his fingers found my wetness with little effort, sliding up into my body, making us both moan with pleasure. "You wanted to suck my cock, Storm. Then fucking suck it."

I moaned at the way his dominant words hit their mark with my kinky side and took as much of him as I could into my mouth and hummed around him, sucking it like a pro. His stomach tensed as he curled up to watch me swallowing his cock as he played with my clit.

"Like this, baby?" I ran my wet lips over the crown of his cock in a seductive but light fashion and then smiled sinisterly, "Or like this, Psycho?" Dragging my teeth over the bulbous head as I cupped his balls, massaging that spot beneath them that made him wild before. I wanted his unfiltered fierceness.

I wanted *my* Psycho.

"Just like that." He thrust his fingers into my body again and then dragged them up through my crack to my ass and circled it before putting pressure against my back entrance. "Are you enjoying this?" He mocked me, repeating my words from earlier, but instead of hiding from the pleasure he was giving me like it could somehow embarrass me, I embraced it.

"Fuck yes," I arched my back and pushed my ass into his hand, giving him better access and he took it, pushing one finger into my ass. "I want to feel you everywhere."

"You're going to feel me blow, baby," He rasped as his body tightened up underneath me. "I'm coming."

I pushed my mouth down onto him and felt him erupt as he roared his manly cry of ecstasy while he came. The entire time he came, he played with me, giving pleasure as he took it like the true Dom that he was. Never were my needs not met and as I pulled off his cock, gasping for breath, I reached with my own orgasm, coating his fingers with wetness and digging my nails into his thighs while I rode the high.

My knees felt weak from the power and the crash of pleasure as I laid my forehead on his thigh but before I could give into my desire to let my body fall to the ground, he swung his legs off the table and lifted me into his arms.

No one had ever carried me before, not even before I started growing a watermelon in my stomach, but Maddox did it with ease and I felt so feminine in his arms like I wasn't a plus size woman.

"Troublemaker." He whispered against my temple as I snuggled into his chest further. He knelt on the bed and laid me down in the center of it and before he could pull away, I wrapped my arms around his neck to make sure he came with me, making him chuckle. "Afraid I'm going to leave?"

"Just making sure you don't." I grinned up at him as he pushed my thighs apart and laid between them.

"I'm not going anywhere, Storm. Ever." Maddox stared down at me before lowering his lips to mine. The softness and sensuality behind the kiss felt off given the indecent things we had just done, but I melted into it, letting his passion ground me. When we finally parted, he rested his forehead against mine and grinned, lightening the mood. "What exactly are these?" Running his hand over my thigh high socks, he played with the lace hem against my inner thigh.

"These are called Maddox kryptonite." I joked, and he nodded sheepishly. "Do you like them?"

His eyes glowed in the dim candlelight as he looked away from the lace and up to my eyes, "I think I'm going to need to do some further scientific studying of them before I can answer truthfully." Sitting up on his knees, he ran both of his enormous hands from my thighs, down my calves and over my feet, covered in the soft white fabric. I watched, fully engrossed in him as he lifted my feet to his chest and then ran his hands back down my legs, opening them and folding my knees out wide as he went. With any other man, being on display in such a position of vulnerability would have driven me nuts. But with Maddox, I simply tucked one arm behind my head to watch him explore my body like it was his right.

Because it was.

I was his.

If he wanted to play and explore me, I had no qualms about it.

"How's the research coming along?" I asked as he ran his hands back up the length of my legs, but kept my thighs spread for him like his good girl would. The growl that rumbled in his chest said he approved as he finally tore his eyes away from my exposed body to my eyes.

"It's proving to be very enlightening." He grinned devilishly. "Now roll over." He used his hold on my thighs to spin me over so I was on my knees with absolutely no effort on my part before giving me a gentle push between my shoulder blades so I was bent over for him. "I think I want to research something else now."

"Oh yeah," I looked over my shoulder, spreading my thighs and arching my back to present for him. "What exactly is the subject of your study this time?"

He slowly lowered his lips to my ass cheek, kissing one before moving over to the other one and then kissing his way in towards the center. "I want to see how many times I can make you come with my tongue in your ass."

"Jesus Christ." I snorted, but it died on a moan when he buried his face in my cheeks and went to work. "Fucking hell, Psycho." I cracked my neck and put my hands on the headboard, arching even more for him and pushing back against his face. "Good boy."

He slapped my ass for the chide and I moaned louder as he added a second and a third while he explored. "I'll be your good fucking boy, Storm. And then I'll be your good fucking psycho. However you want me, I'll be so damn good for you."

CHAPTER 16 - MADDOX

THE LINE WALKERS

I opened Liv's front door and called out to her when I didn't find her in the living space. "Storm."

"In here." Her voice drifted down the hallway from her bedroom and I followed it like a sailor to a siren song, straight into the rocky shore.

When I found her standing in the closet staring at herself in the full-length mirror, wearing only a bra and a pair of panties, I leaned on the doorframe and watched her. There was a lot going on in her head, and the storm clouds were back in her eyes as she finally looked at me in the reflection.

"None of my clothes fit." Her shoulders sagged as she looked back down at her growing belly in the mirror. "And I don't think baggy hoodies are going to hide this from P anymore, either."

I leaned up off the frame and walked into the closet, wrapping my arms around her from behind and laying both of my palms on her very round baby bump. "We can go buy clothes any time you want. Or we can order an entire truck load online and have a fashion show right here in this closet." I kissed the back of her head as she leaned back into my body. "And I think you're far overdue in telling P, anyway."

Thinking her sister's disappointment would overshadow Liv's joy from her first OB appointment, she began with the same evasive line she'd been using on me for weeks. "She'll just be—"

"She won't." I cut her off. "She'll be happy for you."

Liv pursed her lips but didn't tell me I was wrong. Truth was, neither of us knew how Peyton would react to the news that she'd be an aunt in just a few short months. But we were running out of ways to keep it hidden *and* time to figure it out.

"Maybe I'll tell her when we go tree shopping." She sighed. "Christmas always sweetens Peyton up." Turning in my arms, she wrapped her arms around my neck and smiled at me, and I could tell my little Storm was up to no good before she even opened her pretty lips. "You know what would distract me from the doomed conversation altogether?"

"Hmm." I raised one brow at her skeptically.

"Work." She whispered and widened her eyes dramatically. "I can help, you know."

"No." I shut down the notion before it even began.

"I could do something simple, like monitor accounts or trail searches and underground conversations."

"No." Pulling her arms free of my neck, I backed up and tried to create space between us as the conversation instantly made me sick to my stomach. We'd hit a dead end with tracking down the last two names on the list, Damon Kirst and his primary investor. We didn't even have a name for the mysterious silent partner yet, but we were getting closer. All we had was a callsign for him.

Fang. Stupid fucking callsign if you ask me, but whatever.

We knew they'd go underground and hide for a while, which was what I had wanted. Because if they were hiding, the Velvet Cage wasn't operating.

It would make them desperate.

It would make them slip up.

And when they slipped up, we'd find them. Dane and I had been working around the clock to find any trace of them. Until we did, I wouldn't take a deep breath again.

"Madd." Liv put her hands on her hips and cocked her head to the side. "I have to work. I can't stand just sitting here anymore."

"You're not sitting here; you're growing a human being." I snapped, tired of the same old conversation. "And you are safe here."

"I'm suffocating here." She snapped back and my blood ran cold at her words. She must have seen the effect because she dropped her hands and sighed, "I didn't mean it like that, I'm just not used to being so idle. I feel like I'm losing my mind."

"I can't." Shaking my head, her shoulders sank even more. "I'm sorry, but no, Storm. No work. We can't risk them tracking you through it."

She gritted her teeth, and I watched a look of utter defiance slide over her features. "Fine, but just remember that you are to blame for this."

I squinted in speculation as she reached behind her and undid the black bra that barely contained her massive tits that had grown each day with her pregnancy. I was a total fucking sucker for those fun bags, and she knew it. "What are you doing?" I growled as she pulled the fabric free, letting her tits fall with their weight and she sighed like the relief was overwhelming.

"I'm going to take a bubble bath." She slid her fingers into the band of her matching panties and pushed them down, and then kicked them at me with her painted toes. I caught them and felt the silky fabric that had been against her pussy, still warm with her body heat, with my thumb. Almost every day for the last month, we bathed together in her ensuite's giant soaker tub, but her look as she turned and walked away into the bathroom made me assume she didn't want me to join her this time.

"Do you expect me to sit this one out because I won't let you have your way?"

"That's exactly what I expect." She turned the tap on and then poured her favorite bubble bath in. Somehow, she had turned my ruthless killer self into a fucking simp desperate to soak in a tub filled with jasmine scented bubbles in the middle of the day. I couldn't tell which version of myself was crazier.

Her psycho, either way. Which was exactly how she liked me.

So, as she sank down into the water with steam rising out of it and sighed as the weightless sensation she loved so much took her over, I did what any good crazy boyfriend would do.

I stripped out of my clothes as she peeked up at me through one cracked eyelid until I was naked, and hard, standing next to the tub.

But instead of doing what I'm sure she expected me to do by bullying my way into the tub or begging for her to let me, I sat on the edge opposite of her, letting my feet and legs sink into the delicious water.

Sitting up, Liv put both arms over the lip of the tub to stare at me in challenge. The water was just up over her belly and her huge fucking tits were starting to bob with the waves from the jets as I turned them on for her.

I spread my knees, loving the way her eyes dropped to my hard cock and heavy balls as I leaned back on the ledge and slowly wrapped my hand around my aching length. Her lips parted as she finally caught on to what I was doing, and then her eyes snapped up to mine. "You want to play dirty, Storm?"

"Looks like you take the cake there." She argued through tight lips as she tried but failed to keep her eyes on my face.

She was just like a man when faced with something sexually appealing laid out in front of her, unable to resist the temptation.

"Be a good girl and invite me in." I challenged, "And I'll make you feel so fucking good."

She reached up with her toe and turned the tap off as I kept slowly stroking my cock for her. "I can play with myself, just like you can."

"True," I admitted, "But can you fill that sweet little pussy so good that you come repeatedly?" I leaned forward and tilted my head to the side, "Then can you carry your relaxed and sated body into bed and tuck yourself in for your second favorite pastime?" Fire danced in her eyes. "And *then* can you cook that cheesy chicken and broccoli Alfredo you've been begging me for the last two days and feed it to you, fork by fork until you're so fucking full and happy you can't find the energy to be angry with me anymore."

"I'm not angry." She pouted, and I knew I had her, so I slid down into the water on my knees and leaned over her body until my lips were right above hers as she laid her head back against the lip of the tub. "I'm frustrated."

"Then let your dirty Psycho fuck the frustration right out of your sinful little body until my sweet and loving Storm comes back."

I rolled my body under hers and molded her back against my chest as she willingly relaxed into my body, accepting her defeat. Bubble baths were better with orgasms, and she was obsessed with the orgasms I could give her. There was never any question whether I was getting in the bath with her or not.

"I want to have a purpose, Madd." She sighed as my hands roamed over her body, laid out for me. As soon as my fingers slid below her belly, she spread her thighs, hooking them over my knees as I widened them, opening her to me.

"And I want to protect you from any more pain." I bit her ear as I rolled her clit between my two fingers, making her arch into my touch. "I need to protect you, and our baby Storm." I'd taken to calling the baby mine, because it was. The DNA didn't matter, nature and nurture would have to battle it out, but our baby would have me as its father. Even if I didn't have a fucking clue how to be a good one to it, I'd learn.

"I know." She moaned, taking my other hand and bringing it to her breast, manipulating my fingers until I started pinching and pulling her nipples the way she was obsessed with. They were so sensitive, some days I'd lay her out like this in the tub and play with them to make her come, never even touching her with my mouth or cock.

And she fucking loved it.

"Let's table it for right now, and we can discuss it again after you come for me."

I could feel her smile as I spread her pussy lips with my fingers and lined my cock up with her tight, hot entrance. She arched her hips and angled herself just right so I could slide up into her body. The sigh she gave me every time I fed her my cock felt like the biggest thank you in the world. Like without me inside of her, she'd been missing something.

I used both hands on her hips to rock her back and forth, impaling her with my thick cock in a slow and almost torturous pace that drove us both wild but was gentle enough for her at the odd angle. After a while, she was panting and clawing at me for more, which was why I chose that moment to stop. She gasped when I held her still, with my cock filling her up but holding off her orgasm like a bastard. "Maddox." She hissed.

I kissed her neck and then bit it before whispering in her ear, "Make me a promise, and I'll let you come with me to Hartington tomorrow and work on a few things."

"Anything." She panted, palming her bare breast that I wasn't holding in my other hand. "I just want to help, baby."

I gently strummed my finger over her swollen clit under the water, and she mewled and tightened around my cock. "Promise me you'll tell Peyton tomorrow while we're there, and I'll let you come."

"Maddox," She whined, hating the condition I put on her pleasure. "Fine."

"Good girl." I bit her neck and thrust up into her as I rolled her clit around just how she liked. "You're my perfect, beautiful girl, Storm."

"God!" She arched, gripping the edge of the tub as she shot off with a massive orgasm that had her body tightening around my cock so much, I saw stars and could not hold off my release. "You're so evil." She gasped and relaxed back into my body as I slowly kept thrusting into her spasming pussy.

"No." I kissed her shoulder over the mark I left with my teeth, "I'm perfect for you and you know it."

"Hmm." She hummed, laying peacefully in my arms until the water cooled. "I have to get out and moisturize." She sighed and sat up begrudgingly. "Or my zebra stripes will get worse."

I ran my hands over her stomach and the faint lines that were there long before she got pregnant that she hated. She was obsessed with moisturizing her skin to avoid more marks on her skin from this chapter of life.

Helping her from the tub, I wrapped her up in a pre-warmed towel thanks to the new heater I installed for her after we started taking these daily dips. If someone had asked me last winter if I'd be taking daily bubble baths, and installing fancy things that made my pregnant girlfriend smile and swoon happily simply because it made something in my chest vibrate and tingle like it was alive, I would have beat the question off their face before they were done asking it.

Yet it was my life. And I fucking loved it.

"Tell me something about your past." She said as she sat down on the end of the bed while I grabbed her lotion from the top of her dresser.

I sank to my knees in front of her and pulled her towel open, revealing her lush body to my gaze. "It's not as exciting as you probably imagine it to be." I pumped the lotion into my palm and then rubbed them together, warming it as best as I could before I touched her.

"Tell me anyway." She watched me as I started rubbing the lotion over her round belly. "I need to know who you are outside of these walls and how you got to be him."

"Why?"

"Because you're going to be my baby's father." She replied firmly, "And I think I should know something about you besides your name, and that you're hands down the most devoted man I've ever met. Even if you delivered fingers to me once."

"Hmm." I pursed my lips and rubbed my hands around her sides to her back and then up to her shoulders as I tried to figure out what to tell her. True, I had dived deep into her personal life via Dane's hacking skills, but she knew little about me. Maybe she was right that with the baby coming, there were things she should inherently know about me. "Well, I'm thirty-four."

She snorted and rolled her eyes but mimed locking her lips shut when I glared at her.

I got more lotion on my hands and started rubbing it over her thighs as I went on. "Would you prefer it if I told you I was eleven the first time I killed someone?" I asked, and her lips parted in surprise. "Or that I was fifteen when I lost my virginity to a woman almost three times as old as me?" Her eyebrows dropped, and I could feel the outrage shining through her eyes at me, but she stayed silent. "Or that I've never been in love, or even understood it, until now?" A barely audible sigh escaped her lips as her shoulder relaxed happily, but I went on. "I didn't have some incredibly tragic upbringing at first, but it wasn't great. When I was eleven, I made a choice to take care of myself and pave my way through life, how I wanted to, and it cost me a lot over the years. But I'm here today," I slowed my hands, cupping them over the back of her hips as I leaned up on my knees to be eye level with her. "And I have you, and it all seems worth it now."

"Well shit," She sighed, "My journey to you feels far less philosophical now." A teasing smile danced on her lips.

"You're a pain in my ass." I smirked, and she ran her hands over my cheeks, pulling my face flush to hers.

She whispered, "I'm falling in love with you, Maddox."

"Good, because I'm already head over heels in love with you." I replied without hesitation. "And it would have been a little embarrassing if you didn't feel the same."

She snorted and kissed me, "You know I may have given into your seduction earlier if you were a little more romantic."

I leaned forward, forcing her backward until I leaned between her naked thighs. "Oh yeah? Like something corny from your movies?"

"It wouldn't hurt to try sometime." She challenged against my lips.

"Hmm," I hummed, running my towel covered hard cock against her bare center, open and exposed for me. "So the next time I take body parts from someone in your honor, I should deliver them with a romantic note attached?"

She tipped her head back and laughed as I kissed my way down her neck. "Oh yeah, something like that."

I sucked on the skin of her throat and grinned, "Something like *Roses are red, violets are blue, I took these off him, because I like you*?"

She cackled and dragged her nails over the back of my neck when I lowered my lips to her nipple, sucking one deep into my mouth and rhythmically feasting on it just how she liked. "Mmh, maybe something like, *Roses are red, violets are blue, that fucker's stiff now, and so is my dick?*"

I bit her nipple and delighted in her gasp as I moved to the other one, "I'll try to come up with something witty next time." Reaching under her legs, I folded her knees back and looked down at her pussy with the white evidence of my orgasm in the tub pooling at her entrance as I held her open. "But right now, I'm more worried about making you come again, and then tucking us in for a nap."

"God." She moaned, palming both of her breasts and playing with her nipples as she watched me intently lower my mouth to her clit to flick my tongue across it. "I don't think I've ever heard anything sexier before."

"Stay here." I pulled away from her sweet body and stood up over her. My cock was rock solid again and tenting my towel, so I pulled it off as I walked back around her bed.

"Where are you going?" She called out after me, but I just finished my journey to her bedside table and found the hidden object I stumbled upon yesterday when I was looking for her extra phone charger.

"Bringing in my assistant." I said as I rounded on her. Liv was still reclined in the center of the bed with both of her feet on the mattress and her legs spread wide around her rounded abdomen. She grinned at me seductively as she sucked on her two middle fingers while I walked toward her. When I got right in front of her, she lowered her wet fingers down to her glistening pussy and circled them around her swollen clit, keeping her eyes locked on mine the entire time. "Tell me how that feels?"

I dropped back down onto my knees, pushing hers wider for a better view as she surprised me by gently slapping her fingers against her clit with a dirty grin on her face.

"Like I didn't just come on your cock twenty minutes ago." She hummed, playing with her nipples with her free hand as I fought to decide which act I wanted to watch more. "Like I can't think of anything else besides how full I'll feel when that big, thick cock is deep inside of me again."

"You want my cock, Storm?" I pulled my eyes away from what she was doing to her clit and up to her eyes. "Then show me how you use this, and I'll give it to you?"

I pulled the sex toy out from behind my leg and clicked the button on the end, waking the thing up and bringing it to life between us. She grinned as she stared at the ruby red thing and started rubbing her clit faster. "You found my toy? Do you want me to apologize for having one?"

It looked like a normal vibrating dildo, but where there were usually little ears or something to tickle a woman's clit while the dildo was deep inside of her, there was a cup-shaped dome with something inside that looked suspiciously like a tongue. With enough imagination, I could guess what it did for her, but I wanted to watch her use it. "I've already told you what I want you to do with it, Storm. I want you to use it for me while I watch."

"Do I get to make myself come with it? Or will you edge me and torture me if I agree?"

I slid my hand around her ankle and pulled her foot to my face, biting the inside of her arch and drawing a sexy moan from her lips as she rubbed herself faster again. "I want you to come with it. Come all over it so I can fuck you hard when you're done." I held the long dildo vibrator up for her between us. "I want to fuck you so hard, Storm."

"You haven't done that yet." She took the toy from my hand and clicked another button on the end, and I watched in fascination as she flicked the tip of the tongue thing against her finger. "You're always so gentle with me."

"Not tonight. Not if you do what I say."

"I want it rough, Maddox." She purred, lifting the tip of the thick dildo to her lips and spitting on it before rubbing it down the length of the toy. "I want you to fuck me like a man possessed." She spread her pussy lips open, drawing my eyes there as she pushed the toy deep in one smooth motion. She moaned and closed her eyes as the tongue-like part of the cup played with her clit while the thick rod filled her. "I want you to fuck me like a Psycho would."

"Be careful what you wish for, Storm."

"No." She shook her head back and forth with her eyes closed as I lost my hold on my restraint and cupped her ass, pulling it off the edge of the bed until she was positioned exactly how I wanted her. Liv pulled the dildo from her pussy and we both stared at the vibrating thing, now covered in her wetness, before pushing it back in deep. "Give me what I want, Psycho." She purred, took my hand, and guided it around the toy's end. She then pulled it out and pushed it back in hard, pressing the tongue against her clit. I could tell there was a suction feature working it by how puffy her lips had been when she pulled it off the first time, so I held it in deep as she started trembling under its pleasure. "That's it, baby." Her eyes opened as she panted while I pulled the toy free and then started thrusting it into her over and over again, drawing moans from her lips as she led me with her hand over mine. "Make me come."

"Hands above your head." I growled, pulling the toy out of her body completely as she eagerly grabbed the top of the blankets above her head and held on. "Don't fucking move, do you hear me?"

"Yes, baby." She hummed, licking her lips as I pushed the toy back into her. Fuck, she took it so well too, meeting me thrust for thrust as I gave it to her. "Fuck, that feels so good."

"Do you fuck yourself with this toy like this when I'm not here?" I growled, running my fingers through her wetness that pooled at the bottom of her pussy lips when I pulled the toy out. "Am I not giving you what you really want, so you're using a toy to satisfy yourself."

She snorted mockingly, "I bought that toy over a year ago, big guy. I can't help it just so happens to look a lot like your massive dick."

"Answer me, Storm." I pulled the toy out and dragged the vibrating dildo tip over her nipple, making her breath catch and a new fire burn in her eyes. She wanted the suction part on her nipples, but she'd never ask for it. She hated how much pleasure she got from nipple stimulation, like it should embarrass her.

But my pretty little Storm was about to come harder than ever before if she gave me what I wanted first.

"Sometimes." Liv mewled, wiggling on the bed now that her body was empty and needy. I pushed two fingers deep, loving the wet noise they made as I twisted and turned them inside of her. "Fuck, Maddox." She hissed, arching into my hand and rocking against it. "Yes, okay. When you are off doing your dark and dangerous shit and I'm alone and horny, I play with myself." Her eyes were a fiery green as she snapped them up at me. "What now? Are you going to yell at me about coming without you and how having toys is cheating?"

I chuckled and twisted the toy, so the suction part landed directly over her right nipple. Through the clear cup I could see it sucking her nipple forward against the tongue and she screamed in ecstasy, dropping one hand to my chest and digging her nails in. "No, baby girl." I lined my cock up with her wet hole, and spread my fingers wide, so she took my cock with my fingers still inside of her as the toy sucked her nipple. "I'm going to insist that you use this thing for me every single day while I watch. And every single night that I'm gone, I want you soaking it with your come for me, Storm." I thrust into her hard, making her big tits jiggle as she took me with a look of absolute bewildered awe on her face. "And if you don't, then I'll make you do it twice in front of me before I give you my cock again."

"Jesus fuck, you're not human." She shook her head back and forth. "You're not normal."

"You're right, Storm." Pulling my fingers from her body, I wrapped my hand around her throat to hold her still as I really started fucking her, switching the toy to her other breast. "I'm a fucking psycho. And I'm going to show you just how fucking psychotic you make me with this sweet, supple body." I slammed into her, holding her still by her neck even as I kept the pressure off her windpipe. "The dirty and depraved things I'm going to do to you, now that I know you like it like that, Mmh," I growled, leaning forward to bite her free nipple and she tightened like a rubber band snapping around my cock as she started orgasming, screaming for me to fuck her harder still. So I did. "Take that cock, baby. Take it, you dirty little minx."

My skin burned as her nails dug wounds deep into my flesh, but even so, she wrapped her ankles around my hips and begged me for more.

I had been treating my troubled little Storm cloud with gentleness and caution because she was pregnant. But she didn't want that, at least not all the time.

No, my Storm wanted to feel the brand of my psychotic darkness on her skin, just like I wanted to feel her loving warmth on mine. And as blood dripped down my chest from under her nails and smeared into my skin against her palm, I filled her up with my come, knowing I'd never be whole without feeling how I felt in that very moment.

She embraced *me*.

The real me.

And I'd never hide it from her again.

CHAPTER 17 - OLIVIA

THE LINE WALKERS

"I hate this." I hissed as we walked up to the front door of Peyton and Dane's house.

Maddox smirked at me and slung his heavy arm over my shoulder, pulling me into his side. "The reward I'll give you when we get home will be so worth it."

I elbowed his side in indignation before contemplating it. "Give me a hint."

He chuckled and leaned down into my ear, "It has to do with orgasms. And food."

"Mmh." I moaned and lost the fight, holding back my grin. "I accept those terms."

"Good." He opened the door, and we walked into the foyer. Instantly, I adjusted my heavy cardigan over my stomach. I lived in leggings these days and luckily for me, winter was swirling all around us, so it gave me a good reason to layer up to hide my bump. But it wouldn't be fooling anyone for long, so I was out of time. Even without Maddox's ultimatum in the tub yesterday, I knew I needed to woman up and tell Peyton and Dane the truth.

As we walked through their expansive house, Maddox tightened his hold around my body like he could feel the nerves building inside of me.

"Oh, hey!" Peyton called from the kitchen as we rounded the corner. "I didn't know you were coming over today, I planned to come to see you in the morning."

I smiled awkwardly with a shrug and then took a seat on the barstool at the large island. Maddox lingered right behind me with his hand on my shoulder as Peyton finished putting a pan into the oven and then turned and wiped her hands on a towel.

She must have been able to sense the anxiety rippling out of my body, because she paused and looked between the two of us. "What's going on?"

Dane came into the room through the pantry and nodded in greeting, "Hey guys."

"Shh." Peyton waved him off as he paused at her side with a perplexing look on his face before he caught onto the mood in the room. "Liv." She pressed on, "What's wrong?"

"Nothing's wrong." Maddox answered confidently, "But Liv has something to tell you."

Peyton's green eyes flicked back and forth between us rapidly as I opened my mouth to say the words, but they were stuck in my throat. "I—"

"You what?" Peyton looked so worried as more silence fell between us. Jesus Christ, I was fucking everything up.

"I'm pregnant." The words hung in the air after I blurted them out, and the nausea that burned in my throat only intensified as I wished I could take them back. I didn't want anyone to know because I didn't want them to make me feel worse for it.

My baby deserved to be cherished and celebrated, not to be regretted.

"You're—." She stammered and then looked at Maddox as she shook her head. "Oh, my god!" A huge smile split her face as she clasped her hands together in front of her. "Congratulations, you two!"

"No." I shook my head, halting her celebration, and her smile fell when I didn't return one. Maddox rubbed his thumb over the back of my neck, lending me his silent support as I ripped myself open to my sister and her husband. "It's not Maddox's."

Peyton's mouth opened and closed and then her lips pursed tight as she tried to decipher what I said. "What does that mean?"

"P." Dane put his hand on hers and I could feel the way he was trying to lower her reaction before she let her emotions build up.

"What?" She snapped at him and then turned back to me. "Whose is it then?"

I shook my head, unable to say the words out loud.

"Damon blackmailed her into more than just her involvement with the Velvet Cage." Maddox replied.

"Damon." Peyton gasped and her eyes fell to where the counter hid my stomach. "Liv." She shook her head in horror as tears filled her eyes. "Oh, Livvy."

She brushed Dane off her and rounded the island, pushing past Maddox and swallowing me in a bear hug as we both started crying. I didn't realize until that very moment just how much I needed her support. And once I had her arms around me, I broke.

I finally let go of all the fear, and the shame, and the uncertainty. And Peyton absorbed all of it, holding me and reassuring me in ways I didn't know I'd ever have.

When we finally pulled apart and wiped at our tears, Maddox pulled out another stool for her and we sat down with the guys lingering around us.

She spoke first, staring at me like she'd never seen me before. "Why didn't you tell me?"

I shook my head, taking a deep breath, "Because I was so ashamed. I didn't think I was strong enough to keep it."

"Keep it?" She gasped and then her eyes fell to my stomach, still hidden behind all the layers, "But you did, right? You kept it?"

I nodded and wiped away the tears, forcing myself to take another deep breath. "Maddox kind of forced me to pull my head out of the sand and face reality."

She looked at the big guy standing at my back, "How did you know?" And then her eyes snapped back to me, "Did you tell him before you told me?"

I grinned at her outrage. "He figured it out."

"Intuitive." Dane grumbled with a smirk, and Maddox grunted in some wild man's response.

"Maddox made me an appointment with an OB and went with me so I could at least figure out what to do with the help of a medical opinion." I shrugged, "Turns out I'm already over halfway through."

Her eyes widened, and she looked back at my stomach. "That's why you've been living in baggy shit, isn't it?"

I chuckled softly and nodded, "I was still struggling with it. And I wasn't ready to admit it to you."

"I'm so sorry." She got a weepy look in her eyes again, "I'm so sorry that I gave you any indication that I'd be anything but supportive and loving to you if you told me. I'm so sorry, Liv."

"It wasn't you." I reassured her quickly, taking her hand in mine and squeezing it. "I had so much guilt for getting myself into this situation and so much fear about having a baby by a man I hated."

Her eyes rounded, and she looked up at Maddox and then over her own shoulder to Dane. "You plan to kill him, right?"

Dane raised one brow at her like there was any question to that at all, and Maddox replied for the both of them. "He's earned himself a very long visit from us."

Peyton went on, "And *you* plan to—" She nodded to me and tilted her head knowingly.

"I'm not going anywhere." He leaned down to kiss the top of my head. "As far as I'm concerned, this baby is mine."

Her eyes rounded even more, and her lips parted, "Ooh, I like it." And then she snapped out of it. "Wait, you said you're halfway through the pregnancy already. Do you know what it is? Boy or girl? When are you due? Jesus Christ! I have to plan a baby shower." And then she gasped, "What are you going to tell Mom and Dad?"

"Ew." I rolled my eyes and shook off the thought. I truly believed that my parents tried their best with us as kids, but that didn't mean it was ever enough or the right thing. As an adult, I didn't talk to them even though they still lived in the house we grew up in and had the same phone number. There was just something that broke between us when I realized they always loved the idea of us more than us personally.

So, as an adult, I chose not to have them in my life.

Maddox answered those questions for me, knowing that thinking too far ahead stressed me out. "We have the gender in an envelope we haven't opened yet. Liv wanted to wait until you knew before we celebrated with finding out the gender. And she's due at the end of March."

"March!" Peyton screeched, "It's already almost Christmas!"

"I know." I sighed, "Just stop stressing it and simply be happy for a moment. Please."

P's smile held a hint of understanding as she pulled herself back. "You're right. Let's enjoy this right now. Because this can be a good thing, Liv. You're going to be a mom!"

"Hey," Dane held his hand out to Maddox, "Congrats, Dad."

I looked over my shoulder and caught the massive smile Maddox gave his friend as he shook his hand and the last little bit of doubt I'd been having faded away. These were our people, our family. And if they were happy for us, then I had no reason not to be.

"Let me see your belly." Peyton started pulling at my clothes and I laughed and obliged, standing up and pulling open my layers and releasing the hold I had on my muscles to relax my baby bump. "Oh, my god!" She gushed, laying her hands on my stomach like she was holding the most precious thing in the world and cooing to it like a crazy lady.

Maddox kissed my temple as I soaked in the happiness around us and looked up at him. "Thank you."

He winked back at me.

CHAPTER 18 - MADDOX

THE LINE WALKERS

> **How are my sloppy seconds?**

M y blurry eyes fought to focus on the words as I sat up in Liv's bed, untangling her naked body from mine as I stared at the nameless text that popped through my phone. Not only was there no name or number with it, but it broke through my do not disturb feature too.

Which meant it wasn't accidental. I looked down at Liv as she turned over on her other side, seeking comfort in my absence, and snored softly as I put my feet on the floor. Another ghost text popped up, pushing the first up.

> **Return what's mine, and I'll let you live. Keep fucking around by killing men I don't give two shits about, and I'll use every contact in my book to get her back.**

> **And if you make me work hard for it, I'll take it out on her when I get my hands on her.**

> *Then again, she always liked it more when I slapped her around while I fucked her.*

Bile rose in my gut from the cowardly words across my screen seconds before it blacked out and they disappeared. Damon knew where she was. He knew I had her.

Which meant she wasn't safe until he was dead.

"Maddox." Liv's breathy voice called from behind me as her soft fingers brushed across my back. "Everything okay?"

I hit the power button on my phone and hit the internal kill switch under the back cover, completely deactivating it and any track that might be on it.

"Yeah, Storm." I replied, dropping it onto the floor and rolling back over behind her, wrapping her in my arms. "Everything is fine."

"Good." She sighed, snuggling deeper into my hold and lacing her fingers through mine, laying our hands on her baby belly that was hardening by the day. "Goodnight."

"Goodnight, Storm." I replied, staring at a spot on the wall across the room as she fell back to sleep in my arms while my mind raced and my heart spasmed at the idea of any harm coming to her because of my faults.

THE LINE WALKERS

"T alk to me." Dane snapped when I turned on a burner phone and called him.

"He knows." I replied, "He texted me last night."

"Fucker." He growled, "Bring her here."

"No." I sighed and ran my hand over the back of my head. "She hates it there."

"Who fucking cares?" He yelled, "She's safer here than she is in the city. There are too many people milling around there."

"And if a blitz attack hits there in the middle of nowhere with only the two of us around, who are you going to protect? Liv or Peyton?"

"Damnit!" He roared, knowing he'd always protect his wife first. Which was fair. "So, what are we going to do?"

"I'm calling in reinforcements to protect her while I'm gone, and then we're going to hit the ground harder."

"There are only six names left on the list, Madd. Maybe fuck the rest of them and just focus on him."

"No." I clenched my teeth, "That's what he wants us to do. He knows if the other four men die and all that's left is him and his silent partner, then he's going to be a fucking wanted man, by far more than just us. They'll all turn on him once they figure it out."

"I don't like this."

"Me either. But we don't have a choice. We stick to the plan, eliminating the remaining four Johns, and then we'll focus on Damon and his partner. Until then, just work on finding out who that is. It shouldn't be this fucking hard to find out a name on the scum bag funding Damon Kirst's Velvet Cage."

"I know. It's almost like I designed the smoke screen myself and that's why I can't see through it."

"Figure it out. Until we do, she's at risk."

"Got it."

THE LINE WALKERS

"M add." Liv's voice cut through my thoughts as we walked down the busy city street, "Earth to Maddox."

"Sorry." I tightened my arm around her shoulders, and she snuggled into my side further as we weaved around the other people out on the streets. It was unseasonably warm for January and even though I didn't want her outside of my building at all, I couldn't lock her down without telling her why.

And I couldn't take away her peace like that, so I hid it.

"You're regretting letting me out into the world, aren't you?" She stated plainly.

"No," I lied and then turned us down the sidewalk "I just can't wait to get you back home."

"I'm not buying it, Renner." She sighed but held back from re-torting it further as we got to the door to the maternity clothes store. When I held it open for her, she hesitantly walked in and then looked around in awe.

"What?" I asked after a bit. There were clothes in nearly every inch of the place, including pregnant mannequins showcasing dozens of different outfit styles. The boutique wasn't designer, but it was high end. Peyton had done some research and recommended it when she noted Liv's tight shirt the other day. It would cost a pretty penny to get Liv an entire wardrobe that would fit her comfortably now and after the baby was born.

Good thing I had lots of pretty pennies saved up for such an occasion.

Spending my entire adult life as a mercenary, working for rich and powerful clients, did more than just entertain me with bloodshed; it had lined my bank accounts well, though I had never spent much of it.

Until now.

"I don't know," She shrugged and walked over to a display table covered with fuzzy warm sweaters that looked like they could be the softest things in the world. Leather jackets hung on the rack at the end of the table and velvet pants adorned the other side. "I guess I always imagined maternity clothes were going to look like a bad curtain from the 90s."

I scoffed and followed her, noting the way she touched things as she passed by them, but didn't pick anything or even hold it up to appraise it. "Dawn of a new era." I mused, catching the eye of an employee milling around and calling her over. I waited until Liv was out of earshot and murmured to the smiling woman. "My wife is playing hard to get with finally buying a new wardrobe to fit her changing body growing my baby," I watched as the woman looked over at Liv and nodded knowing, "I'll add a twenty percent tip to whatever we buy today if you make sure she leaves here loaded down with new things." The woman's eyes rounded excitedly and she nodded once professionally. "Anything she touches, pick out her size and have it put in a dressing room."

"Yes, Sir." She nodded again and skirted me to pick up four dresses that Liv had just teased her fingers across as she kept walking.

Liv noted the woman moving around, but didn't pay enough attention to her as I caught back up. I gave the employee credit; she was discreet and incredibly efficient as she picked up each item and handed it off to other employees as Liv moved through the store.

"I don't know," Liv sighed after a while. "It's not like I actually go anywhere." Shrugging her shoulders, she looked up at me, "Maybe I'll just get some bigger pajamas."

"You sleep naked." I deadpanned and Liv's eyes flashed around the store like she was embarrassed, but I knew her better than that. "What would you need pajamas for?"

"I don't know," She hissed, and looked over at a rack next to us she had circled three times already. I knew without her saying anything that the black cashmere sweater had lured her in, even though she still refused to pick anything up. "It's expensive stuff here."

Tucking my knuckle under her chin, I forced her to look up at me instead of the mysteriously entrancing spot on the rack of clothes she was staring at and spoke firmly, so she'd have no choice but to understand my meaning.

"I am buying you new clothes, Storm." I motioned around us to all the racks, "You can either pick them out, or I will. But either way, we're loading my truck with full ass bags." Leaning down, I brushed my lips over hers, "And then we're going to the baby store to stock the nursery."

"Jesus, Mary, and Joseph." She sighed, "What kind of cave dweller, Fabio, romance novel alternate universe have I landed in?"

I smiled and kissed her again, loving the twisted humor she used in place of revealing her genuine feelings sometimes. Then I replied, "The kind where you finally let me take care of you the way you've always deserved to be taken care of." I kissed her once more, ignoring the lurking employees and other customers as they all watched, "And where you repay me by letting me ravage your sinful body and give you orgasms for breakfast, lunch, and dinner for the rest of your life."

"Yep," she leaned into me with her eyes closed and a cheerful smile on her face. "Alternate universe, but damn it if I'm not going to live blindly in it for the rest of eternity."

"Good girl." I added, and she simpered even more and then pushed away from me and looked around.

"Okay, I guess I should start picking some things." Her eyes danced to the dress again on the rack and the enthusiastic employee gently slid into our space with a warm smile for Storm.

"Actually, your husband has already taken care of everything." The woman said and then held her hand out, "My name is Teresa, and I've already picked everything that you've admired off the racks in an array of sizes per his instructions, and they're all waiting for you in our VIP fitting room in the back."

"My—" Storm stuttered and looked at me in confusion, "How did you—?"

"I know you." I answered plainly and herded her forward so she could shake the woman's hand and follow her to the back. "And I knew you wouldn't pick out nearly enough, so I picked for you."

"Madd." She said cautiously, eyeing the woman as we followed her to the luxurious fitting room, with an extra-large seating area outside of a curtain partition. "You've already done so much."

"Hush." I commanded and then slid her jacket off her shoulders and laid it on the back of a velvet couch as I removed my own. "Now go put on whatever you feel comfortable trying on here and show me." As I sat down, she stood frozen. "Either way, one of everything at least is coming home with us, regardless if you think you'll ever wear it or not, so get to it. Chop chop."

She chuckled, shaking her head in defeat and walked into the separate room, eyeing up the dozens of options already hung up and styled into full outfits for her, and she glanced back at me briefly before they closed the curtain. "Thank you, Madd."

"Mmh-hmm." I hummed, rubbing my fingers over my beard as I forced myself to relax the anxiety that bloomed as soon as she was out of reach and out of sight. "Start with that black sweater you drooled over out there."

I heard her scoff and giggle as she embraced the way her afternoon had turned out, which gave me a bit of peace while I waited to see her beautiful face again.

She could have this afternoon of fun and excitement toward her pregnancy, like a normal mother to be with a doting partner at her side. But when we got back home, my extra security team would have finished making the changes I was implementing, and her small freedoms would be restricted even further in the name of safety.

She'd be angry whenever she found out, but at least she'd be protected.

The safety of her and our baby would always be my number one priority, even if it meant her happiness came second. Because if anything ever happened to either of them, the earth would crumble under my boots as I lost control of the shadows inside. They'd cover the world around me and I'd destroy everyone in her wake.

CHAPTER 19 - OLIVIA

"What is this thing again?" Peyton asked from the floor of the nursery in my apartment. Even though I still referred to it as mine, it was Maddox's, too. He only went to his to work, as he said he wouldn't bring that darkness into the space our baby would live in.

Whatever that meant.

I just hoped he wouldn't be delivering anymore body parts to my door, and instead, he'd keep them in his own fridge.

"Uh," I blinked away the image of brains on a platter in his fridge, like some gross Jello mold jiggling and wiggling around when he opened and closed the door to grab a beer or something. "Nose sucker. For when the baby has boogers."

P's eyes rounded as she swung the straw looking thing around and then cringed. "Yummy."

She was surrounded by the massive bags full of baby stuff Maddox insisted we buy a few weeks ago that I hadn't brought myself to put away yet. Perhaps, in a way, my lack of ambition to put it all away was because part of me was still in disbelief that I'd be raising a baby in Maddox's fancy home with him standing by me, supporting me every step of the way. Or maybe it was the fact that I was thirty-one weeks pregnant and feeling like a whole ass whale.

More than likely, it was that.

I was still waiting for the deep-seated doubt to just kick rocks and stay away for good, but it still hadn't. Never mind the fact that Maddox had been working around the clock to find the last names on the list and finish it.

All of my alone time had been giving me time to think. And when I sat around in solitary confinement, with just my raging hormone induced brain to keep me company, anxiety and paranoia loved to join in on the fun.

The other day I had been walking by the window in the living room, and I swore I saw someone walking across a rooftop across the street from us. But it wasn't like a construction worker or something; the figure that made me stop dead in my tracks was dressed in full black military gear.

The dark figure disappeared before I could even release the scream trapped in my throat, almost as if it hadn't been there at all. I stood in that fucking window all damn day long, waiting, watching intently, almost hoping to see it again just to prove to myself that my brain wasn't going soggy with a lack of stimulation. But it never reappeared.

And now I don't open those blinds.

"So," Peyton called my attention back to her from her spot on the floor as I kept rocking in the beautiful new rocking chair that had appeared yesterday morning. "Which set am I putting in the dresser and which set am I putting in the storage tote for the next baby?" She held up two identical onesies in contrasting colors.

One pink.

One blue.

I sighed, looking over at the envelope tacked into the corkboard on the wall with my baby's gender identified inside. "Maybe we should skip doing the clothes for now."

She laid them down on her lap and tilted her head at me, "You know, I could peek if you don't want to. Then I could always just put away what needed to be, and you could just not open the drawers until you want to know."

I rolled my eyes and ran my hands over my enormous belly, knowing Peyton would literally knock me over to get to it if I told her she could look in that damn envelope. She was chomping at the bit to find out what her first niece or nephew would be.

"I don't think I want to know." I shrugged.

"But why, though?" She watched me intently and challenged me when I simply shrugged again in response. "I think I know why you don't want to know yet, but you won't like it if I'm right."

I knew why I didn't want to look, but I knew she didn't. Even if she thought she did.

The reason I didn't want to look burned my gut with guilt and shame every time I even dared to think it. I was afraid if our baby was a little boy, that I wouldn't love him because he'd remind me of Damon. I was terrified of feeling grief upon meeting my first baby, so I refused to dwell on it, even if she asked me in some way every time she came over. Which was almost every day, since I still could not leave. I didn't think it was possible, but somehow Maddox had gotten even more serious about me staying in the building than he was when he first moved me in.

"Then keep it to yourself." I replied firmly and stood up from the chair, not wanting to dwell on it anymore. "I have to pee."

"Someday you're going to have to stop using that sweet baby pushing on your bladder as an excuse to avoid uncomfortable topics." She deadpanned and then smirked when I glared at her.

"Then I'll be able to use the fact that it used my bladder as a trampoline for nine months and I will still have to pee every five minutes as an excuse for the rest of my life." I called over my shoulder as I left the room.

I didn't have to pee.

But she didn't need to know that.

THE LINE WALKERS

Hands covered my throat, cutting off my air as I swiped my hands out, desperate to break their hold. It was dark, and I couldn't see who was on top of me, but the softness of the mattress beneath me gave little in the way of leverage for me to fight back from. "No!" I screamed, but it came out with the last hiss of breath before fire erupted in my lungs.

Right as the pressure built to where I was sure my chest would explode from it, light broke through the darkness and I sat up straight, swinging out against the figure in my face as it disappeared with the shadows.

A dream.

It was a dream.

With a strangled gasp, I raked my nails across my skin, battling the phantoms in my mind and desperately trying to control my ragged breathing as my eyes darted around my dark bedroom, searching for a sense of stability. Glancing at the clock, it was half-past two in the morning, and the other side of my bed was cold and empty where Maddox should have been.

Where he was missing from when I finally fell asleep a few hours ago. His nights were getting later, and I missed his presence more and more on these nights when I fell asleep alone.

"Madd." I called out as I swung my legs over the tall bed and slid to the floor. I'd never sleep on a bed that wasn't as tall as his beds ever again, because there was something really fucking joyous about sliding out of bed with gravity's help rather than climbing from it under the weight of the world and a watermelon on your chest.

I wrapped my bathrobe around my naked body and peeked in the bathroom on my way out to the hallway, finding both empty. A glow from the bedroom down the hall beckoned me as I tiptoed across the plush carpet. Peeking in through the open doorway, I took a deep breath when I spotted the man of my dreams sitting in the middle of the serene room, tightening a screw into the side of the crib as he built it.

He wore only a pair of red plaid pajama pants, and his hair was damp from a shower he must have taken in his old apartment before he came in. Which meant he had killed someone tonight.

The darkness of it surrounded his aura like a black cloud of danger, and it kept him from settling and coming to me like he should have.

His tattooed skin rippled as he reached across the sage green area rug for another part and worked on tightening it into place. I watched him, leaning against the doorframe, carefully assembling the crib, each movement precise and deliberate, yet his shoulders slumped with the weight of his unspoken burdens.

Piece by piece, he put it together and when it was whole; he sat back on his feet and stared at it like it held answers to something he sought after.

"Maddox." I whispered, and he didn't react, but I knew he heard me. Walking in, I cautiously ran my hand over his tense shoulder, up his neck to the hair at his nape. He leaned into my touch and took a deep breath as I gently stroked his scalp, just how he liked as we both stared at the crib. "It's beautiful."

When he spoke, his voice was hoarse, "It's hard to imagine it being worthy of holding such a precious being." Even though I knew he'd have to help me up, I lowered myself to my knees behind him and wrapped my arms around his torso, clinging to him while I pretended to offer him support. I kissed his shoulder, and we both basked in the silence again until he broke it, "I killed an innocent person tonight."

A searing pain shot through my nose, tears blurring my vision before his words even registered, his voice thick with such sorrow it felt like a physical wound. I tried to level out my voice as I fought to speak, "Was it an accident?" I whispered, and after a long pause, he simply shook his head no. It felt like my heart would break for him and whatever had happened to him while he worked to protect me. "What happened?"

"I lost control." He admitted in a pained voice as he kept looking at the crib as I held onto him from behind. "And I've never cared before. But tonight, I did something heinous simply because I'm a monster and could do it. And I can't shake it."

"Shh." I squeezed him tighter as the tears pooled between my lashes for him and his soul. "It's okay."

"What if our baby was here?" He vibrated in my hold, but I wouldn't let him go. "What if I did what I did tonight, and then came home and came in here and—" His voice broke, and he dropped his chin to his chest. "How am I supposed to look that innocent little baby in the eyes knowing what kind of man I am?"

I crawled around his body in a rush and forced his head up to look at me as the tears in my eyes broke free and ran down my cheeks. "You are going to look our baby in the eyes knowing you're the only man in their life that will ever do everything you can to protect them." I urged, clawing at his face when he tried to shake me off in his own grief. "You look our baby in the eyes knowing you're the only man that will ever love them the way they deserve, Maddox. The rest does not matter, because they will feel your love. Regardless of anything you've done to get us there, they will know that. Just like I know that."

He shuddered and his face screwed up in agony as he pulled me into his arms and clung to me. "I've never cared before." He muttered angrily. "I've never cared about life and death and who meets their maker or when. But now I do and I fucking hate it."

"Shh," I tried soothing him with my touch and voice, even as my mind spun with the endless possibilities of things that could have derailed his peace so heavily. "Tell me what happened."

He took a deep breath and loosened his hold around my body to pull back and look at me, "Not in here."

"Let's go then," I backed up from him and got to my knees as he stood up and helped me to my feet. Even at his deepest peril, he still saw to my needs. He wasn't human. He was heaven sent, even if he did evil things.

Instead of leading him into our bedroom, I turned down the hall toward the living space and turned on the soft ambient lights as we sat down together on the couch. He pulled me onto his lap and buried his face in my chest, so I covered our bodies with my favorite comfort blanket, like it could help shake the bad things from his skin and let me comfort him in their wake. He kept his lips pressed against my neck as he spoke, and I held him through it.

"We found Simon Miles tonight." He hesitated briefly, but kept going, telling me about the last name on the list besides Damon's and his money man. Simon was the last piece to eliminate before Maddox got to the men who orchestrated my entire kidnapping.

"What happened?" I asked cautiously.

"I needed answers from him. Answers about who Damon was getting the funds from now that the Velvet Cage wasn't operating the way it used to." Maddox leaned back finally and rested his head on the couch cushion behind him, but kept me held tight. He wouldn't look me in the eye, but he was talking at least, so I didn't take it personally. "But Simon knew he was dead, either way. The only mercy I offered him was the method I used to kill him, based on his cooperation."

"What did he do?"

"Refused to give me any information. We tortured him for hours, nevertheless, he held firm." His eyes got a faraway look in them as he stared at the ceiling, and I knew he was remembering whatever he did. "I thought we hit a brick wall. Until his girlfriend showed up."

My stomach rolled, putting together the pieces in my head. "And you found the tool needed to get him to talk."

He nodded solemnly. "I didn't even think twice before using her, neither did Dane. We needed the information, and he was our last link to the Velvet Cage." He blinked away the memories and finally looked over at me. "But when we were done, and they were both dead, I saw your face on her body for a second. And I think it put into perspective just how much danger you're in by being with me. Someone could use you to get what they want from me."

As I ran my palm over his cheek and tried to soothe some of the pain in his black eyes, I told him, "Baby, my days had been numbered long before I ever met you."

"You don't get it though, Storm, I wouldn't survive losing you or this baby." He shook his head, and I felt sincerity in his words. They weren't pretty words of affirmation or empty promises, they were raw and honest, laced in harshness.

Nodding, I reassured him. "I know you wouldn't, Maddox. Without me, you'd burn the world to the ground before giving in to the devil himself, I know."

"You're changing me, Storm."

"You're changing me, Psycho." I tried to smile, but it was more of a grimace. "Tomorrow we can both revel in that change, because I don't regret how loving you is softening me, just like it is you, Maddox. But I know that right now, that softness is making you second guess your true nature. So tonight, we'll just hold space for the danger and what it means to have weakness and vulnerability. And tomorrow we can try to find peace knowing that even if this life is the reason we die before our time, the time we'll get together will forever be better than a lifetime of what we had before."

He simply laid his hand on our baby and a small sad smile kissed his lips when the little one answered his touch with a bump back of their own. "Tomorrow." He whispered. "Tomorrow we'll be okay."

"Yes, we will." I laid my cheek on his head, and he leaned us into the corner of the couch, reclined. "Because neither of us deserved this kind of peace, so we'll enjoy it for however long we get to have it."

"Forever, Storm." He used the remote on the end table to turn the lights off and blanket us in the darkness we both found such familiarity in. "Because even in death, I'm yours."

CHAPTER 20 - MADDOX

THE LINE WALKERS

P ulling into the parking garage at nearly six in the morning after yet another long night of hunting, I ached for nothing more than Liv's calming touch on my skin. I never craved another human being the way I craved Liv, it was visceral, and it was vital; I couldn't go without it.

But as soon as I parked my truck, my internal alarms started screaming when Chris, my head guard, came out of the shadows in a rush.

Throwing my door open, I bolted from the truck and met him in the elevator corridor. "What is it?"

"She found T-bone in the hallway outside of her apartment."

"Fuck!" I roared, slamming my fist into the button as the man rushed on.

"She gouged one of his eyes pretty bad. I wouldn't be surprised if he's blind."

I ignore anything else he had to say as I hit the button for the top floor of the building, panicking with each passing second of Liv being upset and scared from finding armed men in her space without me telling her first. As the elevator came to a stop, I could hear her screams before the doors even opened.

And as soon as they did, a ceramic mug flew at my head that I barely avoided before it smashed into the back of the elevator. "You son of a bitch!" Liv screamed at me with fire in her eyes blurred with tears. "You lied to me!" My vision was tinted red at the thought of her in nothing but a tight long sleeve shirt and booty shorts for my paid guards to enjoy the sight of.

I dodged another mug as she threw it out of our apartment door as three guards watched silently. Three men hired by me to protect her at all costs, who watched as she gave me a tongue lashing. "Leave us!" I bellowed, catching the next mug in the air as her red hair flashed through the opening, no doubt on her way for more ammo. "Now!"

With a hard shove, I crossed the threshold, grabbing her arm before she could land another blow. The door slammed shut behind me, a heavy, satisfying click sealing us inside, away from their prying eyes and ears. "You bastard!" A sharp screech tore through the air as she thrashed against my grip, her fist a blur before connecting painfully with my jaw. She gasped, a ragged breath hitching her chest, her fist trembling with a mix of fury and pain.

"Stop it!" I commanded and took both of her arms, crossing them over her chest and then turning her so her back was against my chest. I needed to calm her down, or she'd hurt more than just her hand. "Storm, calm down."

"Don't tell me to calm down, you dick licker!" She screamed, fighting me anew. "You made me think I was crazy! Those fucking men have been lurking for weeks and I thought I belonged in a nuthouse, but it was all because of you!" Her voice was manic as she swung around, kicking and fighting me for every inch of space she could make, but she wouldn't get away. "I thought I was going insane, and it's all your fault!"

"Shh, Storm. Just calm down for a second and we can talk."

"I don't want to talk to you!" Her voice broke and then her teeth bit into my forearm, instantly breaking through the skin as she held nothing back in her attempt to gain her freedom from me. "I want to hurt you!"

"Then hurt me." I growled as blood ran down my arm. Gently as I could, swept her legs and pulled her down onto my lap on the floor, twisting my legs over hers so she was sitting on her ass with me wrapped around her like a cobra. "Here." I held my other arm out and her teeth sank into it just like the first when she realized she couldn't move anything else to fight me with. When she broke through the skin, she spit my blood out and hissed in anger, but didn't go back in for another bite. She huffed and I could feel her heart racing under my arm across her chest, but she remained silent finally. "I'm sorry."

It wasn't like those words would do any good, but they needed to be said.

"I'm angry." She sneered and shook against my arms like she hoped I had loosened them up since she stopped fighting the last time. "Really fucking angry, Psycho."

"I know." I held my arm out and eyed the puncture wounds, "You have every right to be. But above all of that, you need to calm down for the sake of the baby."

"Fuck you." She hissed, but followed it up with a deep breath. A long stretch of silence came after that, and I let it linger as she obviously tried to collect herself. "Who are they?"

"Guards." I replied honestly, "To protect you when I'm gone."

"To keep me imprisoned, you mean." Liv shook her head, "Let me go. I want to get off the floor."

"No," I kissed her temple, "But I will let go of your arms if you promise not to go for my eyes."

She sneered under her breath, something that sounded a lot like *fuck around and find out,* but didn't go right for my vitals when I loosened my hold on her wrists. "Why didn't you tell me about them?"

"Because I knew it'd upset you."

"And finding an armed militiaman in the hall wasn't upsetting? I thought he was a hit man here to kill me! Kind of how I did when I saw one on the rooftop last week, Maddox. I deserve to know who's existing around me!"

"Storm, I already told you that you were right. You won't hear me counter your claims on it. But you need to lower your heart rate and relax so you don't go into labor."

"I'm fine. But I want to get off the floor."

"Why is being off the floor so important to you?" I argued, annoyed with her repeated request when she wouldn't do the first thing I asked of her.

"Because!" She fought anew, elbowing me in the chest and cried out when I recaptured her flailing limbs. "Because it reminds me of that fucking room!"

My mind raced to catch up to her, and when it did, my heart sank. "The storeroom." The place I found Liv months ago, cold, beaten and unconscious, with nothing around her but the cold concrete floor.

"I want to get up!"

Getting onto my feet, I lifted her into my arms and off the cold floor, carrying her across the room to her favorite spot on the couch. As soon as she was within reach of it, Liv grabbed her prized blanket and covered herself from nose to toes, glaring at me over the hem.

I sat on the coffee table in front of her and slid my hands under the blanket to cover her bare, cold feet. She didn't immediately kick my teeth in, so I tightened my hands on them and gentled my voice. "Tell me what you're feeling."

"Anger—" She snapped instantly but pursed her lips when I glared at her.

"We know you're boiling with rage aimed in my direction, Storm. Tell me something I don't know. Tell me about that room."

She huffed and held my gaze before blinking and staring off at a spot on the wall as she whispered her trauma out loud, "There was no heat." Shivers wracked her body like she could feel the cold even now. "The concrete floor had a way of making the cold seep into my bones until I didn't think I'd ever warm up."

"That's why you're always bundled up now." I replied, feeling foolish for thinking it was simply a comfort thing. It was a trauma response, and I had triggered one with my lack of tact. "How long did Damon have you there?"

She shook her head sadly, "I don't know. Days. Maybe a week. He pulled me out when it served him to, but I lost track of the time." Her voice died off, and I knew what she meant. The only time he took her from the room was when he used her body for his pleasure.

"Do you know who his silent partner is?" I asked, breaking my vow not to involve her in Damon's death. "He seems to be the missing link to finding Damon."

She slowly shook her head, "As far as I know, he's kind of a myth. I only ever heard whispers about him. Some good, very little bad."

"What does that mean?"

Shrugging, she burrowed deeper into the blanket. "I never heard his name, which I think was Damon's plan. But the girls made up a nickname for him." She rolled her eyes, "They called him The Duke.

Something about him being royal blood or something. Either way, they never had much in the way of bad things to say about him."

"He used girls from the Velvet Cage? And they talked nicely about them?" That made no sense.

"I wasn't privy to any actual information, but a few of the girls talked near me sometimes at the Hell Eaters Lounge before I was," She swallowed, "Blacklisted. Rumors said he didn't come to Boston often, once every few months, and when he came for a visit, he would always hire a girl for his stay. Usually a few days at a time."

"Was that normal?"

"For girls to take multi-day jobs? No. Damon always said girls made more per night than they did multiple nights lumped into one. But I guess for his money man, he had no choice but to allow it. What was weird, though, was some girls lined up for the chance to spend a few days with him. And they always looked so—" She shrugged and grimaced, "refreshed when they got back. I don't know if that's the right word, but they sure looked better than they usually did after a job, especially one that lasted a few days. And he paid well. Very well."

"Hmm." I hummed, processing her info. "When was the last time he visited?"

"A few months before I got blown in," She tilted her head to the side, "My guess is he would have been due for a visit right around the time shit hit the fan. Why? Do you think he's coming back sometime soon or something?"

"I think our best chance of finding out who he is, or even getting hands on him, is here when he visits. But enough talking about all of that—"

"You really don't get it, do you?" She sighed, "In the last two minutes, I've felt more useful than in the last two months, all combined. I need this, Madd. I need to be valuable."

"I don't want you in it, though." I pleaded, begging her to under-stand my point, "The memories of what happened to you there aren't worth reawakening just so we can have some inside knowledge. We'll get it another way."

Liv covered my hand with hers under the blanket and squeezed it. "Knowing that Damon Kirst is dead before I give birth to this baby will give me peace. If he's still alive, I won't be able to breathe. So let me help. Let me be involved in my revenge."

She was right; I knew that. If Damon was still alive when our baby was born, she'd never relax. Liv needed that last piece of the puzzle put to rest before our baby was truly at risk.

"Fine." I got on my knees at her feet, and she wrapped her legs around my back, sitting up closer to me. "If you think it's what you need to do, then you can help."

"No more secrets?" She confirmed, "No more armed men peeping through the windows from neighboring rooftops or lurking in the hallways?"

"No more secrets." I agreed, "But the guards stay put. I won't waiver on that."

She rolled her eyes and slid to the edge of the couch. Instantly, I laid a kiss on her belly and sat back up. "I'm sorry I threw a mug at you." A blush covered her face as she played with the whiskers in my beard. "And called you names. And bit you—twice."

"Three mugs." I corrected her, "And I didn't know your mouth knew such filth."

She chuckled lightly and wrapped her arms around my neck, meet-ing my stare. In a breathy, seductive voice, she cooed, "Oh, the filthy things I could do with this mouth for you, Psycho."

I gazed down at her lush tits in her tight shirt and watched as her nipples pebbled up from just my eyes on them and licked my lips.

"Had I known that letting you in would have this effect on you, I may have done it sooner."

"Liar," she giggled and pulled the hem of her shirt up, slowly revealing her body to me as she took it off, keeping the blanket around her shoulders. "But you can take me to bed and trick me into thinking so anyway."

CHAPTER 21 - OLIVIA

THE LINE WALKERS

Hushed whispers woke me up, and I rolled over in a panic to find Maddox's side of the bed empty. My heart raced in my chest as I imagined the voices coming from Damon or someone hired by him to find me. The anxiety was enough to choke the breath from my lungs as I swung my legs out over the bedside.

Maddox had been with me when I fell asleep, but he was gone, and I didn't know where he was.

But I'd be damned if I just laid in bed and hid in fear, so I grabbed my bathrobe and tied it over my body and silently walked on tiptoes to the bedroom door. I held my breath and peeked out around the doorway towards the living space and saw a soft glow lighting up the space from the front door. Pulling back into the bedroom, I let my breath out and chewed on my bottom lip in contemplation.

More than likely, it was Maddox.

But there was a real possibility that it wasn't.

What to do, what to do?

One of the voices rose loud enough that I could make out the words being whisper screamed at each other, and my heart sank in my chest when I realized it was a female's. "Why are you even bothering to get involved, Ren?" The feminine voice hissed, "We both know you don't want to be tied down. You don't want a family."

I finally recognized Maddox's voice snap back at the woman, but I couldn't make out what he was saying.

My stomach rolled as her words circled around in my head, there was no doubt I was the subject of the conversation.

Stupid me, always a glutton for punishment, I tiptoed out into the hallway, desperate to hear more. I also was desperate to see the woman speaking with my own eyes.

The female spoke again as I got to the end of the hallway and took a deep breath before peeking my head around the corner enough to just see the front door. She was tall and had the body of a swimsuit model, skinny waist, mile long legs, complimented with a nice ass and big tits. Great. She wore black leggings that hugged her body like a second skin and a gray long sleeve shirt that was fitted and cut deep over her breasts. Was she one of the guards that Maddox had hired? A female? She carried weapons like a guard.

She spoke again, "I just don't want to see you trapped in something you didn't think through completely, Ren." She brought her hand up and laid on Maddox's naked chest like she was saying something heartfelt in the middle of the night to a man that wasn't hers. He wasn't, was he? "You know how much I care about you."

Jesus fuck. I had been so pre-occupied with studying the woman I didn't even realize that Maddox stood in the middle of the hallway in only a pair of black boxer briefs, that showed off exactly what he was packing south of the belt.

And she was touching him.

And he was letting her.

Jealousy thundered deep in my gut as I watched him patting her hand, still pressed to his bare chest with his own before removing it.

"I'm sure." He replied in a whisper. "I appreciate your concern, though, Mack."

Even across the room eaves dropping I could hear the lack of conviction in his voice when he said, *I'm sure*. What I did hear in his voice, though, was affection, but only when he told her he appreciated her concern.

He moved back toward the door, and I hurriedly ran back down the hallway to the bedroom as the front door clicked shut.

I tossed my robe off and jumped back in bed, trying like hell to calm my breathing, but unfortunately, I was so fucking pregnant I got winded just talking these days. I turned away from his side of the bed and pulled the blankets up over me, hoping they'd cover up my gasps as my mind spun in a million different directions.

Did he regret getting 'tied down' with me?

Who was the woman and why was he so openly comfortable with her when with literally everyone else, even Dane, he was a dark mime who hardly even spoke if he didn't have to.

What the fuck was I doing?

I bit my knuckle when I heard his soft footsteps come up to the bed before I felt his weight slide back into his side.

I prayed he wouldn't come up behind me and hold me, or my racing heart and tense body would give me away. Yet, when he stayed on his side of the bed, choosing not to cuddle with me like he normally would, my heart sank a little further in my chest.

Maybe she was right after all. Maybe Mack knew Maddox better than I did.

THE LINE WALKERS

I t took me hours to fall asleep again, and when I woke up the next time, Maddox was gone from the apartment completely.

I tried to tell myself that it wasn't a sign, but pregnancy hormones were a bitch on a good day and today, they were wreaking havoc on my mind.

So I had sent an SOS text to Peyton, asking her to pick me up and take me to Hartington for the day to take a deep breath. Of course, there was a note about keeping it between the two of us.

And exactly one hour later, Peyton walked through the front door with a concerned, gentle smile on her face.

And a Starbucks cookie the size of her head.

The day was already improving.

"Come on," She wrapped her arm around me, ignoring the oversized purse I carried with me stuffed with a change of clothes just in case, and led us out to the hallway. "Let's go have a girls' day."

I had never left the building with Peyton before, and in a way, I didn't know if I was even *allowed* to. But I had to try.

I needed to take a deep breath and get my head on straight, and I couldn't do it surrounded by everything Maddox and this baby. I just needed to focus on myself for half a second, so I could think.

As we reached the elevator, she asked, "So, what kind of food are we getting on our way back?" However, I noticed her pressing the elevator code slowly and ostentatiously, then making eye contact with me before looking at the small camera in the room's corner and continuing the conversation. "Mexican? Italian? Greek?"

"Uh," I stammered, realizing what she was doing and memorized the six number code she used as I entered the elevator. "Italian?" Shaking my head to focus, "Cheesy Alfredo sounds great."

"Done," She went on as we rode the elevator down, both of us once again aware of the security camera in the elevator staring at us like a beady little eye of control. "We'll order from Marco's and pick it up on the way." At the bottom of the elevator, there was another code to enter to make the doors open up again, and as before, she punched a separate six-digit code in, number by number, like she was trying to memorize it herself. And I memorized it in turn.

"Perfect." I replied calmly as the doors opened up, revealing her car waiting in the loading zone, not even parked in a spot. Like she was planning a fast getaway.

Getting into the passenger seat, I tossed my bag in the back seat and wrung my hands together in my lap, struck by how eerily similar my escape was to the night they took me to Damon's jail cell for my involvement in his scheme.

My heart raced, my stomach rolled, and my hands sweated as Peyton locked the doors to her top-of-the-line car and drove off through the underground garage. I half expected someone to stop us, one of the guards perhaps that I now knew lurked in the darkness. Did they not intervene because Peyton made it look so normal and casual?

But as we crossed through the final gate at the end of the building and out onto the crowded street, I caught a face staring at me from the shadows.

Mack.

She stood against the exterior wall, with a full uniform of weapons strapped to her and a smug smirk on her face as she watched us leave. Was she happy I was leaving so she could have Maddox to herself? Or was she excited by the idea of getting me in trouble with him and proving I was too much trouble in the end?

CHAPTER 22 - OLIVIA

THE LINE WALKERS

"Alright, lay it on me." Peyton mumbled, wiping pasta sauce from her face with her last mouthful. To my surprise, she held back from asking throughout the drive to Hartington and during our meal.

Dane wasn't home, probably out somewhere with Maddox, but I still felt stupid saying any of my thoughts out loud.

"It's probably just pregnancy brain." I brushed it off, washing down the last of my meal with water and hoping she'd let me just rest.

"Well, tell me what happened, and I'll help you figure it out." She tried again, "Because I can see through your tough girl exterior, Livvy. And I can tell you're hurting." When she put her hand on mine, I pulled away. "Let me in."

"I'll cry if you're nice to me." I took a deep breath, steeling my spine against the emotions trying to take over my body. "And I hate crying, so don't do that."

"Okay," Peyton tried another tactic. "Tell me what the fuck that limp dick mother fucker did to my baby sister, or I'll hunt him down and sick the post office lady on him."

I simply raised one eyebrow at her from across the table. "The post office lady?"

"She's terrifying. Even Dane won't walk in that building. And he's a fucking monster." She shrugged like that was all the answer I needed.

"Hmm." I hummed, "Who knew you were such a badass?" I deadpanned, and she broke character and smirked.

"Was I convincing?" Leaning forward on her elbows, Peyton gave me a silly smile. "Did I ever tell you about the time I tasered Dane? Well, twice now I've done it, actually."

I snorted and covered my face in absolute disbelief as she clucked her tongue like she'd save that story for another day.

After a long stretch of silence, I knew I owed her some explanation for my SOS text, so I ripped the band aid off and tried to make sense of all my thoughts and feelings. "I don't think Maddox wants a family after all."

Her brows knitted over her eyes in disbelief, "Did he say that to you?"

"No." I picked at a string on the placemat under my dish.

"Did he give you hints? Make you feel like that?"

"Well, no."

"Then how are you determining that then? I haven't seen even a second of hesitation in him this entire time."

"I did." Whispering, "Last night, when he was having a secret conversation with a woman in the hallway." Peyton's eyes bulged as I word vomited the story, "She was touching him, and he was letting her. She said she cared about him, and he said, *I know*. And that he appreciated it."

"Whore ass dead beat, who?" She stood up in a flurry and stared at me. "You're joking."

I shook my head sadly, realizing deep down that the whole situation seemed bad if she could get outraged in ten seconds flat. "I woke up in the middle of the night, alone, and heard whispers." Tears welled in my eyes as I stared at the placemat, shoulders slumped. "I thought Damon had found me and was there to—" I let out a shuddered breath. "But instead, I found Maddox in his underwear talking to some Swedish supermodel as she outright questioned why he'd want to be tied down to me. And he didn't tell her to—"

"To fuck all the way off?" She screeched in outrage. "He's such a standoffish guy, and he let her touch him?"

"Even touched her back." I replied, and then groaned. "And now I'm fucked in the head and I'm out of time because this baby is going to be here in like point two seconds flat and I don't know what I'm going to do." Hysterics bubbled up, and I hiccupped as despair tried to pull me under again.

"Shh," Peyton hushed as she pulled me to my feet and walked us over to her couch. We sat there, with her arms wrapped around me, and I just cried. For the first time in—forever, I just cried.

I didn't have any answers. I didn't have any plans.

I didn't even have a last name to give to my baby that was due soon. So, I cried.

And Peyton held me while I let it all out, even though I knew it wouldn't give me any answers when I finally wiped away the tears. But it felt good to just let it go in the moment.

"We can figure this out. You and me, Livvy." My sister's soothing voice and touch calmed me, the tears eventually subsided, but a heavy feeling of sadness settled over me.

"I thought I already did." I sighed, "I can't believe I thought Maddox was going to just step up and take care of something that wasn't his responsibility. That was stupid, P!" I hissed as anger replaced the sadness in me. "*We* don't do stupid. We're Everett's, and we always have a plan, and we always think three steps ahead, so we don't get into these situations. Ugh!" I cried out and huffed, forcing fresh air into my lungs as hysteria tried to take its place.

"Talk to him, Liv." She squeezed my hand, grounding me. "Because you're right, we are Everett's, and we take care of ourselves and sometimes that means facing things head on. If at the end of that conversation you don't feel convinced that he's in it for the long haul, then we'll reassess and make the moves necessary to give you the peace you so dearly deserve." My sister put her hand on my stomach and gently patted it, and on cue, my baby kicked back in greeting. "The peace that both of you deserve."

I took a deep breath again and laid my head on her shoulder. "Yeah."

Was I convinced I was going to speak to him about it? No.

Was I convinced that I was going to get to the bottom of who the hell the blonde bombshell was and why she was so touchy feely. Yes.

"Do you have a computer?" I peeked up at my sister as she raised an eyebrow. "One that isn't Dane's?"

"There's one in my office." She squinted, "But he programmed it."

"Damn." Mumbling, I already knew that the second I tried to do what I needed to on that computer, Dane would be notified.

"But I have the old laptop I used before I moved in here." She smirked with a mischievous glint in her eye. "I haven't turned it on in over a year, but I'm sure it will get the job done. Whatever the job is that you're thinking of doing, that is."

I grinned back and finally felt like I was in the driver's seat again for the first time in months. "Perfect."

CHAPTER 23 - MADDOX

A s soon as I opened the front door, I knew she wasn't home. "Storm!" I barked, flipping on lights as I walked through the living space and down the hall. "Olivia!"

The nursery, the guestroom and the primary bedroom were all dark and empty. My heart raced in my chest as I dialed Chris, the man on guard while I was gone today. Luckily, he answered on the first ring.

"Where is Liv?" I snapped in greeting.

"With her sister." He replied. "They left this morning."

"And you didn't think to tell me?" I roared back, walking back through the apartment on my way to my truck.

"Mack was on duty and reported it to me when I took over a few hours ago. She should have communicated that with you."

"Got it." I hung up on him and dialed Liv's phone in the next breath, but as I shut the door behind me, I heard her ring tone in the other room. "God damnit."

I dialed Dane's number next. He had been with me most of the day, but never said anything about Liv and Peyton being together, which meant he didn't know either.

"Yeah." He answered.

"Liv there?" I punched the buttons in the elevator, pulling my truck keys out.

"Bingo." He replied, and I heard Peyton's melodic laugh in the background like he was walking away.

"She okay?"

"I mean," He hesitated as I got to my truck, "There are ice cream containers in my trash and they're watching Hope Floats. What did you do?"

I rolled my eyes, not a hundred percent sure what Hope Floats was or why that paired with ice cream would mean I did anything wrong. I found Liv eating ice cream at four am the other morning when I got home late. And she had tossed it to the side and rode my cock like a pro the second I walked in the room. "I'm on my way."

"What did you do?" He repeated, and my nerves jarred against each other as my hand tightened around my phone. "I don't know."

"Well, I recommend you spend the drive reflecting on whatever happened the last day or two. Because by the looks of it, guard dog Peyton is on duty and you're not going to be welcome if you don't prepare before you get here."

"Got it." I snapped and hung up as the actual object of my anger stepped into the garage from the private entrance, almost as if my mood summoned her.

"Hey, Ren." Mack smiled at me as she walked toward me. "Heading out again, didn't you just get home?"

"Why wasn't I notified that Olivia left today?"

She raised one brow at me, but I could tell my tone did not surprise her. "Peyton Bryce is on the approved list of visitors." Her response was an answer, but not the answer to my question.

"Why wasn't I notified she left?" I repeated with a lethal tone in my voice as the door opened again, and Chris walked out with two other guards who were on perimeter duty today.

She shrugged nonchalantly, crossing her arms over her chest, "I didn't think—"

"It's not your job to think." I barked, "Your job is to protect her and notify me immediately of anything that goes on when I'm not here!"

"Why didn't she notify you?" She cocked her head to the side, "Trouble in paradise, Ren?"

"Fuck you!" I sneered as the other guards got near, turning my attention to them. "If Liv leaves this building, I am notified immediately. Got it?"

"Got it." Chris replied with a nod, eyeing Mack.

"What's the big deal, Ren?" Mack put her hand on my arm, and I shook her off with a growl.

"It's your fucking job, that's what! You were hired to do a job and you're to do it the way I tell you to, or you can get the fuck out. Period. That's how it goes!"

"We got it." Chris stepped in again, "It won't happen again."

I glared at Mack again as I ripped open my truck door and got in. When I got to Liv, I was going to redden her ass for leaving like she did.

And then I was going to get to the bottom of why she did it in the first place.

THE LINE WALKERS

I tried using the drive to calm down, but it only took about ten minutes in the truck to realize that my anger wasn't anger at all, but fear.

Fear of coming home and finding Liv gone.

Fear of not knowing where she was at that very moment.

Fear of not knowing what made her leave without telling me in the first place.

Fear.

A fucking foreign four-letter word for me.

I feared nothing before I met Liv, yet now, I was nearly crippled with it when I thought of all the ways the world could harm her.

And our baby.

Jesus, fuck. The world was cruel to grown adults, let alone, defenseless little babies.

By the time I walked in Dane's front door, I was nearly vibrating with the need to wrap Storm up into my arms and smother her with my love. But when I found her, sitting on the floor of Peyton's closet surrounded by a massive pile of ball gowns, laughing her ass off, as P strutted around in a bright pink fluff ball, I paused.

Dane stood at my side, leaning his shoulder into the door frame with a huff. "They've been at this for a while now." Peyton did some Rockette's style high kick and Liv cackled, clapping her hands as tears of laughter rolled down her cheeks. "What the fuck did you do, man?" He hissed.

"I. Don't. Know."

"Well, I'm no expert, but in the last few years being with P, I've learned two things." He turned to look at me as Liv picked up a lime green frock and tossed it at P, demanding she put that one on next. "One," he lifted one finger, "Everett women are notorious for keeping their feelings to themselves, but when they're mad, they like to yell." He rounded his eyes and raised his eyebrows, "But two, is that when they go silent, they're past the point of mad and have hit a full raging inferno inside and there's only two ways to put the fire out." Dane dropped his hands and looked back over at the girls, "Groveling and sex. But the sex can't be just normal sex, it must be one hundred and fifty percent all about her sex."

"Isn't that the only kind of sex to have?" I deadpanned at him, and he pursed his lips and rolled his eyes.

"You *would* be a pleasure Dom."

Liv heard him and looked over her shoulder, finally aware of my presence in the room and her smile faded as did her giggles.

Something in my chest ached, knowing whatever happened today was my fault.

"Hi." I tried, feeling like I was balancing on a tiny piece of ice in the middle of the freezing cold ocean. One small move in the wrong direction and I was a fucking goner.

"Hi." She replied, looking back over at P who in her own right glared at me. "Help me up, Pey."

It felt incredibly unnatural to watch Peyton help Liv to her feet as I stood by idly, but it was obvious that she didn't want me to touch her. Which fucking hurt.

Dane and Peyton lingered, adding to the unnatural feeling between us as Liv turned to face me. I tried to break the ice, "Can we talk?"

She didn't answer right away but looked at the clock on the wall and sighed, "It's getting late," my heart sank into my gut as she glanced back up at me. Was she kicking me out? "Are you going home or back to *work*?"

The tone in her voice when she said work grated my nerves even further.

"We're going home." I replied, holding her stare, almost hoping she would challenge me on it.

"Okay." She stated flippantly and gave her attention back to her sister. "Thanks for today."

"Any time." Peyton replied firmly and then grabbed a large tote bag off the floor. "Don't forget your bag."

I eyed the change of clothes and toiletries sat on top of the bag, like she wasn't planning on coming home with me originally. Silently, we both walked out of Hartington, and even though she let me help her up into the truck, Liv didn't speak.

Liv was chatty on a normal day, referencing movies or shows I knew nothing about, commenting on random bits and thoughts she had and making small talk constantly.

But as I drove back down the long driveway, she stared out ahead of us with her hands resting on her belly, rubbing them back and forth over it.

I didn't know how to break the silence, but with each passing second, the rift felt bigger, like it was growing and making my skin boil under the pressure of breaking it.

Opening my mouth to blurt out something stupid, she beat me to it with an audible intake of breath as she leaned to the side.

"What?" I looked over at her as her brows pinched together in the middle. "What's wrong?"

"Just a twinge." She whispered like she couldn't let her breath out normally while she pushed on a part of her stomach. "I think he's pushing on my spleen."

She had taken to calling the baby he or she intermittently like she was trying them on for size, even though she still refused to open the envelope and find out what she was carrying for sure.

"Can I?" I held my hand out, hovering over her stomach as I drove. I couldn't remember the last time I asked to touch her and our baby, but at that moment, it felt appropriate.

She guided my hand onto her bump where the pain was coming from and instantly the baby flipped and rolled around, pressing against my palm. "I think I ate too much ice cream and now he has a sugar high."

Glancing over at her as I drove down the road, a soft smile graced her lips as she peeked over at me. "Maybe." I held my hand against her belly even after she dropped hers because I ached for the connection. "Tell me what I did wrong, Liv."

She peeked over at me and sighed, readjusting herself in her seat, dislodging my hand. "You didn't do anything, Madd."

"Then why did you leave today without telling me? Why didn't you take your phone?" I looked over at her as she stared up at me. "And why did you take clothes with you when you left?"

She swallowed and looked back out the windshield, chewing on her bottom lip before finally speaking. "I'm lonely."

I scowled into the darkness, "Lonely?"

Out of my peripheral vision, I noticed her shrug, "Yeah, I spend a lot of time alone, Maddox. It tends to make people lonely. Especially people like me."

"What does that mean? People like you?"

"People who like to be alone but want people around at the same time. We get lonely in the solitude we create around ourselves."

"You sound like Dane." I deadpanned as I tried to mull it all over. "But I guess that makes sense. It's not like I leave because I want to—I'm working."

"I know." She agreed calmly, "Doesn't mean the silence doesn't get to me at times, though. Therefore, I called P and had a girls' day."

I tapped my thumb against the steering wheel in contemplation as we drove through the wilderness. "Were you mad at me when you left?"

She was silent for a second or two longer than I would have hoped, giving me my answer.

"Yes." She admitted, "But I think most of it was just in my head, made up by the silence and the distance between us when I went to bed and when I woke up again."

She was right.

I was always gone.

"I'm sorry."

"Don't." She replied instantly. "It's part of our arrangement. I knew that."

Why did her tone sound so accepting and so dismissive in the same breath?

Riding in silence the rest of the way back to our building, I replayed everything that had happened since the first day I met Liv, rescuing her from the Hell Eater's Lounge and bringing her home with me.

Every single day since then, she had been told when, where, and how she could live. Sure, it was for her own protection, but the facts remained the same.

She was at our mercy, a woman who, before the Velvet Cage, had been independent and living on her own for years.

Liv was unhappy, even if she was trying to pretend, she wasn't. And that was my fault.

But no more.

CHAPTER 24 – OLIVIA

THE LINE WALKERS

T here was something incredibly innocent and inviting to that feeling of bliss when you're in between awake and asleep, in that space where rules don't matter and all that exists is the sensations.

The pleasure. The delight. The lack of inhibitions or worries to cloud those pure sensations for what they are.

Good.

God, it felt so fucking good to orgasm in that in between space with darkness blanketing you from the world and cocooning you in safety.

"Yes." I moaned, giving myself over to the ecstasy, uncaring of the implications of it.

"Come for me again, Storm." Maddox's deep voice echoed through my haze as I pinpointed the pleasure and its source as his thick cock slid into my body again.

"Make me." Moaning, I arched my back and pressed into his chest as he thrust again. I was on my side in bed, and he was behind me, with my leg pulled up and supported by his big hand under my knee so he could fuck me.

He changed the angle of his hips and pushed in deeper with the next thrust, his grin against my neck. He had been just giving me the tip before, like he was enjoying the fact that I was on the precipice of sleep while he fucked me. But now that I was awake, he was giving it all to me.

Every fucking inch and I loved it.

Even if each second of consciousness returned the feelings from the day before, I'd take whatever he gave me. At the end of the day, if he regretted tying himself down to me, that didn't mean I regretted him for even a second.

I was so pathetically in love with the dark psychotic man, I'd take the bad for even a moment of good. And right now, with each push and pull of his hips, it was so fucking good.

"I love you, Storm." He growled, reaching between my thighs to play with my clit as I clawed at him for more. "I can't breathe when you're away. I won't. Not anymore."

"Maddox." I hissed, as his words gave my stupid, helpless heart hope. "Don't."

"I mean it." He bit my shoulder with enough strength to break the skin and I cried out as the pain took me closer to orgasm again. "I know what you said yesterday, but I don't believe you." Thrusting deeper as he rolled my clit between his fingers and sucked on my neck, marking me. "I fucked up, somehow, but I'm here and I'm going to make it right, Storm. I promise. Just let me make it right."

"Fuck!" I screamed, turning my face and biting his arm in response to his own markings, leaving mine in his skin again.

"I'm done leaving you. I'm here. I'm right fucking here, Storm."

"You don't want to be." I screwed my eyes shut and buried my face in the blankets as I admitted it out loud. "You don't want to be tied down."

He growled so powerfully I felt it in my chest as he rolled us over until I was on my knees with my upper body pressed against his chest, sitting on his thighs as he kept lazily fucking me.

"You misunderstand my devotion to you, Olivia." Something about the way he used my full name instead of the nicknames for me made it more powerful. "I love you."

"I heard her—" I cried out, "I heard her question everything because you never wanted this."

"I never imagined myself wanting a family before I met you." *Thrust.* "I never imagined myself in love with someone before I met you." *Thrust.* "I never imagined how it would feel like I couldn't exist without another person by my side before I met you. But now," *Thrust.* "Now I'm fucking addicted to you and I need you more than you'll ever know, Storm."

"Maddox." I sobbed as another orgasm crashed over me and I moaned in a delirious tone for him as it washed over me. "I need you. I love you."

"Good." He slowed his thrusts and then pulled out of me, lowering us both back to the bed and wrapping himself around me, covering every inch of my skin with his. I ended up with my head on his chest and his rock-hard cock was standing erect before he pulled the blankets over us to cover himself.

"You didn't come." I looked up at his face in the darkness, in confusion. "Why?"

"Because you still don't believe me. Because of words you heard a jaded woman speak. And until I can prove myself to you, I won't find pleasure in your body. Not until your heart knows my truth, Storm."

I lowered my gaze again, feeling so torn inside my heart about everything my head was thinking. "That feels like a punishment toward me."

"It's not." He kissed my temple and tightened his arms around me. "But I can't stomach the thought of orgasming until you feel secure and safe in my love. So now I'll work on proving myself to you. After you get more sleep."

"You woke me up in the first place." I murmured as his words swam in my brain.

"I know." He chuckled humorlessly against my hair as he stroked it. "Someone told me that there were only two ways to quiet the storm brewing in your mind, but I guess I chose wrong in my endeavor to apologize. Now I'll try the other way by using my words and love to prove it."

I relaxed into his hold, trying like hell to trust his words for face value and believe in him blindly. It wasn't like he'd ever done anything but show me exactly how honorable he was toward me.

But for some reason, the disconnect between my brain and my heart was just too strong. So I snuggled deeper into his arms and took comfort from his touch.

"I love you, Psycho." I whispered, tracing the lines of his muscles over his stomach as my eyelids grew heavy. Because I trusted my words, even if I couldn't trust his.

"I love you so much more, Storm."

CHAPTER 25 - MADDOX

S he looked at me.

    I looked at her.

She looked away.

I smirked and shook my head, gazing back at the directions on the back of the package in my hands. Feeling her eyes on me again, I glanced back up and found her staring at me over the top of her book from the other side of the room.

I lifted my head fully, staring back at her.

She looked away. Again. This time, she huffed as she did it.

I smirked again.

My plan was either going to go off without a hitch and make her fall even more in love with me, or Storm was going to kill me with a blunt butter knife in my sleep.

It was anyone's guess which direction it would go, to be honest.

Four days ago, she ran away to Hartington Estate to get space from me after she overheard Mack trying to tell me what I did or didn't want in the middle of the night.

And every single second since I got her back home that night, I was just within reach of her.

No more late-night hunts. No more long hours in front of a computer working to find Damon or his mysterious money man. And sure as fuck, no more unattended Storm left to entertain herself in my absence.

No, I was making sure she was well and entertained with me under foot twenty-four seven.

Which was why I wasn't sure if she was loving it or plotting my death as she once again looked over the top of her book at me.

She looked at me.

I looked at her.

She looked away.

This time, she slammed her book shut and grumbled at me, sending daggers my way as she tossed her book down on the table next to her. "You're insufferable, you know that, right?"

I shrugged, ripping the package open as I decided to just give the foot peel mask thingy that Peyton had delivered a shot in the dark.

How hard could it be to put a Ziplock on a foot and find something to entertain her for an hour while her toes marinated in it?

Ideas had been shooting through my mind since I read the line on the directions that said, 'Do not walk with bags on, as they are tripping hazards.'

Which meant once they were on, she'd be at my mercy.

Again.

Just like she was in the shower this morning when I held her body up and made her come with the handheld wand. And before that when I laid her out on the kitchen table and slowly fed her my cock until she came four times before I fed her the eggs I made her. Or last night when I bent her over on the couch, propping her up on the back of it so her stomach was free, and ate her from behind for an hour straight.

Storm was cynical and doubted everything she dared to believe in suddenly, simply because of Mack's words and her wild hormones. But what she couldn't deny was how fucking right it felt when I touched her.

Or how badly her body ached to give in to me when I offered her pleasure that her mind tried to pretend she didn't want. I knew her better than that.

"Do you know what else I am?" I carried the slime filled bags over to her as she squinted her eyes at me. Unbeknownst to her, I had filled both pockets of my sweatpants with things to make the next hour of her immobilization much more fun. Lowering myself to my knees in front of where she sat, bundled up in her blanket, in the reading chair. "I'm also incredibly prize motivated." I pulled her blanket up, revealing her bare feet and legs, but tucked it around her knees, giving off the illusion that everything still under that fluffy blanket was safe from me. Wrong. But she didn't know that yet.

"You're psychotic." She deadpanned like I was supposed to be repulsed by her words. In reality, they made my cock hard.

Rock, fucking hard, thanks to the hardcore edging I'd been doing to myself for the last four days.

Even though I had fucked her more than a dozen times, I hadn't come once.

Not once had I given into the insane urge to fill her body up or coat it with my release as she begged me to repeatedly.

But I was losing my hold on that control, because I was only a man, and Storm's body was heaven. And when she stuck her bottom lip out and begged me with sweet conviction to come deep inside of her, she made a credible argument.

I'd fill her up continually when her last bit of doubt in me had washed away from her mind. When she no longer expected me to walk away from her, or at the very least, feel obligated to stay, I'd give her whatever she wanted.

Until then, I'd keep proving to her just how dedicated I was to my mission.

"Do you want to know what prize I'm after this time?" I asked, as I lifted her bare foot up and bared my teeth, gently nipping the top of her big toe. Did I have a foot fetish? I didn't know. But what I did know was if she wanted me to, I'd suck her toes and come all over them. It didn't matter how she let me touch her, I just had to.

"I'm afraid to ask." She speculated.

"Mmh," I hummed, tilting my head to the side and kissing my way down the inside of her arch before running my tongue up it. Nope, pretty sure I had a foot fetish if they were her feet. And by the way her lips parted, and she shifted in her seat, she wasn't unaffected by it either. "I think that's a lie."

She licked her lips when I dragged my teeth over the arch of her foot, careful not to put too much pressure on the sensitive nerves there but enough to draw a small gasp from her lips before kissing my way up and sucking her toe into my mouth.

Yep, I had a Storm fetish.

"Madd." She moaned, letting her eyelids flutter closed for half a second before snapping them back open like she didn't want to give in to the pleasure I was teasing at.

"Yes, Darling?" I joked, lowering her foot and sliding the bag up over it, peeling the tape, backing off and securing it.

"You're driving me nuts."

"I know." I admitted, picking up her other foot and mirroring the same teasing touches on that one as she melted further into the chair until I was securing the second bag into place. "Do you ache for me?"

"You know I do." She hissed, wiggling her feet around in the bags on the floor, testing out their slipperiness. "Why tease me and then ruin it with these?"

"Oh, these won't ruin it, baby." I slid my hands back up her calves and under the blanket to her thighs as she stared at me. "Do you want me to touch you?"

"You know I do." She repeated, "But you won't give me what I really want."

"My come?" I questioned, pushing the blanket up higher, revealing the sweet little cotton panties she wore under one of my shirts and nothing else. It wasn't as if she had much use for clothes as many times as I'd taken them off her the last few days. "Is that what you want? You want me to come deep inside of you, fill you up and brand your body from the inside?"

"Fuck." She tipped her head back again like she was fighting for control. "Yes, you fucking psychopath, that's what I want."

"Mmh," I pulled the blanket apart and hooked my fingers under the band of her panties, "Do you trust me yet?" She opened her mouth, no doubt calling me another sarcastic name, but I cut her off. "Don't lie to me, Storm. We both know I can tell."

She screeched in annoyance, giving me the answer she hated to admit. No, she didn't fully trust me yet.

I moved on with my original plan. "Fine."

"Maddox." Her pouty lips puckered as I gently pulled her hips to the edge of the chair before pushing her shoulders back into the cushion. "What's your plan here, Psycho?"

"Tsk, tsk." I chided, slipping my fingers under the hem of her panties again and ripping them to pieces before pushing her legs wide, revealing to me what I already knew I'd find. "A serial killer never tells his victims his plan before he does it."

As I hooked her legs over the arm of the chair, keeping them open, her tight little hole clenched and released more wetness.

"That's a lie." She rocked forward as I watched, enticing me as best she could without openly begging me. "A lot of serial killers hold their victim's hostage to play with their minds before they kill them. They even sometimes eat parts of them before they're dead."

I paused, raising my eyebrow at her in challenge, "Why did my dick just get harder?"

She licked her lips and opened her blanket, revealing her upper body to me as she shimmied out of my shirt. "Because you're insane, and me talking about insane things makes you feel right at home."

"Hmm." I hummed, reaching up to palm her massive breasts and pinch both of her nipples. She was so incredibly responsive to nipple play she melted from the simple touches before I even really got down to business.

"Would you ever kill a person?" I questioned, lowering one hand and running my fingertips through her wetness as I kept playing with one nipple. "Would you tie them up and do depraved things to them if you felt they deserved it?"

"Yes." She moaned without hesitation. "Fuck yes."

"Yes, to killing someone, or yes to the sexual pleasure?" I pushed two fingers into her waiting hole, and she moaned louder, pushing against my hand.

"Both, baby." She hummed, "Depending on who it was and what they did, I'd let you fuck me while I did it and get both highs in one."

I scissored my fingers as a mischievous grin played across her lips. I wasn't sure how much of her words were the truth and how much of them were just bravado from the height of her sexual pleasure, but it didn't matter.

Someday, I would fuck her overtop of someone taking their last breath. It was just a matter of time, really. But until then, she'd have to settle for my current plans.

So, turning the topic to something I was more interested in, I pulled my wet fingers from her pussy and pushed them against her asshole. I didn't give her time to consent or prepare, instead, I just gave her my entire finger, deep into her ass as I toyed with her nipple.

"Fuck!" She screeched but rocked against my hand. I knew what she wanted, clit stimulation. But I wanted to drive her mad before I gave her the release she sought. "Again."

Leaving her hard nipple, I pulled a bottle of tingling lube from my pocket and squirted it directly onto her pussy, starting on her clit and pouring until it dripped down over her lips and down to my finger buried deep in her ass.

The lube would ruin the chair, but I didn't care. By the time I was done with her tonight, the carpet would be trash too.

And I'd happily buy her new ones, knowing that they were destroyed by her inability to tell me no.

"You want me to fuck your ass?" I questioned, as I withdrew my finger and pushed it back in, letting the lube soften the sensation.

"Yes." She nodded with a dreamy look in her eyes, "I think it's time, don't you?"

"I do." Agreeing, I pushed another finger into her ass, giving them a twirl and then withdrew them. Her wet little pussy clenched again. "But I think this cunt needs to be filled too, don't you?"

She moaned in wonder as I reached back into my pocket and pulled out a toy I ordered just for this occasion.

After how well she took to the suction toy, the last time we played with it, I got her another one, but this time it was a wearable kind that wouldn't get in the way as she wore it when I fucked her ass.

Or her pussy.

But she'd get that surprise another time.

Tonight was about claiming her somewhere new.

Taking something else from her until I owned everything.

I needed her to feel me everywhere.

With her pregnant belly in the way, she couldn't see what I was doing as I lubed up the toy and started sliding the flared, almost squid shaped head into her tight pussy, but she could feel it. "Oh yeah, Madd." She moaned, palming her breasts in my absence as she took what I gave her. What was the alternative? It wasn't like she could run away at the moment with her feet immobilized. "That's new."

"Turns out I have an obsession with buying you things." I stared down at her body as I pushed the curved part flush against her body until the suction cup landed against her clit. I flicked my eyes up to her as I turned it on at full speed and watched as they rolled back in her head. "Things that make you drool and your pussy throb." I was mesmerized, watching her whole body respond to the pleasure I was giving her.

Her brows pinched, her lips parted, her knuckles turned white where they gripped the chair, and her toes curled in the stupid little bag socks she was wearing.

"I'm coming." She gasped after a good thirty seconds of finger fucking her ass and using the sucker on her clit with the vibrator in her pussy. "Fuck, yes I'm coming!"

"I know." I praised, watching her pussy clench around the toy as her ass did the same around my finger. "I can feel you."

"Feel it with your cock." She gasped, "Because if you don't shut up and fuck my ass right now, I'm going to kick your teeth in and ride this toy while you're forced to just watch."

Biting my lip to keep from daring her to do just that, I pushed my pants down, freeing my cock. If she wanted it, she'd get it.

Coating my cock with lube, I lined up with her ass, and pulled my fingers out until they were barely still inside and used the pressure of them against the tight ring of muscles at the opening as I fed my cock in. "Jesus Storm, I wish you could see what I see."

"My ass swallowing your cock?" She hissed when I pulled my fingers out and pushed deep. She wasn't new to anal, but she was new to anal with me. And my thick cock was going to make her sweat before it made her come. "Christ."

"Mmh, I usually relate to his counterpart more." I joked, but my humor didn't land when I was completely inside her, because it was the most heavenly feeling in the world. "Okay, never mind. I see the pearly gates."

Liv moaned and dragged her nails down my stomach as I pulled out and pushed back in. "Don't leave me hanging again, Maddox." Her green eyes intently held mine as I slowed my thrusts and pushed the toy firmer against her clit. I knew she was close again, and I knew she wanted me to come with her. "I need you to orgasm."

"Do you trust me yet?" I questioned the same thing I had been asking her all week. Not that I was trying to blackmail her into suddenly believing me again, or even lying to me for the sake of pleasure.

I *needed* her to find her faith in me again in her own way, in her own time. But I couldn't give in until she did.

I had to hold out.

"Damnit, Maddox." She cried out, arching her back so far that her body changed angles, and my cock pressed upwards as I picked up speed. She started coming around my cock, strangling it with her ass as the toy continued to play with her clit and G-spot. My cock rubbed the toy against her G-spot in rhythm with my thrusts because her body pressed against mine. Her glorious chest flushed as she screamed, tipping her head back in ecstasy, as her pussy flooded around the toy.

"Fuck yes, squirt for me, Storm. Cover me with it, while I fuck your ass."

I slammed in hard as the proof of her massive orgasm coated my abs and thighs until she quivered beneath me, convulsing with the intensity of it all.

"Shh," I hummed, slowing my thrusts and then stopping all together as she gasped for breath, blinking at the ceiling like she was fighting to stay conscious. "Easy, Storm."

"Don't stop," She cried, clawing at me, even as tears ran down her temple into her hair. "I need you to come."

"Shh," I repeated, withdrawing from her body and pulling the toy free, so she was at peace as she recovered from the high. "Don't worry about that right now. Just ride the ecstasy, enjoy it."

She huffed but closed her eyes as I gently lowered her feet to the floor and laid gentle kisses all over her body, working my way from her thighs, over her sweet belly, to each breast and up her neck until I blanketed her body with it.

"I love you," she whispered, turning her face to kiss my lips. "But you just made me ruin my favorite chair."

I shrugged, "Carpet too." She pursed her lips and glared at me. "But the way I'm going to remember the first time you let me in your ass for the rest of my life will make it all worth it."

"You're vulgar."

I wrapped my hand around her throat and sat up, towering over her so she understood the power I had over her. "Would you prefer if my romance was cute and sweet instead of raw and scarring?" Her eyes flashed and her lips parted, "Would you rather I pretend to be something I'm not, Storm? To fit myself into the role of one of your movie boyfriends who romanticizes their flaws to hide them?"

"We both know I'm addicted to your flaws." She whispered as she twisted my thumb away from her neck, releasing my hold on it. The move surprised me and caught me off guard, but it shouldn't have. Storm had never been defenseless, but seeing her fire made my body flare to feel more of her power. However, instead of breaking my thumb with another twist, like she was more than justified to do, she sucked it deep into her mouth, hollowing out her cheeks with her eyes locked onto mine. "But this is where you stop using your flaws as smoke screens to keep me pleasured, but not satisfied."

My brows rose in indignation, "I don't satisfy you?"

Shaking her head slowly, she sat forward, reaching down to grip my cock and then lower to my tight, swollen balls. "Not the way I need to be. And it stops now. I don't orgasm again until you do."

"Storm." I warned, as she tried to top from the bottom.

"Shut up." She snapped, tightening her fingers around my balls and stroking them in a way that made my eyes cross and my cock weep. "We're done with this little experiment where you edge yourself until I tell you what you want to hear." She lowered her fingers and pressed them against my taint and I hissed, gripping the arms of the chair so hard the wood beneath the upholstery creaked. How the fuck did she top me after what I just did to her? "I trust you, Maddox. Okay?" She rubbed her fingers in a come-hither motion against my taint as I stood ram-rod straight and still for her. If I moved even an inch, I'd blow. "Just because I'm hormonal and angry that you let that woman near you to begin with, doesn't mean I don't trust you to my core. It means I have doubts because that's *my* fucking flaw in life. I doubt that you want this because you're the catch and I'm the baggage and no amount of watching you suffer is going to change the way my brain sees it."

"Storm." I whispered again, staring down at her. I wanted her to stop, and I wanted her to keep going all at the same time. Her words made sense, but there was no blood in my brain to process them the way they deserved to be as she continued massaging me the way she was.

"I. Trust. You." She repeated, and I screwed my eyes shut, trying to stay in control of myself. I was a disciplined man, but with her hands on me and her words circling around in my brain, I was losing my edge. "Do you hear me, Psycho? I trust you."

"Fuck!" I roared, tipping my head back as she pressed harder on that spot she was torturing me with as her other hand wrapped around the base of my cock as I erupted.

"That's it, good boy." She purred, milking my cock as I came all over her chest, coating her skin with it. "Come for me baby, don't stop. Give me what I want."

"Storm!" I hissed through clenched teeth as my head tipped forward when her teeth latched on my tight peck muscle, biting me and forcing my cock to spasm in a way it had never done before. "What the fuck!" I cried when another wave of ecstasy burned through my spine and more come shot free from the head of my cock in a second orgasm. "Stop." I begged, "Please."

She loosened her hold on my cock, gently teasing her fingers up the length of it as she scooped some of my come off her chest and returned her hand back to that spot behind my balls. The pads of her fingers were silky with my release, making them glide over the skin as my toes curled and my cock throbbed still hard in her hand.

"Tell me just how raw you feel now, Psycho." She stared up at me with defiance in her eyes as her silky fingers brushed against my asshole. Every fucking thing inside of me wanted to push her away and force her to stop. But I was entranced by the fire in her green eyes, as she dominated me and pushed me past boundaries I never once wavered on before her. "I want you to wear my scars so there's no doubt in the world who you belong to anymore, Madd. Be raw and scarred with me, baby. I love you. And I trust you." She pulled both of her hands away from my body, releasing me and the invisible hold they had on me as I sagged against the chair. "But if you ever let another woman touch you again, I'll cut her fucking touch from your skin."

I grinned down at her like a nutcase as her words excited the insane part of my psyche.

My pretty little Storm was perfect for me.

And I was going to enjoy watching her bloom into the menace she hid from the world.

CHAPTER 26 – OLIVIA

I eyed the envelope tacked onto the cork board for the fourth time since waking up. I walked in and out of the nursery all morning, putting away extra items we didn't need that Peyton insisted on buying, and tidying up the already spotless room.

Was I nesting?

Or was I just bored?

I was pretty sure it was impossible to be bored when all you wanted to do was sleep. It was probably nesting. Or maybe it was just going stir crazy since Maddox insisted on being up my ass for the last two-weeks straight.

Okay fine, I didn't hate the way he insisted on smothering me with his love since the whole blonde super model drama. In fact, the constant pampering and coddling didn't even rile me up like I would have thought. It was nice being—important to someone.

But I knew that with him being at home every day and night, the task of finding Damon was at a pause. And that was weighing on me.

"Madd." I called out as I came down the hallway, intent on sending him to work for the first time in weeks.

When I found him, though, kicking him out was the last thing on my mind. Wearing only a pair of athletic shorts, he hung from the metal beams in the living room, doing pull-ups like they required no effort at all.

He grinned when he saw me, but never broke his stride as he continued lifting himself up into the ceiling space and then lowering himself back down. "Yes?"

"How often do you work out?" I mused, leaning my head to the side when he did some fancy thing with his hands, turning himself around to show me his back as he lifted himself up again.

"Every day."

"When?" I countered, "And why have I never had the privilege to watch before?"

He chuckled and dropped onto his feet like an agile cat, hardly making a noise. "Because you usually have your eyes closed in ecstasy when I hit peak cardio heart rate." I rolled my eyes at him as he walked toward me with the grace of a predator circling around its prey. "Which I've been doing a whole lot of lately."

"Speaking of which," I forced my eyes away from the rivets of sweat sliding down his thick torso to the waistband of his shorts so I could focus on my task at hand. "I need a girl's break today."

He paused and his dark stare intensified, "Explain."

"You've been the perfect boyfriend, pampering me and keeping me entertained for the last few weeks, just like you said you would."

"But." He crossed his arms over his massive chest, and my mouth watered as his muscles bulged from the motion.

"But I miss P and want to spend the day with her."

"You have an OB appointment today, you can't."

"I can." I fired back, having already thought it through. "She's been begging to go with me to one so she's going to come over and pick me up, we'll go to my appointment and then grab lunch and come back." He didn't look convinced, so I tried to sweeten him up a little, "It will give you a few hours to go do whatever dark and dangerous boy stuff you've been neglecting so you can keep my eyes closed in ecstasy." I joked as I slid my hands over his enormous arms, up to his shoulders. "A few hours, max."

"I don't know—" His eyes squinted slightly, "I haven't missed an appointment yet."

"I know. But it's my last one before I start going every week and Peyton will absolutely gush for a chance to see the baby in real time on the ultrasound."

"My baby." He countered like a Tarzan replica.

"It will still be your baby, even if you don't go to the appointment for once." Still, he looked unmoved by the idea, so I went for the kill shot. Sliding my hands down his arms and to his abs, I teasingly dragged my nails over the ridged muscles until they found their way into the waistband of his shorts. His nostrils flared, but he didn't move a single muscle as I slowly pushed them down his legs. "You know you want to let me do it."

"What are we talking about at the moment?" He asked as I cupped his thickening cock, slowly stroking it as it hardened for me in my hand.

"Let me go out for a few hours, and I'll give you what you want most." Slowly sinking to my knees in the middle of the plush area rug as gracefully as possible until I was face first with his massive prize.

"I'm still wondering what *exactly* you're offering." He dropped his arms and instantly threaded his fingers into my hair as I laid wet kisses up the length of him. I didn't suck the man's dick, nearly as much as he deserved.

"How does a blow job sound for right now?" I laid the flat of my tongue against the base and licked my way up to the head, twirling around. "And tonight, when it's just the two of us again, we can open that envelope you stare at every single day."

Baiting him with the gender of our baby was probably cruel and over the top, but I really wanted an afternoon out so I could wash off some of the guilt I had from keeping him hostage.

"Storm." He growled, tightening his fingers in my hair. "Don't offer something you won't follow through with."

He wasn't talking about the blowy, considering I was actively sucking the head of his cock and tasting his pre-cum. And he was right, because I had been dragging my feet with the gender reveal out of fear.

But he desperately wanted to know what we were having, and I was out of excuses to wait.

"I promise." I looked up at him from under my lashes as I hollowed out my cheeks and took him deep. "Now be a good boy and fuck my throat like the big scary psycho we both know you are. And stop trying to hide it from me so you can go to work for a few hours."

"Fucking hell." He growled but thrust his hips forward, pushing himself down my throat as his hands went to the back of my head, holding me still.

There he was.

My beautifully dark and depraved psycho, who tried to pretend he was a good boy on the inside. The problem was, I only thought he was a good boy when he showed me the dangerous side of his nature.

So, I dug my nails into his bare thighs and stuck my tongue out flat as he pushed back in, forcing me to take him how he wanted.

"That's it, Storm." He growled, staring down at me darkly as he came unglued, "Beg me with your mouth, baby."

I hummed, I gagged, and I sucked him like a prize-winning whore in a brothel. I even did that tricky little reach around thing he hated to love where I massaged that spot behind his balls as he orgasmed, intensifying it while he choked me with come.

And when he finally pulled free of my mouth and stood over me, gasping for breath as his muscles flexed and pulled from the exertion, I licked my lips and moaned from the flavor of his pleasure on my tongue.

Sucking him off was no hardship at all, but I would not let him know that because it was my secret weapon against him.

A girl had to keep some secrets to herself, after all.

THE LINE WALKERS

"Tell me again how you managed lunch and shopping alone with me?" Peyton asked as we walked back to her car after overindulging ourselves on pizza and salads following a trip to the toy store for some secret items I picked up for Maddox.

Toys that would restrain a big guy like him so I could play without him taking over and taking control.

"Let's just say he's very persuadable when I'm on my knees." I grinned, walking around her car and getting in as she cackled.

"Well, how very selfless of you to sacrifice your morals and comforts in life so we could spend the day together." She joked before sobering up a bit. "I can't believe that soon there's going to be a little one attached to your hip twenty-four seven."

I snorted and rubbed my hands over my belly. "Regretting your upgrade to Auntie status already?"

"Not at all." She snapped, grabbing the sonogram photos my doctor printed out specially for her during my appointment earlier. "It just seems unfathomable."

"What about you guys?" I asked, broaching into uncharted waters between us. "Have you and Dane made any plans for kids?"

We had never talked about their plans, which I kind of thought was weird, but her choice to stay silent on it felt like enough of an answer.

She sighed and laid her head back against the seat. "Dane can't have kids." I turned in my seat and looked at her as she stared unseeingly out the windshield. "Something happened when he was a kid, I guess. And part of me is okay with that path for our relationship. A huge part of me is at peace with it, without feeling like it's wrong or broken in a way."

"But—" I whispered, knowing where she was going with it.

"But there's this small, little, tiny voice in my head that wonders sometimes what it would be like to be a mom." She turned her head to look at me as her eyes dropped to my belly. "I'm not jealous or sad about your pregnancy, but sometimes I just wonder if *I'd* be a good mom or not."

"I think you'd be a wonderful mom." I replied honestly, and she smiled.

"I think I was meant to be Dane's wife instead, because to be honest, I don't think I want to be a mom." She smiled and rolled her eyes, "I just need to find a way to get that little voice to understand that."

"There's a lot of self-awareness in knowing that it isn't something you want and being okay with that. I also think it's human nature and simple biology to wonder what it would be like to procreate and create life."

"I think raising you ruined the idea of parenthood for me." She laughed, and I rolled my eyes at her statement. I wasn't offended because I remembered all the pressure our parents put on Peyton to be perfect and set a good example for me.

"I wasn't that bad." She nodded in agreement at my deadpan expression.

"No, you weren't. At least not when we were kids." P sat up in her seat turning the car on, "Your teenage years, on the other hand," She widened her eyes dramatically, "Were enough to scare me celibate."

"Ha. Ha. Ha." I droned on.

"If it makes you feel any better, I'm fucking ecstatic to be the best aunt out there. I even turned one of the empty guest rooms into a baby room so I can keep this little one overnight occasionally when you and Maddox need a break." My heart swelled at the devotion and support she'd shown me every step of the way since telling her my news. "Oh, and Mrs. Straight said she'll put her retirement into hiatus to come spoil a new baby in the family. I think she just misses Dane's surly attitude and needs a fix."

I tipped my head back and laughed, remembering the way Peyton described the relationship between Dane and his older housekeeper before she went on a trip to England a few years ago. That trip was the reason that Peyton met Dane and when Mrs. Straight found out how the two of them got on, she announced her immediate retirement, choosing to stay in the UK with her family instead of returning to Hartington to endure more of Dane's crabby nature.

"Oh, I'd love to see how she handles that man in person one day. I'm all for a visit."

She pulled out of the parking lot of the shopping center and turned us back towards the other side of the city as I rested my head back on the seat. I was exhausted, and I could feel my ankles swelling from being on my feet all day.

Maybe Maddox was right to keep me locked up all the time in comfy clothes and warm blankets while we lounged and enjoyed the down time before we had a newborn to care for. I could almost feel the softness of the new fleece lined leggings I planned to change into when I got home.

I started to tell P not to stick around once we arrived—I was desperate to relax and open that envelope with Maddox to find out the sex of our baby—when a violent, explosive sound shattered my thoughts, throwing my body violently against the seat.

Peyton's screams were the only thing I could hear over the terrible noises surrounding us as her car careened onto its side and then onto the roof. Glass, metal shards, and debris rained down on us as we came to a forceful stop.

"Liv!" Peyton's screams echoed through my foggy brain as her hand grabbed my arm, where it hung limply next to my head. "Olivia!"

I tried to move my arm to see her, but it felt like it was dead, hanging there, no longer attached to my body as vertigo set in from being upside down.

Slowly, things started orienting themselves in my brain as it finally stopped rolling around in my head and Peyton's voice cleared up in my ears so I could finally understand her.

"Run!" She screamed.

"What?"

"Run! Now!" She reached for my seatbelt and clicked the release, causing me to slide down the seat onto the roof in a heap, but she kept shoving at me. "Olivia, they're coming! Run!"

"What are you—" I asked, looking over at her where she lay pinned in her seat with the car crushed in around her. "Oh my god, P." I clawed at the roof of the car trying to get my body to cooperate with me but still my one arm wouldn't work as I tried to get her. "Peyton!"

"They're coming!"

Suddenly, Dane's dominant voice echoed through the car's speakers. "Peyton! What happened?"

"They found her!" Peyton screamed, reaching for my hand and pushing it off her leg while I tried to pry the steering wheel out of where it was wedged into her thigh. "They hit us!"

"Get out of there!" Dane roared.

"P's trapped!" I cried, pulling at the wheel, trying desperately to get her leg free, but it wouldn't move. "She's bleeding!"

"Liv, leave me, go!" She shoved me again and then reached for her bracelet that she wore every single day and ripped it off before shoving it at my chest. "Take this, it's your only chance. They'll find you from it." I couldn't process what she was saying, or what her golden skull bracelet was going to do for me as I kept fighting with the mangled metal impaling her. Peyton shoved it down the front of my shirt as a hand wrapped around my ankle, where it hung out of my broken window and yanked. "No! Liv!" Her blood-curdling scream matched mine as I was forcefully dragged across the glass out onto the pavement next to the car. "Let her go! No! They have her, Dane!" Free from the wreckage, I rolled onto my back, the cold ground seeping into my clothes as I stared up into the eyes of the devil himself; his glare burned into mine like a familiar threat.

"Well, well, well," Damon stared down at me as I cowered beneath him. "Why didn't you tell me I was going to be a daddy?"

CHAPTER 27 - MADDOX

THE LINE WALKERS

My blood was cold, moving through my veins in slow motion as my brain locked out everything else but lethal focus.

Damon had Liv.

Dane had been at the loft working on some things while the girls were out for the afternoon together when he got an alert on his phone.

Crash Detected.

As soon as the chime from the alarm ended, the audio connected with the interior of Peyton's car through his system. We were out the door before Peyton's manic words registered through the speaker.

"Olivia, they're coming. Run!"

But it was too late. All we could do was listen while I drove us across the city at breakneck speed as Damon Kirst kidnapped Liv right from Peyton's crashed car. The way my body processed the news, in real time, and even now that she had officially been missing for eight hours, was familiar, yet new all in one.

I was used to having a lethal edge when it came to work, the ability to separate feelings and emotions from my job, it was a skill that made me the most desirable mercenary on the East Coast. But having Liv be the subject of this job ramped those skills up another ten levels.

I was going to find her.

And when I did, the earth would quake with my wrath.

CHAPTER 28 – OLIVIA

God, it was fucking cold. My teeth chattered; the jarring noise echoing off the brick walls around me. I didn't have many details about where I was, or even what type of room I was in, thanks to the pitch blackness surrounding me. But I knew it was fucking cold.

I sat on the floor, leaning against the wall that I thought was farthest from the door I had been thrown through, but the same familiar cold seeped through my clothes and into my bones. Flashbacks of the last time Damon Kirst had me in captivity assaulted me nonstop since he threw me in the room and locked the door behind him.

When Damon had picked me up off the ground and dragged me to a waiting van, I fought him with everything I had. One arm was useless, the sickening grind of my dislocated shoulder echoing in my ears every time I moved it, along with the sting of other, hopefully minor injuries. He easily overpowered me, and the screech of tires was the last thing I heard as he sped away. The only slight relief I had from the mental and physical torment of pain rushing through my mind and body was when my baby would move or kick like normal, reassuring me that it was still with me.

The crash had been so violent that when I felt the baby move for the first time after, I silently cried in relief.

I screamed for Peyton so loud as they dragged me away, my vocal cords ached and burned with each breath, and the only noise that would still come out sounded like a dying cat.

I had no idea if my sister was alive. All I knew was she had been covered with blood, pinned and trapped in the car when I was dragged away from her as we both screamed each other's names.

The longer that time passed in the blinding darkness, the more I worried I'd never see her again. I would accept any punishment Damon, or his rich associates planned for me if her death was my fault. I'd deserve it.

She didn't deserve to get wrapped up in my shit like that. I should have just stayed home like a good girl; like Maddox had wanted me to.

Maddox.

God, even thinking about him made my chest ache and eyes burn with tears I couldn't hold back.

If Damon won this whole thing, Maddox's soul wouldn't survive the fallout. In his revenge, he would shatter Hell's crust and be lost forever.

A loud, jarring noise from somewhere else in the building made every nerve in my body convulse like I was being electrocuted by fear alone. Minutes later, the door opposite of me opened and a blinding light mixed with the blinding darkness, burning my eyes as shadows crossed through the opening.

I cowered away. Again. I didn't care; I was woman enough to admit that I feared what was to come. Damon's cruel voice echoed from behind my scrunched eyelids across the room. "I know she ain't much to look at, but she's smart as fuck."

"Hmm." Another voice hummed from the other side of the room, and I dared to crack my eyelids open enough to catch the spark of a lighter as the second man lit a cigarette. I forced myself to sit up taller as the other man sucked on the cigarette, illuminating the outline of a chiseled jawline and dark eyebrows, but nothing else thanks to the poor lighting. "A lot of trouble you've caused."

His accent was British, and a chill ran down my spine when I figured out who he was.

The Duke.

Damon's money man.

The man that Maddox and Dane had been hunting for months along with his snively counterpart.

"Wasn't exactly my choice to be troublesome." I stated, hoping that maybe the man would show some of the decency he apparently showed the women from the Velvet Cage when he visited. I shifted on the floor, wrapping my good arm further around myself and my belly as they both stood over me.

"You're pregnant?" The Duke asked, taking another long drag off his cigarette, billowing smoke out around him.

I tried but failed to keep my eyes from flicking over to the monster standing to his right before answering. "Another thing that wasn't exactly my choice."

My eyes finally adjusted to the two different amounts of light in the room, and I could make out some more of his features as he stood there smoking.

The first thing that I noticed, aside from his marble cut jawline, was how tall he was. Like God himself would have had to look up at the man because of how tall he was. The next was the expensive cut of his suit, even if the smell of the cigarette told me they weren't some cheap American brand that my grandmother used to smoke at family dinners.

The longer I dared to stare at him, the more I felt he was staring at me through the darkness while Damon paced and kicked the toe of his shoe into the concrete like he was bored.

"Are you hurt?" The Duke asked after a while and I subconsciously rubbed my hand down my jeans again, over the stains of Peyton's blood, making me shiver in regret.

"My sister's." I whispered, forcing my eyes back up to him, still hoping and praying he was merciful. "My shoulder is dislocated."

The man looked over in Damon's direction and then back at me. "Did you call a doctor?"

Damon scoffed and flicked his wrist at me dismissively, "She's fine."

The Duke flicked his cigarette directly at Damon's face and leaned off the wall, "She needs her arm in working order if she's going to use her particular skills to fix your enormous mistakes."

Brushing the ashes off his cheap suit jacket, Damon looked over at me and I shrunk back into the concrete again, shivering.

"Get her into a proper room." The Duke said, walking toward the door, "And if there isn't a doctor here to treat her arm before I light my next cigarette, I'll break your arm to match hers." With that, he walked out of the room and disappeared around the corner, leaving Damon and I alone in the room and I would have preferred to be left alone in darkness and pain than face the man who could help me, but would probably hurt me instead for the fun of it.

"Don't go anywhere." He mocked, walking out and slamming the solid steel door shut behind him and locking it.

And once again. I was left with darkness and pain.

But a small smidge of hope dared to bloom in the same shadows from my short interaction with the Duke. Maybe I'd be able to talk myself out of the whole thing if he could be persuaded.

After all, Maddox and Dane were far better to have as allies instead of enemies at the end of the day.

CHAPTER 29 - MADDOX

THE LINE WALKERS

My fingers flew over the keyboard, hitting dead end after dead end as my phone rang next to me. I was in my old apartment at the loft because I couldn't stomach walking back into the perfect space I shared with Liv without her.

The shrill sound of my phone continuing grated on my nerves, and I glanced at it and saw Dane's name.

Taking a deep breath, I answered it as calmly as possible, given the hell he was currently living at the moment. "Any news?"

His own answering sigh made him sound years older than he was, "Peyton's out of surgery, but still asleep. They had to recreate her entire leg bone out of metal, but she might walk on it again someday."

"She's tough, she'll own that son of a bitch in no time."

"Yeah, maybe." I faintly heard the beeping of monitors behind him and imagined him pacing around a small hospital room where his injured wife lay unconscious in a bed like a caged animal. He wouldn't leave that building without her, I knew that. If the roles were reversed, I'd be the same way.

Liv.

My chest ached, not knowing if she was hurt or not. If she was scared or being hurt as I sat around helplessly only fueled my inner demons and eventually they'd break free and control me for good.

"Maddox, focus." Dane interrupted my thoughts, and I grunted in response. "I listened to the audio repeatedly while P was in surgery and pulled every camera angle possible of the attack. Something that I missed the first few times of listening to it through all the chaos was something Peyton said right before they took Liv."

Olivia's terrified scream from when Damon pulled her through the wreckage echoed through my brain like a horror soundtrack stuck on repeat as I held my head in my hands. "What was it?"

"I think Peyton tried to give her the bracelet I got her. But I don't know for sure since P's still unconscious and I haven't been back to the car to check. I don't know if they took it off her when she went into surgery or if she managed to give it to Liv in time."

"What's special about the bracelet?"

"The tracker in it." He replied, "I've tried pulling the location of it up, but it's coming up blank. So, I don't know, maybe it was just broken off in the crash. But maybe,"

My mind spun as I tried to figure out how to use that information to my advantage in finding Liv. "Send me the code for it, and I'll see what I can find."

"If Liv has it, then they have a system in place, blocking its coordinates from transmitting to me."

"But if she has it, we have our first actual lead in hours." I challenged, "And there isn't a digital hurdle we can't get over between the two of us."

"Okay, yeah, you're right. I'll send it."

"Thanks. Keep me updated when P wakes up. Maybe she remembers something, anything."

"I will." He paused, "Madd?"

"Yeah?"

"Peyton won't survive losing her sister like this. It'll kill her even if the crash and surgery don't. And I won't survive losing my wife. We both know if anything happens to either of these girls, you and I are better off being put down. Promise me if Peyton doesn't make it, you'll—"

I nodded my head, overcome with emotion by the overbearing weight of so many lives on my shoulders. My only loyal friend was asking me to make sure I killed him if he lost his wife before he could destroy the rest of humanity in his grief. "Right back at you, D."

"I promise."

CHAPTER 30 - OLIVIA

THE LINE WALKERS

"Show me how you did it." Damon barked, standing over me where I sat at a desk with a laptop. "I want to know how you redirected the money to your own account without us knowing."

The Duke stood in the corner watching me with intense eyes that were burning a hole in the side of my face. I glanced at him as Damon dragged me into the office and threw me into the chair, and he was even more intimidating in full light.

But there was something about his laser-like stare that called to me. Was there humanity in it? No.

Kindness? Definitely not.

There was only darkness there. But it was a darkness I recognized.

A darkness I had fallen in love with.

The same darkness that Maddox's gaze held when I met him.

The Duke, whatever his actual name was, was more than likely familiar with the same lifestyle that Maddox and Dane were. And maybe I could speak to that, create some kind of connection. But I couldn't tell him who I was attached to, because that would make them targets.

"Are you listening to me?" Damon roared, slapping the back of my head and making my teeth clatter.

"I can't feel my arm." My reply was as calm as I could make it. "I can't type if I can't feel it. And we both know I didn't move that money."

"Stupid bitch." Damon reared back and slapped me again, this time to my face. Even though I braced for it, familiar with his favorite type of communication by now, I still teetered on the chair, nearly falling off. "Lies!"

The Duke's critical stare at Damon caught my attention, but he didn't intervene.

"I only did what you said to do. Following your instructions, I transferred the money from the John's accounts in small increments to the designated accounts to avoid raising suspicion. That's it."

"You stole it!" Damon roared, hitting me again, "I want it back!"

"It won't save you." I changed tactics, forcing myself to be brave and look up at the monster standing over me as blood trickled down my freshly split lip. "They've started the hunt, and they won't stop until you're dead." I turned to face The Duke head on, "Your name is on their list too."

"Who, your big, scary boyfriend? You just couldn't do what you were told!" Damon screamed, his facade slipping from the power-hungry egomaniac to what he really was deep down inside. "You had to go and fuck it all up for everyone!"

A scared little bitch.

Mentioning the long list of men that Maddox and Dane had killed was exactly the right move, even if it cost me my life. Because judging by the look The Duke was aiming my way, he knew nothing about the others.

"He didn't tell you, did he?" I addressed the actual power in the room, drawing his darkness back on my skin. "There are monsters out there that are hunting down the men involved in this scheme. The ones with a hit on my head. And one by one, they've eliminated them. Moving their way up the list to you and Damon. The only two names left, out of thirty-two."

"Who?" The Duke asked cooly, almost like the threat of being hunted didn't scare him. Although he was usually the predator, not the prey, he had probably been on that side of the list before.

I wasn't brave. I wasn't fearless.

But I had to pretend I was.

"It doesn't matter." I replied, "You'll never see them coming until it's too late. That's their specialty." I shook my head and gave a little shrug. "Your only bargaining chip is keeping me alive and offering me back in exchange. And even then, you might not survive."

"Why?" He asked, keeping everything so short and to the point.

"Because my sister was in that car." I glared over at Damon, where he paced back and forth. "And Peyton is the wife of The Ghost." I used Dane's nickname, eluding information to the man, hoping maybe he ran in the same circles to at least be familiar with his reputation. "And I have no idea if she survived. But if she didn't, then you can bet your ass that the ground will open beneath your feet and swallow you whole. Even if my boyfriend spared you, The Ghost never would."

The Duke's face didn't change for the longest time as he stared at me, but his eyes roamed over my face and down my body, where I sat behind the desk with my crippled arm and giant belly. And then a small smile pulled up one side of his face and my blood ran cold.

Oh no. No, no, no.

I misjudged him.

He wasn't familiar. He wasn't sane.

His darkness would make Dane and Maddox's look like sunshine.

"You've given me quite a gift here tonight, Olivia." He walked across the room and leaned down with his fists on the desk in front of me. "Because I've wanted Maddox Renner dead for decades." He tilted his head, speaking the name I didn't give, and I swallowed audibly. "I'm going to enjoy making you watch as I do it, too."

He stood up to his full height as my heart raced wildly in my chest. The Duke turned to Damon, "Call the doctor. Get her arm set and put her in a room. We're going to need her whole if we're going to use her as bait."

And with that, he walked out of the room again, just like before, leaving me alone with the slimy monster who made the big mess we were all in to begin with. The way his own smile grew made my skin crawl and my stomach roll.

I was so fucking fucked.

THE LINE WALKERS

If I thought getting hit by a car hurt, getting my arm snapped back into place without a drop of pain medication was even worse. The doctor had been friendly enough, but he didn't have any drugs that were safe for me in my heavily pregnant way, so I had to endure it dry.

That was hours ago, and I laid on my side, cradling my arm over the swell of my belly because it still throbbed from the violent jarring of it being replaced. But at least I could feel it again. Which was reassuring.

And at least I was warm in a bed, instead of on the cold concrete floor again. In a way, I suppose the Duke was to thank for that. Though I didn't feel particularly lucky.

I had misjudged him so badly, which was out of character for me. As I lay in the darkness as sleep avoided me, I replayed as much as I could remember of the terse conversation, trying to figure out where I went wrong.

Also, trying to figure out what I was going to do to get myself out of the situation I was in. Not even knowing where I was didn't help. There were no windows in the van that Damon used to kidnap me and all I knew was that we were still in the city somewhere, but I had no clue where.

Confined within the windowless room, a sense of claustrophobia pressed in, broken only by the faint smell of damp plaster. It was just four walls and a bed with a thin blanket and one flat pillow.

The longer I laid in the dark, the more times I replayed the crash in my head. Peyton's screams tore my heart to shreds as I remembered the way she didn't even seem to notice the metal and debris impaling her while trying to get me to leave her behind.

"Please, God. Let her be alive." I cried quietly as my shoulders shook with sobs. "Please let her survive this."

As if a lightbulb clicked on in my head, I remembered her last words to me before someone ripped me from the car.

Fishing in the cup of my bra, I found the forgotten gold bracelet that she had forced down my shirt as the men surrounded us.

Pulling it out and holding it up in the tiny sliver of light from under the door, I ran my thumb over the glowing eyes on the skull jewel in the center.

Take this, it's your only chance. They'll find you from it.

Was there something in the bracelet that Dane gave to her that would help them find me? If so, why the fuck was I still laying in the icy darkness? Did they leave me in captivity because of what happened to Peyton? Was she dead, and this was my punishment?

Would Dane do that? Yes.

And I'd deserve it.

But Maddox—would he abandon me? I tucked the bracelet back into my shirt and rubbed my hand over a spot on my belly where my baby was pushing hard as more tears fell from my eyes. Into the fear of the unknown, they fell. They fell for the pain I'd endured and what was yet to come my way. They fell for the loss I felt being away from the literal love of my life, not knowing if I'd ever see him again.

Maddox had promised me he'd be there for me for the rest of my life, yet now I was alone. Our baby was alone.

And it was my fault.

The turning of the lock startled me upright as the sliver of light from the hallway grew as the door opened, revealing an ominous shadow blocking the big doorway.

The Duke.

He flicked a switch outside of the room, bathing the room in the harsh light from a single light bulb hanging from the ceiling above me and I squinted my eyes, but refused to close them as he entered the small space.

He carried a folding chair in with him and stared at me as he shook his arm out and opened the chair before silently lowering his massive frame down onto it.

I swiped at the tears still clinging to my cheeks and swung my feet off the side of the bed to face him, unwilling to be a submissive victim lying down as I stared at the man who pulled the rug out from under me earlier.

Neither of us spoke, simply staring at each other for a long time like we were stuck in some weird power struggle, and the first one to break the silence would lose.

He pulled a cigarette from his pocket and lit it up, leaning back in the chair, staring at me with judging, scrutinizing eyes before he finally broke his silence.

"Why did you tell me about the list?"

I raised one eyebrow at him in outright surprise. Out of everything he could have said, I wasn't expecting that. Mentally, I was playing chess with the man. If I could figure out how to play his game to my benefit, I might stay alive long enough to give Maddox a chance to rescue me. Which was what I was betting on, doubt be damned.

I trusted Maddox. I told him that, and I had to believe it.

"Because Damon is a rat." I replied with indifference, even though I felt those words to my very core. "And the things I heard about you from the girls made me believe maybe there was something honorable about you."

He grinned slightly, but it wasn't friendly. "You tempted your fate based on gossip of whores who like the way I fuck them?" Blowing out a puff of smoke, he shook his head. "I heard you were smarter than that."

"From Damon?" I scoffed, "I guess we both ended up disappointed in each other's character in the end."

"No," He squinted his eyes, "Not from Damon." He took another drag off his cigarette and I fought the urge to tell him to stop blowing his cancer stick at me but refrained. "From your sister."

My blood ran cold as I stared at the mysterious man, "You spoke to her?"

He grinned again and took another drag and blew it out before speaking, though he ignored my question. "It wasn't just gossip from prostitutes that made you take that chance to get into my good graces. Tell me what it really was."

I curled my hands into fists at my side as he avoided what I needed to know the most, reminding me who was in the position of power, and who was at the mercy of the other.

"Your darkness." I replied stupidly, desperate to hear about Peyton. "The evil in your eyes. It's familiar."

"To whom?" He leaned forward and rested his elbows on his knees to stare at me powerfully. "To your precious Maddox Renner?" His eyes fell to my stomach and then came back up to my face. "That's Damon's baby though."

My hands splayed out over my stomach, covering as much of it as I could over the thin fabric of my black sweater. "To Dane." I replied, trying to turn the conversation away from Maddox, considering The Duke already told me he planned to use me to fulfill his blood thirst for Maddox's life.

The man in front of me was a psychopath, I was sure. But as he stared at me as I spoke Dane's name, he gave me a sign that there was something deeper in his soul than he wanted me to know as a muscle in his tense jaw twitched.

"The Ghost." He replied, leaning back in his chair, but some of the menace in his eyes left his bright blue eyes as he stared at me.

"Dane." I corrected again, given that he seemed to be triggered somehow by my brother-in-law's actual name. "He's a fucked-up monster who runs by no moral code and does whatever he wants to do without a second thought." I sat up straighter and looked down my nose at him slightly, "That's what I recognized in your eyes."

"And you thought to align yourself to a monster like that?" He challenged, "You must be pretty desperate."

That pissed me off, and I envisioned Maddox cutting his heart out with his knife and holding it in his hands, still beating, as he handed it to me for the disrespect.

"Less desperate than you are." I lobbed back, no longer worried about my life or my soul. I was desperate, that was obvious. But I was also anything but a pushover. And the man before me wouldn't scare me or bully me with his callous words. "I may or may not die at the end of this." I shrugged, "That's obviously not something I can change at this point. But I know for a fact that you're just a normal man with a big wallet, walking around on borrowed time. Because you're going to die for sure at the end of this nightmare. The only thing that changes is the how."

The fucker in front of me smiled again and leaned over to snub his cigarette out on the floor before standing up, towering over me. "Is the baby okay from the crash?"

His question caught me so off guard, I had no sarcastic or snarky response to give him as my hands clung tighter to my stomach, staring up at the man. "I don't know."

The Duke's blue eyes fell to my stomach and his head angled to the side. "I'll have a baby doctor here in the morning to check."

"Why?" I squinted back in speculation, wondering why he even cared to be kind.

He shrugged, walking toward the door as he slid his hand into his slacks pocket. "Because if it's dead inside of you, then your value to Maddox and Dane goes down." If I had something nearby to throw at his skull, I would have. But he was lucky the room was bare of projectiles, because I was just manic enough to try. "Oh, and Little Hacker?" He turned, using a stupid nickname that the girls from the Velvet Cage had given to me when we interacted. "Don't tell Damon about this little visit. Better yet, refrain from speaking to him as much as possible."

"Why?" I repeated, hating how he seemed to have all the answers but gave me only crumbs to survive off.

"My chances of getting you and your baby out of here alive dwindle every time you raise that scumbag's temper. Which you do often." He gave me a pointed stare. "Be a good girl, and I'll get you home before you do something stupid like go into labor."

As he walked back out of the door and locked it behind him again, I sank back onto the bed as the same back ache pain I'd been having on and off hit me like a brick. "You'd better move fast then." I whispered into the darkness around me as I tried to figure out the secretive man's motive for *literally* anything.

CHAPTER 31 - MADDOX

"The tracker isn't pulling any data and hasn't since right after the crash." I replied to Dane over the phone.

Liv had been taken yesterday, and every single second that passed without knowing where she was or if she was okay, gutted me. If I didn't have the task of finding her on my plate, I would have lost my grip on reality within the first hour.

"I didn't find it in Peyton's belongings. She had to have given it to her. That's the only explanation."

"Then why can't I fucking find her by it?" I snapped, rubbing my forehead as I rested my elbows on my desk.

"Have you slept?" He asked in place of an actual answer.

"Have you?" I replied, knowing he wouldn't have rested either, given that Peyton still wasn't awake.

Would she know anything we don't about where Liv was taken or was I just grasping at straws.

"Take an hour or two, Maddox." Dane countered. "Your mind won't work clearly under sleep deprivation."

"Yeah, okay. Call me with any news on P." I hung up and stared at the computer screen, lost, begging for an answer.

I had a map up on the screen with points of interest plotted out like where the crash happened and known hangouts of Damon and his Hell Eater Crew, but nothing spoke to me as a place he'd be hiding her.

I didn't even know if she was still in the city or not.

But I couldn't stop searching for sleep. I'd never forgive myself if she was being hurt while I was sleeping.

I'd never forgive myself anyway for everything else that had already been done, but there'd be no redemption for me if I stopped trying.

She'd never forgive me.

CHAPTER 32 - OLIVIA

THE LINE WALKERS

"Good morning." A middle-aged man with a bright cheery smile walked into the room as two men followed behind him with two rolling trunks. The men were Hell Eaters, Damon's minions, but behind them was The Duke.

Conveniently, Damon was missing. Was that the Duke's doing? Why did he not want me to talk to the man who was responsible for the entire shit show we both seemed to be trapped in?

I didn't reply to the first man, choosing to give a curt nod as I sat up on the uncomfortable bed against the wall where I spent the rest of my night after my conversation with the Englishman.

"My name is Dr. Stein." The new man went on, as the lackeys propped his cases up against the wall and walked out. "I'm an OB and I'm here to check you and your baby out." He looked normal and friendly, but I couldn't get over the oddity of his presence, like he was out of place somehow.

Again, I didn't reply. How could a doctor walk into a place like this, to do his kind of job, and act as though everything was okay?

I was a fucking prisoner, after all! It was absurd.

"I'm told you were in a sort of car accident yesterday." The doctor continued, standing in front of me now and forcing me to focus on him. "And that you suffered a dislocated shoulder. Did you sustain any other injuries in the crash?"

I swallowed, prying my dry tongue from the roof of my mouth, and finally replied verbally. "I don't know." I shrugged, "Bumps and scrapes."

"Are you sore today?"

Slowly, I nodded my head. My entire fucking body hurt, especially my back. Was it all from the crash?

"Has the baby moved since the crash?" I nodded again. "As much as normal or less?"

"I don't know." I snapped, a little frustrated with the entire thing. "I've been a little preoccupied with being a prisoner."

He tightened his lips like my outburst was distasteful in his eyes as he weaved his fingers together in front of him. "Well, if you want me to help you, you'll have to be a little more helpful to me. How far along are you?"

"Thirty-six weeks." I spoke through clenched teeth as I forced myself to take a deep breath before daring to look at the tall, ominous figure standing against the wall staring at me. He wore black dress slacks and a black button-up shirt, the latter unbuttoned at the throat and rolled up the sleeves to show extensive tattoos on both forearms. He looked like a proper English gentleman until he smoked or revealed his ink.

Then he looked as menacing as any other crook and criminal I'd met in my time.

"Well," The doctor's eyes widened, and he looked over at the man himself, "Clock is ticking then." Turning back to me, he motioned to the bed. "Lay back and we'll take a peek at the baby with an ultra-sound."

I watched him silently as he moved to one of the large cases against the wall and opened it, revealing all sorts of medical equipment, including a small handheld ultrasound. Unable to let my anger control me, I laid back on the bed, desperate to find out if my baby was okay or not from the crash and the stress of the last day. I could hate the man, but he may be my only chance at reassurance.

I watched from the corner of my eye as he gathered his machine and then came over to the bed, lifting my shirt and pressing on my stomach like my doctor did at my appointments, checking position and growth.

The man smiled down at me and tapped my stomach as he squeezed some gel out onto my skin. "Baby is head down, that will make the delivery much easier, and faster."

I didn't reply, because there was something to the tone of his voice that gave me the shivers.

He ran the wand over my stomach, and my baby moved under it like it hated the intrusion into its space and fought back against it. My baby was a little spitfire and already attuned to stranger danger. And we were most definitely surrounded by stranger danger.

"Ah, here we are." He moved the wand around my stomach, taking a thorough look at everything.

He didn't turn the screen toward me, and there was something about the way he treated me like I didn't matter, that made those shivers turn into alarm bells in my gut. Something was wrong with the man and the entire situation.

I chanced a glance over at The Duke, but he stared at my stomach like he'd never seen a pregnant woman before and couldn't quite make heads or tails of it. I opened my mouth to address him, but the door to the room opened again and Damon walked in with a huff of indignation.

"You started without me?" He snapped, glanced at The Duke and then glared at the doctor and me. "Doesn't the father get any respect?"

"You're not the father." I bit out, pushing the doctor's hand away from my stomach to pull my shirt down like hiding my skin would protect my baby from his disgusting presence.

Damon clicked his tongue and sneered at me. "The math says I am, bitch." He turned his attention to the doctor, who showed him the screen and pointed out something still on there.

"Your daughter is growing perfectly, Mr. Kirst. Thirty-six weeks along and in perfect health to be born anytime."

Daughter.

The word echoed through the room, reverberating through my ears as nausea bubbled up in my stomach over the whole situation.

No. No! I was supposed to find out with Maddox. No!

Daughter. I was having a little girl. And Damon found out before Maddox did. No!

"Perfect." The slime ball rubbed his hands together with a sneer my way again before addressing the doctor. "How soon can you deliver it?"

"What?" I snapped, sitting up and putting my feet on the floor in horror.

"The baby would be early, but very viable any time now," The doctor replied, ignoring me completely. "My recommendation is to induce labor with medications and deliver her here as well. I can have all the equipment necessary delivered this afternoon."

"No!" I cried, flicking my stare from the doctor to Damon and back before finally turning to the Duke. "You can't! It's too early!"

The doctor chuckled dismissively, "You're a big girl, you've grown a big baby." He scoffed and turned back to the man responsible for all my heartache. "You'll appreciate me delivering the baby early if you have any plans to enjoy the act of making another one anytime soon."

The nausea rolled in my stomach even more at the flippant words. This was a nightmare, and I was going to hyperventilate if I didn't get my breathing under control as the two continued making plans about my body and my baby, like they deserved a damn say.

They couldn't deliver my baby, or they'd take her from me. I knew it, even if they didn't say it out loud.

Damon would take my daughter, and I'd never see her again.

Suddenly, my desire to fight and survive burned with a new vigor I didn't recognize in myself.

"Why the rush?" The Duke finally spoke, leaning up off the wall. "Surely it's best to let the baby continue to—" He hesitated to say the words like they didn't come naturally to him, "cook until it's due date."

"We don't have the time to wait." Damon cut in. "The sooner we have the baby out, the sooner the stakes change and fall in my favor."

"You can't do this." I sneered, standing up to my full height to stare down the man who had seemingly already ruined my life until that moment. But staring him in the eye as he prowled across the room toward me, I realized he was just getting started.

"I can do whatever the fuck I want to do." He wrapped his hand around my throat and slammed me into the wall next to us, bouncing my head off it and sneering at me. "And there's absolutely nothing you can do about it. Your future is going to look a lot like this, shackled on your back, growing babies for me. Because thanks to you stupidly getting knocked up, you've broadened my horizons, and I've found a new skin trade far more profitable than whores."

Ice filled my veins as I fought back against him, so he'd stop pressing against my stomach as he choked me. "No." I hissed.

"That's right, smartie pants." He tightened his hold on my neck as I swung uselessly at his face as my vision darkened from the lack of oxygen getting into my brain. "Babies are far more lucrative than whores are." He chuckled, "Though we both know there's a good chance she'll end up working for both black markets before she dies."

I erupted, fighting with everything I had left inside of me, but it was no use. He was too strong and too evil to overcome.

As my body went limp in his grimy clutches, I looked to the side and locked eyes with The Duke, silently begging for help. Begging for what I thought I knew about him would help me in some way in the end.

Although I didn't have long to study it, the look he aimed at the back of Damon's head as I slipped into unconsciousness spoke to that hope in my heart.

It was the look of a madman, ready to tear someone apart.

It was the look Maddox had in his eyes the night he found me on the floor of the storeroom in the Hell Eater's lounge and rescued me.

It was the look Peyton described as Dane having the night he shot his own brother in her guest house when he found him breaking in.

As I fell to the floor in a heap after Damon released me before he killed me completely, I begged God to let that look save my baby in the end. Please let that darkness save my daughter.

CHAPTER 33 - OLIVIA

When I woke up, I was disoriented and confused about what happened before waking up on the bed, but it all flooded back to me when my stomach tightened painfully, making me cry out in pain. I curled myself into a ball, trying to grip my stomach to relieve the pain, but my wrists caught as I tried to pull them away from the sides of the bed. I lay in the middle of the bed, restrained on my back with my arms tied down at my sides.

It was then that I saw the IV in the back of my hand and the bag of fluid hanging above me on an IV pole, feeding something into my body against my will.

"No!" I cried out, feeling like my body was splitting into two as the wave of pain crested and then started diminishing to a dull ache.

I was alone in the room as I cried out again in pure horror, realizing they had induced my labor while I was unconscious.

With my baby's impending birth, a chilling sense of vulnerability overwhelmed me; I couldn't protect her or even myself. I fought the bindings around my wrists, using strength and willpower I didn't recognize to free myself to save my baby. If I got free, maybe I could stop the labor at least, or slow it down and buy some time.

Another contraction hit me like a tidal wave, starting slowly and building until I was crying out again. But I used the pain in my stomach to distract me from the pain in my left wrist as I pulled against the bindings so hard something popped and then my hand slid free. I gasped, biting my lip to quiet my cries as I pulled my arm free and rolled onto my side to try to work the other restraint free.

Which was difficult with a dislocated joint in my hand below my thumb that gave way to allow my hand free, but not impossible. I glanced at the closed door as I struggled to unbuckle the cuff and slide my right hand out. At least I had one fully working hand finally, and the second it was free, I ripped the IV out of my arm, staunching the flow of the medicine they were pumping into me to make my body contract and force my baby out before she was due.

Swinging my legs off the side of the bed, I slid down to the floor, noticing I was on a hospital bed and not the one from before at all, and I was also in a hospital gown instead of my regular clothes. Jesus fuck, I felt like a test subject at some research lab, just free to be poked, prodded and cut to pieces in the name of fun.

There were two rolling carts on the opposite side of the room covered with sterile sheets, but I prayed for what I would find under them as I rushed over.

Tools.

I ripped the sheets from the carts, the scent of antiseptic sharp in the air, revealing an array of gleaming surgical tools—scissors, clamps, needles—a stark collection spread before me, each with a different purpose, but I searched for only one specific instrument.

That's when I finally found my tool of choice. The scalpel.

A chill ran up my arm as I gripped the cold, hard steel, the metal smooth against my skin; I would survive, no matter what the cost.

No fucking questions asked.

There wasn't a person in the building that I'd think twice about killing if it meant I made it out alive with my baby.

My stomach clenched, a visceral warning of the contraction to come. The pain intensified, a searing agony that made me bite my lip until it bled, stifling the scream building in my throat. I leaned on the cart for support as I covered my mouth to stay quiet. I was terrified and alone, and my entire body shook with each contraction.

It wasn't supposed to happen like that. I was supposed to be at the hospital with Maddox. He was going to hold my hand and rub my back as Peyton chatted nervously as I labored my baby into the world.

I needed Maddox!

I sank to my knees as the contraction finally loosened its hold on my body and I wept, grieving what I thought the experience would look like while simultaneously trying to plan how to get out of it alive.

I had no idea what waited on the other side of the door, but I knew if I stayed put, I'd be in more trouble than I already was.

Grabbing a second scalpel off the other tray, I wrapped some gauze around the handles of both, securing them with what I figured was stitching string to make a makeshift shank.

Apparently binge-watching shows like *Prison Break* and *Orange is The New Black* benefited me after all, I couldn't wait to rub it in Peyton's face someday.

With a scalpel in each hand, though my left hand was mildly useless to wield it, I slowly and as silently as I could, turned the handle on the door, praying to any divine nature out there, to help me escape this death sentence.

When the door was open an inch, I peeked out into the hallway, finding it empty but unfamiliar. I had no idea where I was.

Even if I managed to escape the physical building itself, it was February, and I was in nothing but a hospital gown.

They even took my shoes.

It didn't matter, though. My options were non-existent, I had to try.

As soon as I cleared the doorway, I closed it behind me, hoping maybe it'd buy me some time before they realized I was missing. A girl could hope.

I tiptoed down the hall, passing other closed doors and turning corners, trying to find an exit, but it seemed every opening had a closed door in it, and I had no fucking clue what was on the other side of any of them.

Panic burned up my spine as another contraction started, I had nowhere to hide, but I couldn't have another contraction in the hallway if I had a prayer of staying hidden.

Sending another silent plea to any force of nature out there, I picked the closest door and turned the handle, pushing it open quickly and sliding inside as my knees buckled, taking me to the floor.

The room was dark, but there was a window on the far side of the room, and a glow from the city outside lit up the room enough for me to see that it was empty.

I crawled across the floor to the window through the contraction and pulled myself up to see through the dirty glass.

I was at least four stories high, and there wasn't a fire escape to be found. Not that I would chance one in my condition. But that meant I had to go back to the hallway to find an exit.

I silently sobbed in defeat as I tried to muster up the energy and bravery to go back out there, knowing before long I was going to meet someone that expected me to still be tied up in my room.

Right before I turned around, something caught my eye from below the window on the ground.

People.

Two people, to be exact, standing in the empty parking lot below in a passionate embrace. My first thought was to shatter the glass and scream for them to call for help, but as I raised my fist, clutching the scalpel in my palm still, the two bodies took a step away from each other.

And I recognized them.

Damon.

And Mack. That traitorous supermodel.

Jesus, fuck.

I swallowed down some bile as she smiled up at him before he kissed her again and walked back into the building as she turned and walked around the building.

That was when I realized where we were.

The building was only two blocks from Maddox's home. My home.

Jesus, fuck, indeed. She set me up, some way or another. That conniving bitch was part of the reason I was here.

And I was going to use the boiling rage racing through my veins to get the fuck out. As I turned from the window toward the door, the handle turned before I could open it, and the door swung in, forcing me to duck behind it as the doctor entered.

I didn't think.

I didn't process or plan.

I acted.

And I acted like a caged animal intent on enacting catastrophic damage to my prey.

Swinging my right arm in a downward arch, I buried the scalpel in the side of his neck as he walked into the dark room, kicking the door shut behind him and swinging my left hand around the front of his neck, slicing it and soaking both hands in warm blood as I shoved him to the floor.

He rolled over on his back, frantically clawing at his neck to staunch the bleeding as it spilled out through his fingers, staring up at me with wide eyes in shock.

"You deserved this." I sneered down at him as he collapsed flat onto his back, bleeding out faster than he could process, even with his medical degree. Standing over him, I watched long enough to see him take his last breath before I turned and headed back out into the hall.

My blood was cold, and fury filled every cell in my muscles.

Fuck them all for thinking they could just take what wasn't theirs.

They'd pay for it with their lives before I was done.

Every single last one of them.

But as I tiptoed down the dim hallway again, a hand covered my mouth as a strong body ripped me backward into one of the rooms. My arms flailed, slicing skin with the scalpels as the man who grabbed me slammed my back against the wall, grabbing my wrists and pinning them above my head with his hand still over my mouth.

Piercing blue eyes, one covered with blood from a fresh slice to his forehead, stared back at me and I screamed against the palm. My stomach contracted, but I was so scared of the man holding me, I hardly even noticed.

"Well, well, well, Little Hacker." The Duke whispered at me as he held me prisoner. "And to think, I came to rescue you, but it looks like you were well on your way to do it on your own." I fought his hold as the pain of the contraction intensified and my knees gave out. "I think it's time we called in reinforcements to get you out of here alive, don't you? After all, my brother Dane loves when little brother Tamen calls and interrupts his life."

Chapter 34 - Maddox

The Line Walkers

I drove through the city, with my tablet propped up on my dash, running a scan every few hundred yards, hoping and praying that something would come up on the tracker in that damn bracelet.

But with every passing city block, my anger soared higher at the lack of even a blip on the screen.

My phone lit up with a number I recognized as one I never answered willingly. Seconds away from declining, I cursed myself and hit the accept button.

"Feel like dying today?" I asked in place of a greeting.

Tamen's cocky chuckle flowed through my truck's speakers, annoying me before he even spoke. "Funny, coming from the man who lost everything worth living for yesterday."

My blood thickened to lava as my heart rate slowed, preparing my body for battle against Dane's kid brother. He was the only person on this earth that I allowed to walk away from a sure death. That was years ago, and he made me regret it every time we interacted.

"What do you know?" I asked menacingly.

"Well—" He started, but a feminine cry burned my ears, and I instantly recognized it as Liv's pained voice. "I have Olivia."

"Where?" I barked, "Put her on!" Another cry from her lips flowed through my speakers and I slammed on the brakes, sliding to a stop in the middle of the street as Tamen spoke to her, telling her to be quiet. "Tamen!"

"Calm down, big guy. She's in labor. And we're out of time. Get to Fifty First and Tallman St. Abandoned mercantile factory on the south side of the intersection. Don't be seen and text me when you're here."

"Wait." Liv's breathy voice called out and there was a small scuffle on the phone before her voice came through the speakers at full volume. "Madd?"

"I'm here." My voice broke as I heard her pained one, I already turned my truck around and aimed it in that direction, only a few blocks away from my home. "I'm right here, Storm."

"Mack is with Damon. She played you."

"It doesn't matter." I shook my head, imagining Liv in pain and in Damon's clutches.

"It does." She hissed and moaned in pain again. "They drugged me, Madd. They induced my labor to sell our baby into God only knows what. I'm in labor, and the contractions are so close and so painful." She cried, gasping for breath, "He's going to take our daughter, Madd."

"Over my fucking dead body." I promised with lethal calmness as I slid into the role of predator, ready to strike to save her. "I'm almost there, hold on for me." No one was going to touch my daughter or the love of my life.

"Tamen is The Duke. Yesterday, he said he was going to kill you. I don't know who to trust." She hissed, and whimpered, "Fuck, it hurts."

"I'm coming, Storm. I'm right around the corner. I love you."

She groaned something in response and then her cries got louder as Tamen took the phone back.

"On the Tallman Street side of the building, there's a loading dock. Come in through there, we're on the fourth floor. I'll bring her down the west stairwell."

"Anything happens to her, that free pass gets rescinded."

"Game on." His smirk was audible, and I wanted to blow his head off his shoulders for the fucking fun of it.

I parked closer to the building than I should have, but with Liv in labor, she wouldn't be able to walk far. I ditched my truck in a dark alley two buildings away from the one she was in, well aware that it could be a trap set by Tamen. But I couldn't sit by and not try.

As I walked through the darkness toward the boarded-up building, I called Dane, getting straight to the point as soon as he answered.

"Tamen has Liv. He's the Duke. He called, they're a few blocks away from the loft. Damon induced her, and she's in active labor. He plans to take my daughter."

"Like hell." Dane growled.

"Agreed. But it's possible that Tamen set a trap.

"No," Dane stated firmly. "There's little in this life that my brother cares for, but he cares for Peyton. He wouldn't betray her that way."

"He already did!" I barked in a hushed tone as I was nearing the building. "He had Liv and didn't fucking call until now."

"There must be a reason. We'll figure it out later. I'm on my way. Give me five minutes."

The hospital was across town, but I knew Dane would make it in five either way. But I couldn't wait another second. "Tamen said the Tallman St entrance to the old mercantile building on the corner of Fifty-First and Tallman. Loading dock. You can make your way to us when you get here."

"Fuck!" He roared, and I heard his car rev in the background. "Okay, go."

I hung up as I jumped up onto the black dock and pushed the steel door open. I finally had an outlet for all the rage and fear that had been burning in my gut for over twenty-four hours.

Heaven help the souls that I met on my way to Liv, because they were about to experience pain like no other.

I moved methodically, meeting undertrained Hell Eaters on my way and ripping their throats out with my bare hands for the fun of it as I moved up, floor by floor.

Damon never popped his head out of any of the rooms, but I was sure he knew I was there. Death had a way of calling to men like us, announcing its presence and testing which side of it you would fall on.

On the killer side, or on the deceased side.

I heard Liv's hushed cries of pain on the third floor, and I barreled toward it, finding her in the center of chaos as a swarm of Hell Eaters, Damon included, attacked Tamen.

Tamen was a skilled killer, better than even me in ways. But he had Liv behind him, tucked against the wall as he fought off a dozen different men.

And my vision turned red as I bellowed out in rage, tearing men to pieces on my way to her.

CHAPTER 35 - OLIVIA

THE LINE WALKERS

I watched on in sick fascination and horror as Maddox raced down
the hall, taking on the gang of Hell Eaters that had Tamen and
me cornered at the stairwell. He looked so damn good, racing to help
like a man on a mission, but one look at his black eyes as he found me
around the chaos, and I shivered in realization.

Maddox wasn't there, staring back at me. His psycho was in control,
and I was fucking here for it. In a way, I had always wanted to know
that side of him; the man that did the dismembering before he showed
up on my doorstep with boxes filled with the only parts left of the men
who wanted to kill me.

My psycho.

The psycho that looked like he would not stop until every man
between us lay at his feet.

I tried to focus on him and how he and Tamen both almost effort-
lessly worked through the crowd of ten men, spilling blood and tearing
chunks out of them with their bare hands. But my contractions were
nearly on top of each other, and I sank to my knees against the wall,

closing my eyes and trying to close out the noise and smell of death around me as I fought my body's urges to bring life into the world. It seemed insane to birth a baby surrounded by such death, but the harder I tried to stop the pain, the stronger it came.

"Madd." I gasped, clawing at the concrete floor as a scream ripped from my lips. "She's coming!"

A sinister laugh echoed over me, and I looked up in time to see Damon moving over me, blood spilling from his face in multiple spots. "My daughter wants to meet her daddy!" He jeered and my eyes flicked to his hand, where a knife caught the reflection of the dingy light hanging in the hallway's ceiling.

"No." I cried, backing away on my hands and falling to my ass as he got even closer to me, waving his knife in my direction. "Please!"

Even as I threw myself backward, his knife still moved too fast for me to avoid and the tip sliced through the gown and into the flesh of my chest, leaving a searing pain in its wake.

"Storm!" Maddox bellowed, and I clutched the wound as his hands wrapped around Damon's neck from behind. It happened in slow motion, but the fear was paralyzing as I stared up at the two men fighting, eager for it to be over before it even started. Maddox had both hands wrapped around Damon's neck, his fingers dug into the flesh and making it dimple like at any moment, they would pierce through the skin and embed themselves inside. But Damon would not go down without a fight, and I watched in horror as he spun the knife around in his hand and then arched it behind him, and directly into Maddox's stomach.

"No!" I screamed in despair as Damon pulled the knife free and tried to plunge it in again, but Maddox twisted his wrists, and a deafening cracking sound echoed from Damon's open lips seconds before his eyes glassed over and his body went limp. I shook like a leaf on the ground, paralyzed with my eyes trained on the two men standing over me, waiting for it all to end.

Maddox huffed, throwing Damon's body to the side like he was nothing more than a bag of trash as he fell to his knees in front of me. "Move your hands." He demanded, but I just stared at him with eyes wide and my body frozen, watching the red ooze of blood stain his white shirt from the wound in his abdomen. "Storm!" He bellowed, placing both hands on the sides of my face and forcing me to look at him. "Move your hands so I can see the wound."

"Your—" I stammered, letting him pull my hands away and trembling when I saw how much blood coated my fingers over the dry blood of the doctor, "Your wound." I pulled at his shirt and revealed the nasty gash right in his side beneath his rib cage that poured blood out. "Oh my god, Maddox."

"Shh," He hushed, pulling my hands away from his stomach as he put pressure on the slice in my chest. "Stop, we need to get you to the hospital."

"You're bleeding more than me." I got back into motion, pushing him back as Tamen hovered behind him, staring at us with that penetrative stare I had come to hate in the last few days. "God, Maddox, he stabbed you!"

"The baby," Maddox ignored me and, as if on cue, as soon as his free hand touched my stomach through the gown, another wave of agony cut through the adrenaline and hit me like a brick wall. "We're not going to make it, are we?"

I trembled, pressing my head back into the wall as realization dawned on me. I wasn't making it to the hospital before our daughter was born. "No."

"Okay." He nodded and took a deep breath, before forcing a smile to his lips as I trembled in his embrace. "Tamen, she needs a bed. Somewhere far away from this."

"This way." The Englishman nodded curtly and started walking away down the hall as Maddox lifted me into his arms as I groaned an animalistic cry of pain.

"I have to push." I hissed, fighting the urge but giving into it like my body was in control and I no longer had a say. "God, it hurts Madd."

"Shh," He kissed my temple, running through the hallway to a lower floor and into a room behind Tamen. It was a bedroom, and it looked clean enough, as Dane's mysterious brother cleared his things off the bed and paced in the corner as Maddox laid me down in the center of the queen-sized bed as another urge to push took over. "You've got this, Storm." Maddox crawled up on the bed next to me and snapped his fingers at Tamen. "Towels. Blankets. Whatever you can find for this wound and for the baby."

"Yeah," Tamen nodded, rubbing his hands over his face as he moved toward the door. "I'll see what I can find."

"Now, Tamen!" Maddox roared as I dug my nails into his neck and pushed again. "That's it, baby. Just listen to your body and let it work for you. Remember what we learned in those videos, use the contractions to do the work for you."

"It's too early." I gasped when the contraction ended and I could breathe again, "She's not due yet."

"She's going to be just fine," He laid his forehead against mine and took a deep breath, so I'd mimic him in the moment of relief. "We're having a daughter."

Sobs wracked my body as grief of the entire situation overwhelmed me. "It's not supposed to be like this." I cried harder. "What if something is wrong with her?"

"We'll figure it out when she's born." He stated firmly, reminding me of the task at hand. "Let's get her out and we can go from there."

"Ow." I cried, laying my head back against the pillow and arching into the pain as the same overwhelming feeling of bearing down overcame me. "Ow. Ow. Ow." I whimpered and then did as Maddox said and used the contraction to work with me instead of against me.

And then I fucking pushed.

I curled my chin to my chest and silently put all of my energy into the push and felt my daughter be born as Maddox encouraged me and talked us both through it all.

As soon as she was born, it felt as if the pain had just stopped. I took a deep breath and opened my eyes, watching as Maddox scooped her up in his arms, tipping her on her side and rubbing his massive hand over her back.

"Madd." I whispered as our daughter remained silent and still, cradled in his hands that just murdered numerous men to save us both. "Madd." I sat up higher and stared at her, holding my breath, waiting for her to take her first one. "Madd."

Tamen rushed back into the room, with an arm full of towels, and Dane followed him, but they both froze, staring at the unmoving infant in Maddox's arms. "Maddox." Dane walked forward, sliding his hand into mine and squeezing it tight as we all stared at her. "What do you need?"

"I don't know." Maddox replied, rubbing his hand up and down our daughter's back, concentrated and fixated on her limp body as Tamen handed him towels to wrap her up in. "She needs to breathe. She just needs to breathe." The three of them worked together silently as I felt like my heart stopped in my chest, unwilling to beat until I knew if hers did.

I couldn't breathe again until I knew she did.

God, she was so tiny. Too tiny.

"Maddox." I whispered, almost silently. As if that one word was the only one I knew anymore. The only word that would get me what I needed most.

Dane took a towel and rolled it up, pressing it to my chest over the wound and kneeled on the bed beside me, supporting my body against his as Maddox started patting her on the back, rolled over face down in his hand as he progressively increased the pressure he put into each pat.

And then—her arms flailed at her side and a piercing cry echoed from her new lungs, making us all draw a breath for the first time.

Collectively, all three men gasped and their shoulders sagged in relief as I reached for my daughter, taking her as Maddox cradled her against my chest. "Oh, my god." I cried, staring down at my beautiful daughter for the first time and feeling so incredibly unworthy of her as she screamed bloody murder, swinging her fists wildly as her bottom lip trembled with indignation. "Hi, baby."

"Holy fuck." Tamen stared at her, frozen still at the side of the bed. "I can't believe that just happened."

"Fuck off." Maddox shoved him away toward the door and blocked my exposed body with his hulking frame. "Go get my truck."

"Yeah," Tamen moved in a daze, with eyes wide like saucers as he left the room, lighting up a cigarette as he walked out. "Got it."

I looked up at Maddox as he leaned down to kiss my forehead and ran his fingers over our daughter's furrowed brow. "You're incredible, Storm. I've never been so in awe of someone as I am of you."

"I can't believe she's here." I whispered, looking back down at our daughter, "I can't believe I just gave birth in a room filled with serial killers."

Dane snorted and took Maddox's hand to hold the towel against my collarbone. "You're lucky you just gave birth to my first niece, or I might take offence at such a ridiculous and childish title."

I smiled and then froze. "Peyton." I stared up at him questioningly. "Is she—is she alive?"

He gave me a small grin, but it was weak as he nodded. "She's alive. But she hasn't woken up since they took her to surgery." Not once had I ever seen Dane look so broken as he spoke those words, and my heart ached for my sister and her lost husband. "They said it takes time sometimes."

I turned my face to Maddox, "I need to see her." Panic overwhelmed me as I felt her absence in the room like a fire against the soles of my feet. "I have to go to her."

Maddox nodded his head, kissing mine again. "Let's go, but we're going to get you seen and treated first."

"Madd, no!" I brushed him off and then winced as another wave of pain hit my stomach when I moved. "Fuck."

"Exactly." He stated firmly, "I won't waiver on this, Storm. You and our daughter need to be checked out, and then you can go to her."

"He's right." Dane nodded solemnly, "You'll do Peyton no good if you're hurt when she wakes up. You know how she worries."

I deflated a bit, knowing they were both right, but hated every bit of it.

My daughter sniffled and rooted her face around against my chest, reminding me of the most important person in my life suddenly, and I nodded, looking down at her. "Okay. We'll all get checked out, and then we'll go see Auntie Pey."

When we stepped outside of the brick building, Maddox's truck was idling at the curb right behind Dane's discarded sports car where he left it. I nestled our baby into the space between my chest and

Maddox's as he carried us through the frigid night air, but something caught my eye from above.

"Madd, look." I nodded up, pausing the convoy of men from loading us into the truck even though it was colder than a witch's tit outside. The sight above deserved to be seen, even if for just a few seconds.

"The northern lights." Maddox replied, looking up at the bold pink and green hues floating in the star-covered sky above us. Even with the city's light pollution, the glow was visible to the naked eye. "They said it's the first time in a century that they have been so directly visible over Boston."

"It's magical." I stared in awe, having never seen them before in person. "We were meant to see this right now, I think." I looked at him and gave him a soft smile. "With the dawn they'll be gone, but right now, at this exact place, they shined like they were meant for us."

"Maybe they were." He smiled back, kissing my forehead before tucking me into the truck as gently as he could. "Maybe they're just for her."

"Maybe." I wondered, staring down at our sweet daughter, who was sleeping with her plump lips mashed up and adorably snoring softly. "Maybe everything good that happens is for her. Because she deserves it."

"You both do." He replied firmly before shutting the door, encasing us in the truck and driving us away from the building of horrors that almost killed us all.

CHAPTER 36 - MADDOX

When we got to the hospital, the nurses and doctors instantly tried to whisk Olivia and our daughter away to the maternity ward and send me to the ER to have my stab wound examined. Thankfully, Dane already made friends, in his own weird way, with the head of surgery at the hospital during his stay with Peyton. Dr. Debois happily agreed to allow me to stay with Olivia and even stitched me up himself as Liv received the care she deserved from the maternity nurses.

However, when they tried to take the baby out of her arms so they could stitch the gash on her collarbone, something switched in Liv's brain. I watched from the other side of the room, while Dr. Debois finished the last stitch as my pretty little Storm snarled at the nurse who tried to take the baby, baring her teeth and everything.

The room froze, with wide eye glances and whispered breaths as Liv clutched our daughter tighter in her arms. I grinned like a fucking lunatic as I crossed the room, drawing a few more startled glances, while I moved toward them, shirtless and blood covered from head to toe, some mine, some Liv's, a lot of others we weren't going to talk about. "Storm." I warned lightly, holding my arms out, "I think it's my turn to hold our baby."

She swallowed and looked around the room, almost as if she was judging each medical professional near us, weighing if they were her friend or foe. "I don't think I can."

"You can. Because you know no one will get near her if she's in my arms." I spoke to the fear in her heart that was controlling her emotions even now that Damon was dead. The man had tried to physically take the baby from Liv's womb, of course she was going to be possessive.

"You promise you won't—" She started, and I shook my head, silencing her fears.

"I won't let her out of my sight. We'll be right here." Liv's eyes scanned the room again, and she looked down at our daughter, who was snuggled in against her bare chest, wrapped up in the towels Tamen wrangled for us. "Besides, we should get her out of these wet towels and into warm blankets. Then you'll both be fresh and you can have her back."

"Okay." Liv took a deep breath and gently raised our daughter up for me to take.

I didn't have a fucking clue how to hold a newborn, but I'd studied the new parent books endlessly over the last few months enough that I was able to tuck the tiny infant against my chest and settle her down when she fussed at the change of smells. She knew her mommy, but it was time for her to familiarize herself with her daddy, too.

The nurses moved quickly, stripping Liv of the gown she wore and helped her into the bathroom to shower everything off her skin. They quickly checked the baby over, re-clamping her umbilical stump and weighing her after listening to her lungs and giving her a passing grade in all areas. Even though she was small at only six pounds, she was strong. And she would be just fine.

I sat down in the chair facing the bathroom door, holding our daughter so Liv could see us at any time while she took care of her own needs. She deserved to see to her own needs after everything she had been through.

I didn't even know what Liv went through completely, but I could fill in some gaps on our way to the hospital.

However, I was still missing a huge part of the story, and only Tamen could fill that gap. But he was conveniently missing since we left the factory.

After showering and getting the laceration on her collarbone stitched, Liv gingerly settled back into the hospital bed and expectantly held out her hands to me. "Give me that baby, Maddox."

I knew better than to deny her of her demands, and it seemed our daughter was ready for her first feeding if the way she was rubbing her face against everything she could reach was any sign.

"Good, because she's hungry." I nestled her into Liv's open arms and helped her pull her fresh gown out of the way so she could start feeding her. It was such a surreal experience to watch the woman of my dreams nurturing our daughter from her own body in the most basic, yet empowering, way. "You're an incredible mom." I spoke after a while, after the nurses and doctors had all cleared out to leave us in peace.

"I nearly got her killed." Liv whispered, staring down at our daughter as she suckled like she was starving. "I nearly lost you both." Her icy green eyes finally looked away from the babe and up at me, and my heart ached, finding tears pooling in her lashes. "I've never been so scared in my life, Maddox."

"I'm so sorry." Sitting at the foot of the bed, I apologized and ran my fingers along her cheek. "I never should have let you go out—"

"No." Liv closed her eyes, shaking her head as the tears spilled. "I am responsible; you were hurt because of me. Damon almost took her," She gasped and shuddered at the words alone, "He was going to sell her."

"He's dead." I reassured her firmly, holding her stare when her eyes opened back up, "He can't hurt you anymore. There are no men left from that list that can hurt you, Storm."

"Except Tamen." She replied. "How does he fit into all of it? How is he the money man?"

"I don't know." I answered her questions honestly. "I know little about his dealings anymore, but I plan to find out. And I'd wager to say that he wishes you no harm, now that he knows you're Peyton's sister."

She scoffed and kissed my palm before looking back down at our daughter. "I need to see her, Maddox. I can't breathe, knowing she's hurt because of me."

"Shh," I soothed, kissing her forehead as our daughter pulled back and stretched like she was finally full and content. "Peyton doesn't feel that way about all of it, and neither should you. We'll go see her in the morning, Dane said he'd come get us after everyone got some rest."

"We need to name our baby." Liv settled back into bed, bringing the baby up to her shoulder as she started burping her. "But we have to do it right and give her one worthy of her story."

I snorted and winked at Liv, trying to break through some of the tension in her body, "Hostage doesn't have the ring to it I was leaning towards."

"Funny guy." She deadpanned and looked out the window at the dark city skyline for a minute before looking back at me. "What about Aurora?"

"Aurora?" I repeated, trying it out. "As in the northern lights?"

A small smile pulled at her lips as she nodded gently, "Exactly."

"I think that sounds perfect."

"What do you think, little one?" She brought the baby down and talked to her in a sugary sweet voice, "Do you like Aurora?"

The baby burped and covered Liv's fresh blanket with a layer of spit up milk and I tipped my head back to laugh at the comical response. "I think she approves."

CHAPTER 37 - OLIVIA

THE LINE WALKERS

I hummed a tune that I had no recollection of learning; it seemed it had always just been in my brain as I rocked Aurora, or *Rory* as Maddox had already taken to calling her. We were in our regular chair next to Peyton's bed in her hospital room. We visited every day.

But today, they were discharging me and Rory. Yet Peyton remained asleep, like she was trapped in her subconscious and couldn't get out. Leaving her felt impossible, as if they were telling me I had to leave behind a part of my physical body.

I couldn't do it.

So I was stalling. And hiding from the nurse on the maternity floor who told me she'd be around to discharge us in an hour.

Four hours ago.

I wondered if Dane could smuggle in another roll out cot for me to stay with her.

Dane was currently cleaning up some loose ends with Maddox, though I was told there were guards around in their absence, but I was glad I couldn't see them.

The one guard I ached to see more than anything, was that blonde supermodel who two timed Maddox's trust by sleeping with Damon while working to protect me. No doubt, she was the one who fed Damon information about my outing with Peyton that day and led him right to us.

That bitch had conveniently gone MIA after the fall of the entire Hell Eaters Crew the other night. Go figure.

And Tamen. He was the other person I'd give something important up to for some answers.

Real answers, not the vague and veiled ones I got from Maddox and Dane since the entire ordeal. They handled me as though I would shatter.

Tamen never did, not even when I was vulnerable and in harm's way, which made me sure that if he were around, I'd get some real fucking answers out of him.

"Where's the bear?" A deep, rumbly voice echoed from the doorway, surprising me as I looked up to see the Englishman himself, leaning on the frame with a smug grin.

Maddox and Dane assured me he wouldn't hurt me, but they were both unable to hide their distrust and dislike for The Duke from their tone. Which left me on edge as he looked down at my baby asleep in my arms.

"You mean Maddox?" I asked, knowing that perhaps my only real opportunity to get answers was in front of me.

"Do you know any other man as ugly or as furry as a grizzly?" He raised one eyebrow mockingly and then smirked as he leaned up off the frame and came into the room.

Shutting the door behind him.

The hair on my arms stood up as I watched him move with a sort of power that seemed impossible to obtain with his tall build. Yet he moved with grace and ease.

And I was weary.

"What are you doing here?" I questioned, torn between telling him to get fucked and begging him for answers. But when he neared the side of Peyton's bed and gazed down at her slumbering form, the urge to claw his eyes out burned brighter than any need for knowledge.

"You know," He started, still staring at my sister, "When I heard that Dane had let someone into his solitude aside from Mrs. Straight, I thought he intended to torture her with his insanity." He looked over at me fleetingly, "Before he killed her for the fun of it." Returning his almost caring gaze back to Peyton, he continued. "So I traveled to the States for the first time in years, so I could check in on him."

I sat silently, letting him tell the story without interrupting him.

He continued on, "Peyton surprised me when we met. She wasn't what I expected."

"How so?" I asked, never having heard the story before.

He chuckled, "Well, for one she threw two different lamps at my face and had a footstool in her hands, ready to fire again when Dane finally showed up."

I smiled at the mental image of Peyton attacking Tamen, a man bigger than a monster, with lamps. "She's a firecracker." As soon as the words left my lips, sadness followed them, laced with uncertainty whether she'd ever wake up again. "I don't know what I'll do if she doesn't wake up."

He looked over at me again, but his stare was indescribable. "You'll go on with life, because you have to. You have no choice."

I scoffed at his coldness and scowled at him. "Easy for you to say, considering you're technically to blame for most of this situation."

He stood up to his full height and turned to face me, towering over me even from the other side of the bed. "I made you join Damon and The Velvet Cage?" He countered, "I made you steal money from powerful, influential men?" Cocking his head to the side, "I made you invoke the urge for revenge in Maddox and then sit by and simply watch as he eliminated dozens of those powerful influential men simply because he wanted a way in between your thighs?"

"God, you're cold."

"Wrong." He challenged, "I'm English."

"Same thing." I sneered, looking away from him. "Which is saying something, because you share blood with Dane, who's literally unhinged, yet you're the cold brother."

"I don't share blood with Dane." He stared at me, burning a spot on my cheek as I looked at my sister instead of him. "I share blood with Lincoln. Dane is the byproduct of the man who sired us both, turning him into a cold-blooded assassin."

That was the first mention I'd ever heard of Dane's lineage, aside from the occasional mention of Tamen's name over the years.

And to say I was curious was an understatement.

"Your father is to blame for his—" I hesitated, but Tamen went on.

"Insanity, yes." He finished. "In a way, Maddox's too."

Now I was really fucking curious. "How so?"

He grinned, knowing he had me on the hook for information neither man would freely give up. "Has Maddox ever told you how he got his start in our world?"

"No." I admitted, "He doesn't talk about his past much."

"Figures." Tamen tsked his teeth and then sat down on the window ledge, crossing his arms and ankles like he was relaxed while I was on edge and jumpy from his presence alone. Just a few days ago, I thought he was going to be the one to kill me, after all. Those feelings don't just go away. "He was a loner, way too fucking weird to have friends and far too big and bulky to go unnoticed. That kind of attention tends to attract the wrong kind of people."

"What do you mean?"

"When he was a kid, he caught the attention of a scumbag gang that ran in his streets. They wanted to fuck with him simply because he looked like an easy target. He was big and dumb and far more fun to torture than the other twats on the block. So, they started fucking with him." Tamen shrugged like it was no big deal, "Stealing his food and backpack, pushing him around and tormenting his everyday existence for the fun of it."

"He was eleven, wasn't he?" I whispered, remembering how Maddox told me he was eleven when he killed his first person.

"Bingo." Tamen whistled, "He took their abuse for a few weeks before he snapped, which, to be fair, was a few weeks longer than I would have guessed he could last. But one day, they cornered him in the back of their school, after class, and started their same old bullshit."

"What happened?"

Tamen shrugged, "I don't know, details were pretty scarce because of the gore of it all. Supposedly, Maddox fought three of them off at once, but when the adults finally found him, drawn by the animalistic cries of the punks that fucked with him, there was only a red sludge left on the concrete walkway. Even his teeth had chunks in them."

"You're fibbing." I shook my head, refusing to believe that Maddox would have been so—fuck, animalistic.

That was exactly what Maddox was.

It was exactly what Maddox would have done.

I'd seen it with my own eyes as he tore through the Hell Eaters in that hallway, trying to get through Tamen to me the other day.

"The look in your eyes says you know I'm right." Tamen droned on.

"How does that involve Dane? And you?" I snapped, trying to piece the story together in a way that would link Maddox, Dane and Tamen all together in the same universe.

"Easy." Tamen held my stare with that cocky arrogance that made me want to shove my foot up his dick hole to make him sing soprano. "There's no place in the public for boys like Maddox. They're too skilled and too nuts to function around ordinary people. Kids like that end up in special institutions."

"Homes." I whispered in disbelief.

"No." Tamen said, and for the first time since he walked into the room, there wasn't any mirth or crass in his eyes as he held my stare. There was only that familiar darkness. "A home for kids would have been a paradise compared to where we ended up."

"We?" I questioned.

"Coincidentally enough, when Maddox arrived, Dane was already there. They committed Dane years earlier, when he was six."

I shivered, imagining a six-year-old little boy in a place like that, and I hugged Rory tighter to my chest. "And you?"

That bitter grin grew on his face again as he reached into his suit jacket pocket and pulled out a pack of cigarettes, taking one out and putting it between his lips. "Me? I wasn't a prisoner there like them. Though I should have been."

"Then how were you involved?"

He rolled the cigarette between his lips and eyed the oxygen tubes coming from the wall like he was contemplating lighting it up, which was the only sign that he was stressed from the conversation, despite his cool facade. Standing up off the windowsill, he put one hand in his pants pocket and gave off an arrogant air about him. "My dad owned the place."

"Your—" I began, as it started falling in line, "Your father imprisoned little boys who needed mental health help? Dane was his own son; how could he do that?"

"He turned them into tools." Tamen replied, blinking away that darkness, but I could see it lingering right behind his bright blue irises. "He used their rage and their skills and weaponized them."

"Jesus Christ." I deflated in the chair, imagining the horrors that Maddox and Dane endured in a place like that, but then stopped to look up at Tamen. "And you? Were you just a by-product? A casualty of your situation?"

He smirked and pulled the cigarette out of his mouth. "Me?" He scoffed, "No. I was just a little boy who wanted to be just like his strong, big brother."

I trembled at the realization. "You wanted to be a weapon. You wanted to be just like them."

"Bingo." He repeated in the same creepy way he had before. "There are only two types of people in the world, Olivia. Those who are victims, and those who do the bullying. Sometimes it's up to us to choose which side we want to be on."

"You're wrong." I shook my head, refusing to allow him to characterize Maddox that way. He wasn't bad. "Maddox and Dane, they aren't bad people. They didn't choose to do whatever sick, fucked up things I'm sure your dad made them do. They're good men."

He chuckled, "They're insane, Olivia. They'll even tell you that themselves."

I remembered all the times I called Maddox a psycho, after he referred to himself that way the first time. I remembered the way Peyton called Dane a monster and cringed at how we victimized them all over again by agreeing with them.

"No." I sat up taller in the chair and stared down my nose at him. "You're wrong. They have moral compasses. They try to do good, they're—" I hesitated, trying to find the right words as I looked down at my sleeping daughter in my arms, Maddox's daughter. The exact definition of innocence and purity. "They're line-walkers." Looking back up at him strongly, I defended the man I loved against his own descriptions. "They walk the line of good and bad and choose when to cross over to either side, but the fact remains the same; they can cross over the line. They can be good. But you," I cringed, staring at the man, "You gave up that choice. You *decided* to be bad, purely for your own benefit. You don't walk the line; you leaped over to the bad side of it and never looked back."

His face was almost unreadable, but the flicker of anger was there, in that darkness, nonetheless. He wasn't impenetrable. He wasn't immune to it.

"Yet I rescued you." He challenged, tsking his teeth again, "What do you call that?"

"A side effect." I replied honestly, "Of human nature trying to find some footing in your black soul. Because you didn't rescue me." I stood up and faced off with the giant man, clutching my infant daughter in my arms. "You kidnapped me. You tortured me and allowed Damon Kirst to drug me and harm my daughter, forcing her to be born early so he could sell her!" I took a step toward him, glad that the bed was between us, or I might give in to the urge to kick him in the nuts for the fun of it as I remembered how fucking terrified I had been during those hours of captivity. "You only called Maddox at the end because of some fucked up fondness for my sister. But face it Tamen, you're the reason she's lying in this bed, unconscious, fighting for her life. You helped a man like Damon Kirst terrorize us all, simply because you didn't realize who we were until it was too late. If we had been from any other family, though, you would have gone through with it all. But if she dies," I raised my finger up at him with all the indignation I had left in my body, "It will be your fault. And your fondness for her will be the very thing that solidifies your eternity in hell."

His cruel, chilling grin stretched across his face, a grin that made my skin crawl and dredged up memories of his manipulative strategic shifts while I was held captive. When he confessed his unending hatred for Maddox with his voice dripping with the venom of a death wish. Tamen cocked his head, a strange, unsettling tilt that was pure Bryce family evil, and opened his mouth, but a soft, raspy voice interrupted before he could speak.

"What did you do, Tamen?" We both snapped our heads down and stared at Peyton's blinking green eyes as she scowled up at the man before turning back to me and looking at the bundle in my arms. "What the hell happened?"

CHAPTER 38 - MADDOX

THE LINE WALKERS

I could feel the way his neck would squeeze and dimple between my hands when I wrung it as I stared at Tamen's forehead. His spine would crush to dust in my palms until there was finally nothing left of the man on the planet.

It was a long-time fucking coming, after all. But after walking into the hospital room twenty minutes ago, finding him and Liv locked in some silent war fought with dirty glances and menacing glares, I knew he deserved it even more for whatever happened while Dane and I were gone.

There was just no good time to dive into it as we realized that Peyton had woken up right before our return, and all of our attention was on her, rightfully so. But when things settled down, I'd fucking kill the bastard for whatever he did in my absence.

And I was going to kill every fucking guard on my payroll for letting him get near her to begin with. Fucking useless bags of bones.

"And look this way." The doctor instructed, holding a flashlight over Peyton's eyes, scanning them as she looked up, down, all around for the fiftieth time since she woke up. Her annoyance was evident, and the doctor didn't realize how close he was to death the longer he delayed and kept Dane from his wife.

The man looked absolutely feral standing next to the bed, staring at Peyton like she was the Pearly Gates, being granted admission knowing what kind of monster he was in real life.

"Well," The doctor went on, oblivious, "Everything seems in order, but we'll keep monitoring you closely for the next few days and make sure that your memory and abilities return as expected."

"Sure thing, Doc." Dane replied, nodding to the door behind him, leaving nothing to question and luckily for him, the doctor took his leave quickly.

"I suggest lowering the visitor count," The doctor looked around at all of us silently lurking around, "To one or two."

"Got it." I replied, waiting for him to leave before shutting the door and glaring at Tamen. Before I could even open my mouth, though, Peyton interjected from her inclined position in her bed.

"Get in line, Buddy." She pointed her finger at me menacingly and then turned to Tamen, "We'll finish our conversation in a second." Dropping her finger and angry face, she turned her attention to Liv, who sat in the far chair rocking Rory, and Peyton's eyes got misty as her emotions kicked in, "Can I meet her?"

Liv nodded silently as her own emotions ramped up, standing and walking over to Peyton, where she sat with a cast on her left leg and a brace on her arm. She was so banged up from the crash, but she was alive.

And for the moment, that deserved to be rejoiced in.

"What's her name?" Peyton asked, running her fingers over her niece's brow.

"Aurora Grace Renner." Liv replied, sitting down next to Peyton so she could be as close as possible to the baby. "We call her Rory."

"Aw." Peyton's shoulders shook, even though a smile crested her face. "I can't believe I missed it all. She's perfect, Livvy."

Dane put his hand on Peyton's shoulder and kissed her temple, trying to lighten her sadness. "If it makes you feel any better, Maddox almost missed it, too."

Liv nodded, wiping away her tears, "Dane held my hand in your place."

Peyton's eyes rounded as she looked up at her husband with such awe, "You did?"

Dane nodded back gruffly, "Rory came out like a true Renner acting like a drama queen," He shrugged, "Liv needed a hand to hold until we knew she'd be okay."

"Yeah," I snorted, "Had nothing to do with your own fears."

"Gah," Dane waved me off, but the damage had been done. His wife's eyes were all love struck and emotional, seeing her reserved and reclusive husband in a warm light for probably the first time in their entire marriage.

"I love you!" Peyton mushed and Liv rolled her eyes at me as they kissed. "Okay, enough distractions." Pey focused and her lovely face turned scrutinizing as she stared at the only non-smiling person in the room where he stood against the wall all by himself. "What the fuck did you do to my sister?"

"What didn't he do?" Dane mused, taking a seat and letting his wife lash into his brother for his actions.

I still didn't know what had occurred before our arrival, but I chose not to attract Peyton's anger, so I remained silent and listened.

"He was Damon's money man this whole time." Liv answered, after Tamen looked at the floor, clearly intending to ignore the conversation all together. "He held me captive with him and then went along with it when Damon induced my labor to steal my baby so he could sell her."

Peyton gasped and Tamen groaned, finally joining in, "I was never going to let him touch you." He leaned off the wall, "I didn't even know who the fuck you were until right before he went all mad doctor scientist on you."

"Jesus fuck." I growled, fighting the urge to pulverize his neck all over again.

"What?" Tamen flung his arms up, turning away from me and facing Peyton head on. "It's not as if we chat on the phone and tell each other about our days, P." He argued and she tightened her lips, unimpressed. "I did not know your sister was the hacker girl Damon was hunting. It didn't matter to me. She was just another—"

"Human being." Liv snapped. "Say the words, Tamen; human being who didn't deserve to die for your perverse sex trade!"

"Oh my god," Tamen groaned again, "I'm not a pervert, all the women I sleep with are very fucking willing. Even you said they all wanted my dick."

"Enough." Dane snapped his fingers and stopped both Liv and Peyton from jumping on him in argument to that statement. He was a fucking moron for taking the sex worker route against them. "Tamen didn't know it was Liv. He was working with Damon on the Velvet Cage, but didn't know about the money laundering. Believe it or not, T's actually pretty good turning money into sex and then sex back into money. It's a weird skill of his. When he showed up in the states, all he knew was that Damon finally caught the hacker responsible for executing thirty players in their game." I watched as Dane added some sarcasm like only an older brother could, "He should have known if moves on players that big were being made in Boston that I would be involved or would at least know about it, but you know how Tamen is. He's always trying to get that chip off his shoulder and get out of my shadow. Of course, he wouldn't check in to see what I knew about it."

"He hit Peyton with a car!" Liv argued.

"I didn't fucking drive the thing! I wasn't even there!" Tamen lobbed back, and I stood up, stepping between him and my woman and child as I gave in to the urge to dismember him.

"Careful," I warned, leveling the man with a stare, "I would be very fucking careful about whatever else you were about to say."

"Yeah," He hissed, "Big Daddy Maddox can't be tempted." He rolled his eyes, "We all know we'd cut each other's throats given the chance, drop the act."

"Why is that?" Liv questioned, looking away from him to me. "I know the story about how you all—" Her eyes widened dramatically, and she cringed, "*grew up together*. But I don't know why you want to kill each other."

"You told her about Harlow House?" I roared, taking a step around Dane, but he turned on his brother as well, angry and snapping at him.

"That wasn't your fucking Hell to tell." Dane yelled.

Peyton cut us all off with two fingers between her lips and a deafening whistle. "Stop ganging up on Tamen." She ordered.

Every single head in the room whipped in her direction, outraged that she'd stand up for the man responsible for so much.

"I know," She held her good hand up, trying to reason with us. "I get it. You all have every right to be mad at him. But none of you get to take it out on him now." She sighed, leaning back into her bed as fatigue weighed her down. We all shrunk a bit, realizing what idiots we were acting like in front of the woman who just woke up from a five-day coma after being run over by a truck. For fuck's sake, we could have at least taken the arguing out to the hall.

Liv sank back into her chair, using Rory as a shield as she murmured her apologies, and we all followed suit. Except for Tamen, who dared to look smug as his favorite person came to his aid.

Their friendship was so fucking weird.

"Now," Peyton went on in full control of our brood, "Can we all just agree to table this for now? Because I know without a doubt that Tamen wouldn't have done any of it if he knew all the facts." Dane opened his mouth to argue, but she ignored him, "And I know that Maddox is so utterly smitten with this new baby that he's going to let go of the rage and desire to cut Tamen into little pieces and keep him in the refrigerator, so that sweet little Rory isn't subjected to such negative energy." Now it was my turn to deflate; she had a point. "And" But she apparently wasn't done, "Dane wouldn't do anything to upset me, especially right now after everything I've been through. And allowing any more upheaval to our chosen family would upset me." She turned and gave him a pointed look, "Isn't that right?"

He rolled his eyes but nodded his head, "You're right."

"Good." Peyton sighed with a content smile on her face. "Now, I want you two to take that baby home and start living your life." She turned and pointed to Tamen, "And you sir, are going to take Dane to Hartington and—" Dane started arguing but she cut him off once again, "Make him shower. And eat, for the love of all things holy, make the man eat a freaking meal before he comes back."

"I'm standing right here!" Dane threw his hands out in exasperation. "I showered yesterday."

Even I didn't believe the man, and when his shoulders wilted slightly, he knew Peyton didn't either. "Tamen?" Peyton went on, "Stick around Boston for a while this time, will ya?"

I groaned, and Liv pursed her lips, but Peyton ignored us.

Tamen looked at the bossy red head in the hospital bed and shrugged one shoulder, "I've got business here I can take care of for a while. Now that the Velvet Cage has collapsed."

"No sex work!" Liv snapped, unable to bite her tongue any longer.

"Sex work isn't the devil, Little Hacker!" Tamen threw back, "You just have to do it right, so the girls are the bosses!"

"Right," I mused, "Because you've let a woman be the boss in the bedroom. Ever."

Tamen adjusted his tailored suit jacket and winked at me, "You'd be surprised by what I'm willing to let a woman do to me. I bet you're not all that much bite in the bedroom either, you big old teddy bear."

"Ew." Peyton waved her good hand around. "Everyone go home, so I can sleep, and we'll reconvene another day when there is less talk of prostitutes and bloodshed. I've had enough of both lately."

Sullenly, Liv and I left Peyton's room and headed back to the maternity ward where the bossy charge nurse had all of her things packed up and waiting for us. "I guess this means I'm evicted." Liv said, and the weathered nurse smiled at her knowingly.

"You're going to be just fine, girl." Turning to me, the woman nodded her head, "You two have this. Life is crazy on a good day, and babies are just added flare to it all. My one piece of advice is simple, so remember it." She looked back to Liv, "Don't try to fast forward through the hard parts, because tomorrow there will be a different hard. And if you fast forward through them all, it will all be over before you know it and you'll be begging to go back. People come into this world crying and they go out the same way. Enjoy the in between."

"Hmm." I hummed, widening my eyes at Liv when the woman turned and walked away, leaving us and our newborn standing in the hall. "Guess we start the living thing now."

"I guess so." Liv shrugged, and we walked away towards the exit. "Nothing to it."

CHAPTER 39 — OLIVIA

THE LINE WALKERS

"What exactly is all of this stuff?" I flipped open the top of a box stuffed in the corner of Maddox's old apartment closet as he carried some out to the elevator. He was cleaning out junk, but he was being—*secretive* about it.

So, I was being *nosey* about it in return. My vibrators were in his bedside drawer, the man wasn't allowed any secrets anymore.

"What?" He asked, coming back into the apartment where he found me lifting masks out of the box. A whole lot of masks. "Hey, why did you open that?"

He rushed over and shut the flaps of the box so I couldn't see anything else, but the damage was done. I had one in my hand and there was no hiding it.

I held up the plastic mask, dangling it from my fingertips to examine it and dodging him as he tried to steal it back. "Nope," I warned, turning away from him to see the front of it. "Is this a purge mask?" I eyed the neon led light strips under the plastic that created an X over each eye and a gnarly sewn shut look to the mouth.

He sighed and put his hands on his hips, trying to use the fact that he was standing in just a pair of athletic shorts and nothing else to distract me from my current investigation. "You're supposed to be putting Rory down for bed." He said in turn, avoiding my question.

"She's down." I challenged, nodding my chin to the monitor sitting on the old kitchen table across the room, showing our sleeping daughter a few rooms away. The girl knew how to sleep, it was her favorite pastime. Day and night she stuck to a routine and life with a newborn was, dare I say, easy. "Why do you have a box full of masks?"

"Because." He lunged, reaching out with his stupidly long arms and stealing it from my fingertips. "I'm a psycho."

I squinted my eyes at him and looked away from his naked torso and back up to his face. I was four weeks postpartum, and the whole no sex for six weeks was feeling like a life sentence.

And highly unnecessary.

Fuck it, I was willing to risk the pain if it meant I could ride Maddox's dick.

I was desperate, and he knew it.

"You're not." I countered, no longer using that term to define him, even jokingly like we used to, since learning about his teenage years inside of the institution that Dane's father ran. "But you are a dumbass if you think I'm going to let this go."

He tossed the mask on the top of the box and cocked his head to the side as I crossed my arms under my breasts, knowing it would lift them up and draw his attention to the fact that I was wearing just a spaghetti strap nightgown and nothing else.

Two could use weapons of war, even with their allies.

"They're just masks, Storm. Sometimes jobs call for it." He dismissed it, but my intrigue was too strong to ignore.

"Put it on."

"What?" He looked surprised.

"Put the LED mask on." I nodded to the box behind him, unwavering. "Now."

The command crackled in the air between us, just like the sexual tension had been for weeks. He was holding out on actually fucking me, because he thought it was the right thing to do, simply because the doctor recommended it. But all he was doing was pissing me off.

He made me come a dozen times in other ways, but he just wouldn't break the rules and actually give me what I wanted.

Dick.

He stared me down for a minute before finally reaching for the box and putting the mask on. Maddox knew what he was doing and what fantasies he was playing into of mine, so as he put the damn thing on, he clicked a button turning the neon teal and pink lights on and then slowly tilted his head to the side like a fucking—psychopath.

"Fuck me." I replied. There was no need to mince words. No veiled threats to hide behind or smoke and mirrors to use to get what I wanted. I didn't have the patience for it.

"No." He replied authoritatively. "You know the rules."

"Fine." I shrugged and walked past him. "Then the first thing I take inside of me again will be that lovely vibrator you used to use on me. Shame though, I wanted it to be your dick instead."

As I walked past, he spun me around and trapped me in his embrace, his powerful arms pinning mine to my sides. His body heat radiated against my back. Excitement grew in my core as my lower body clenched from just the feeling of his body on mine again.

The entire time I knew him before Rory was born, I was pregnant. And because of that, there was a level of restraint that he used with me. Even the few times we got caught up in the moment before she was born, I knew they weren't him being truly free.

I wanted him in his barest form. I wanted nothing holding him back from me. But still, he refused.

"Careful, Storm." He murmured from behind the mask as his hands tightened around my wrists. "You're playing with fire."

"I want it to fucking burn, Maddox." I hissed, pressing my ass into his groin and rocking back against him. He was hard, unable to hide how badly he wanted to give in to me and my demands. "Do you want me to beg you?" I fought his hold until he moved with me as I lifted the hem of my nightgown up my thighs, using his knuckles against my bare core. "Would that make you give in, baby?" I changed tactics and purred, lowering my voice and playing with his alpha tendencies. "Please, Madd. I need to feel you inside of me again. I need to feel you lose yourself with me. Don't make me wait anymore."

"Storm." He growled, cracking his neck to the side, fighting the urge. "You know what the doctor said."

"Guidelines, Madd." I moaned when he extended one finger from the hold on my wrist and ran it through my wetness to my clit, rubbing it. "They're suggestions. But I'm fine. You won't hurt me."

"You don't know that."

"I hurt right now!" I cried, losing my hold on my own emotions, as my need felt overwhelming. "I ache for you, baby."

"Fuck," He complained and then pulled his finger free of my body and turned me around, pinning my wrists behind my back as he bent me backwards. "You aren't the only one aching here."

"Tell me something," I gazed up at the mask, trying to see his face behind it, but it was impossible with the bright lights shadowing them. "Did you kill someone wearing this?" I could hear the way he clenched his teeth behind it, and I pressed on, trying desperately to push him past his reservations. "You did, didn't you?" I moaned, rubbing my breasts against his bare chest until one strap fell off my shoulder and pooled the fabric of my dress between us. "You were the last thing someone saw, just like this. And now you're here, and I'm begging you to fuck me wearing it." I hooked one ankle around the back of his leg and rubbed my aching center against him shamelessly. "Begging you to be the freest you've ever been with me, finally."

"You don't know what you're asking for, baby." He kept one hand on my back, holding my wrists hostage as he forced my foot to the floor as he started walking across the room. "You don't know how unhinged I can be."

"Show me." I challenged, pulling away so my nightgown could fall free of my breast, and shimmied until the other side followed suit, leaving the fabric tangled around my arms and waist. "Show me how good you can fuck me. You held back every other time, I want to see the real you."

I gasped and shrieked when he pushed me against the wall and lifted my wrists above my head, kicking my feet wide all in one move. The rough cut of the exposed brick wall dug into my back, and I reveled in it as I rubbed against his erection.

His eyes were on my bare chest as I rubbed up and down against him, but the only one being distracted by my moves was me. I didn't notice the way he wrapped something around my wrists in place of his hands until it tightened as he hung it over the edge of a beam in the ceiling. He lifted me and sandwiched me to the wall as he fastened it, effectively hanging me to the ceiling by my wrists with his hips, holding me up enough to relieve the ache in my shoulders.

But not enough for me to mistake the power play as he made it.

I was restrained, and if he backed up, I'd clear the floor, effectively at his mercy.

And my body dripped for it.

"You make it sound like you've been unsatisfied by me this entire time." He cocked his head to the side again, eye level with me as his hands slid up the backs of my bare thighs and held me up by them. "Is that what you're trying to tell me, Storm? Was your sweet little pussy unsatisfied this whole time?"

"Will it get me fucked if I say yes?" I licked my lips.

"It might get you spanked." He challenged, and I laughed.

"A girl can't be picky. I'll probably come from that too."

His fingers dipped back into my wetness between us as I kept rocking against his lower abs, using them for my pleasure until he pushed two into me without warning. "Mmh," He moaned, watching me carefully as he started pumping them into me. I wrapped my hands around the fabric, holding me to the beam for leverage and rocked in rhythm with him, nearly crying out from how good it felt. "Beg me for another."

I grinned like a maniac, "Please give me another finger, Maddox."

"I'm not Maddox right now." He challenged, pushing a third finger into me and stretching me further. Sure, it burned more than it would have before I gave birth, but that was probably from the lack of sex for so long, more than it was from the delivery alone. "You wanted me to fuck this pretty little cunt wearing a mask I wore when I skinned a mayor alive, inch by inch until he wore a jacket of muscle instead of skin." I moaned at the depravity of it all, "Call me by the name that suits that man."

"No." I shook my head, fighting a war in my head. "It was never supposed to be mean."

"It's not." He growled, pumping his fingers into me while holding me up with one large hand under my ass. "It's the truth. Say it."

"No." I cried and swore when he pulled free from my body and backed up, letting me fall until I hung by my wrists. I kicked wildly, trying to use the brick wall to get leverage, but my toes were a foot above the ground and my shoulders burned as I tried to hold myself up. "Madd!"

"Say it." He growled, "Call me what we both know I am, and I'll fuck you."

"Maddox." I whined in protest as he ripped my nightgown down the center, revealing my entire body to his hungry eyes. Even through the mask, I knew he was desperate for me, too. "Psycho." I whispered, and then swallowed and said it louder. "Fuck me, you psycho."

The fucking head tilt nearly made me come alone as he slowly slid his hands back under my thighs and spread my thighs, sliding his cock in deep. He was so smooth; he did it all in one move that sucked the air right out of my lungs, and I hissed from the stretch. "Fuck yes, Storm." He growled, pulling out and pushing back in, feeding me his cock as I anchored my ankles together behind his ass, taking every inch. "You wanted a psychopath to fuck you, baby, not me."

"It's all you." I moaned, nearly orgasming already as he reached between our bodies to roll my clit as he fucked me. "You're both. Good and bad."

"Oh yeah," He chuckled, "This Line Walker theory of yours." He slammed in deep, making me cry out in ecstasy as we both fought that desire to peek, but also wanting the high of the climb to last forever. "You're wrong though, baby. I'm only good for you."

"Yes!" I cried, giving in and falling over the edge of bliss and orgasming. He groaned when I tightened my muscles down on him, forcing his own orgasm to crest as he started pumping himself into me. "God, yes."

He slowed his thrusts, but kept them going, giving me every inch of himself over and over again. Eventually he stilled, pulling the mask off and throwing it across the room toward the boxes. Laying his forehead against mine, he smiled and rolled his eyes when I bit his bottom lip teasingly.

I had won the battle and got my way.

And neither of us felt like he was the loser at all.

"You're the one that's wrong, you know." I spoke after a while. "It's not just me you're good for anymore. I think maybe there's more good in that enormous body of yours than you're willing to admit."

He snorted, pulling free of my body and undoing my wrists so I could finally touch my toes to the ground, though he held my weight against his body as I snuggled into his warmth. "Careful, or I'll put a sibling for our sweet girl inside of you to test that theory out on and start the whole thing all over again."

"Gah!" I cringed, imagining the difficulties of pregnancy starting all over again already. "Maybe we should abstain from sex for a few years."

He tipped his head back and laughed loudly, before gripping one of my ass cheeks in his large hand and shaking it as his fingers dipped dangerously close to my ass. "I don't care which hole you let me fill, Storm, but you've awakened the beast inside of me after letting him lay sleeping for the last month. And I'm never going that long without being inside of you again."

"Hmm." I mused, tightening my arms around his stomach. "Did you just threaten to fuck my ass for the rest of eternity?"

"If that's all you'll give me." He spanked me again, "Damn fucking straight."

Epilogue - Maddox

The Line Walkers

"Are you going to tell me where we're going?" Storm asked, stumbling over her feet as we walked down the long corridor with my hands over her eyes. She wore a skimpy black dress and thigh-high gold boots, perfect for a romantic night, which is exactly what I intended to give her, though in a very unconventional way. Which fit us perfectly.

It was our first night out of the house since our daughter Aurora was born three months ago, and I promised to wine and dine her all night long so she'd relax enough to let our baby go to Peyton and Dane's house for her very first sleepover. If it was anyone else, I wouldn't have felt comfortable with her being out of sight, but I trusted Dane would keep her safe in my absence.

Besides, the evening was about eliminating the last thread of danger left out there from Storm's kidnapping. It was a thread that needed to be cut. A thread that I was going to give Storm the choice to cut herself or allow me to. Either way, tonight was about fresh starts and the end of a bad chapter.

Leaning over her shoulder, I whispered in her ear, "I'm taking you to the train station."

She snorted, "Funny guy," She swung her elbow half-heartedly into my stomach but kept walking as I steered her forward. "It feels like we're in a bunker. But that doesn't feel very romantic, so I'm confused."

"Are you not familiar with my diverse flavors of romance by now?"

Chuckling, she wiggled her butt against my belt and then stumbled. "Did you get me fingers again?

"Better." I growled and stopped us as we made it to the end of the corridor, typing my code into the panel to open the door.

"Better than fingers?" She scoffed and then went silent as I walked us deeper into the room, locking the solid steel door behind us.

"Better." I kissed her cheek and removed my hands from her face. "I got you the whole fucking body, before it was a corpse."

I stepped around to watch her face as she finally saw my present laid out on display for her. Or better yet, chained down on display for her.

"Mack." Storm sneered as her entire body tensed, staring at where my old acquaintance kneeled in the middle of the concrete floor. I sedated her, then chained her, spreading her arms wide and securing chains around her neck and ankles.

The woman was a trained assassin with a vendetta against Storm, there was no way I was going to be leaving anything to chance for this encounter. By the end of the night, Mack would finally be dead for her role in scheming me and selling information to Damon Kirst, leading to the kidnapping of Storm and our unborn baby.

"Better than fingers." I smiled at Storm as she finally looked away from our captive and back at me. "My kind of Psycho romance."

"What exactly is my gift here?" She asked, flicking her glance back to the woman on the ground. "What is your plan?"

"My plan is to let you see to her death; however you see fit." I replied, "Slow or fast, from your hands or mine, it doesn't matter. It's your choice."

"Is she—?" Storm asked, licking her lips, "Asleep?"

"Sedated, but I have the reversal." I walked over to a table filled with tools and picked up the syringe that would bring Mack back to consciousness. There was an array of implements to use, knives, saws, pliers, hammers, and various other weapons of warfare. I was excited to see which one Storm would pick to use; you could tell a lot about someone's soul by their weapon of choice. "But I want to know what you're thinking before I do that. Because I know Mack, and she's going to get into your head if she gets the chance. Therefore, I want you to know what you want to do before she gets to it."

"I killed that doctor." She whispered, staring at Mack. "But I didn't plan it."

"I know." I replied, remembering the things she told me about her time trying to escape, slitting the doctor's throat to do just that.

"I didn't think I could ever hate someone as much as Damon. But Mack," She tilted her head to the side slightly, "She makes a different kind of hate burn in my gut."

"Tell me about it. What does it feel like?" I walked back toward her as her eyes got a faraway look in them.

"It feels like acid. Burning me from the inside out every time I think about how she wants you." Her green eyes flicked to mine, "How she touched you. How she thought she was going to get me out of the way and move right in on you like I meant nothing to begin with."

"So," I held the syringe out between us, "What are you going to do about it?"

Storm's eyes flicked over to the table of tools and landed on an item before she looked back at me. "I'm going to burn her like the acid of hate burns inside of me."

I grinned down at her and uncapped the syringe, taking a step backward toward our captive. "Let me wake her up then."

Storm moved to the table behind me as I stuck the needle into Mack, injecting the reversal into her veins and watching as she moved against her bindings as she regained her awareness.

"Move, Psycho." Storm hissed, and I jumped to the side as she held a glass bottle in her gloved hand, coming closer to Mack. The woman's head lifted as she blinked off the effects of the drugs just in time for Liv to douse the front of her chest in the sulfuric acid. Mack's screams erupted the second the corrosive liquid melted through her clothing, making her fight and strain against her bindings as the acid worked its way through layers of skin and muscle.

Liv set the bottle back onto the table and stood right in front of Mack's writhing body, where she kneeled down to speak to her. "I once told Maddox that if he ever allowed another woman to touch him like you did, I'd cut her touch from his skin." Storm tsked her teeth as Mack's wild eyes shot back and forth between the two of us, "I was wrong though, because it was always you that never deserved to know the feel of his skin on yours. So, I plan to melt every part of you that ever felt it."

"You psychotic bitch!" Mack sneered through painful pants. "You insecure, fat piece of trash!"

"Aww, she thinks I'm fat." Storm mocked her and stood back up, picking the bottle of acid back up with her protective gloves still on as she looked at me. "Where else have you touched this skank?"

I raised my brows at her, already knowing she was going to want to pour that acid on me by the end of her little experiment. But she deserved the truth, because that was how she regained her power.

"Hands." I spoke evenly, and Storm grinned before turning back to our prisoner. "Now, I'm no chemist, but I'm pretty sure this acid would eat through these chains if I just doused you with it." She pouted her pretty red lips out dramatically, "Better be careful then." She cheered and poured the acid on just Mack's fingertips, working from one hand, pouring a trail up one arm, and then down the other one to her fingertips, melting the skin in its path.

I thought for sure after the first wave of corroded flesh met Storm's nose that she would give it up and quit. But she never blinked an eye as she slowly and methodically tortured the woman who helped Damon kidnap her.

"Where else?" She asked me firmly, with a pointed stare. "I've already got her fake tits," She glanced back at Mack who, to her credit, was still conscious and hadn't let the pain knock her out. Yet. "I know you've touched those; you're such a tits man."

I snorted and rolled my eyes. "Ask what you really want to know then, Storm."

"Did you fuck her?" Storm demanded instantly, primed and ready with a hair trigger of control. "Is that why she was so obsessed with you and thought she'd trick you and me both into getting what she wanted? Did you give her that big dick of yours and turn her into a jealous little girl when you told her she couldn't have it anymore?"

I crossed my arms, "I never fucked her." I replied firmly. "She's not my type."

"Mmh," Storm pursed her lips in disappointment.

"But she kissed me once." I added, and Storm's green eyes flicked up to mine with excitement in them.

"She kissed you, or you kissed her?"

"She kissed me," I repeated, "Years ago, on a mission."

"Hmm." Storm turned back around to face Mack, who was looking a little more delirious with each passing second as the acid worked deeper into her body. "Is she going to die from what I've already done?"

I eyed the woman up, knowing that Mack was probably one of the most stubborn people I knew. "Not likely. Not for a long time, anyway."

"You know," Storm took a step toward her, "I've always been told I'm a bleeding heart." She was speaking to Mack alone as she towered over her in her thigh-high boots, "And it's always gotten me more grief than it's worth. But I think this time, I'll choose to help you out, anyway." She kneeled again in front of Mack and waited for the prisoner's eyes to focus on her face a few feet in front of her. "I'm going to erase the proof of Maddox's body ever gracing your fake one, and I'll make sure you find your way to Hell before too long into the process."

And with that Liv stood up and poured the bottle of acid down the front of Mack's face, sure to stand to the side so there was no splashing back onto her as Mack screamed, ingesting the acid and drowning on it as it melted her airway and lungs.

It took only a minute for Mack to stop breathing completely, but I remembered the way those seconds could tick on when I first started killing people, so I remained silent as Olivia simply stared down at the woman until she was long dead.

"Holy fuck." Storm's hands shook slightly as she set the empty bottle down on the table and tore the gloves off, ridding herself of the gear like she couldn't believe what she had just done.

I didn't go to her; I didn't touch her or interrupt her physical space as she processed it, instead speaking in a calm voice to get her attention.

"Tell me how you feel?"

Her green eyes flashed to mine briefly before scanning the room like she was finally taking in her surroundings and surprised to find herself in a chamber used for torture.

"I thought it would be a one-off kind of thing." She whispered, frowning slightly and swallowing as she faced me head on from ten feet away. "I thought the feeling I got after killing the doctor was just a product of the environment, of the fight or flight I was in. But—"

"But?" I prodded, pushing for her secrets.

"But I feel like a fucking billionaire who just doubled all of my money on black."

I grinned at her and her lips split into a cautious smirk, "You liked it?"

"Fuck yes," She nearly moaned as she ran her hands up her thighs over her short skirt and then shook them out at her sides. "It's like taking a hit of a powerful drug for the first time. I feel—invincible."

"You are invincible." I replied, closing the distance between us and sliding my hand around the front of her neck to anchor her to my chest. "You are powerful, Storm. And you deserved every second of that."

She licked her lips and took a deep breath, "I have one regret."

I raised my eyebrows in surprise as she smiled up at me seductively, "I told myself if you ever caught her, I wanted to fuck you in front of her and make her watch how you fuck a real woman before you killed her." She pouted slightly, "But I got carried away and killed her before I took your cock."

Her hands slid down my body, and she gripped my dick through my jeans, tightening her hand around the shaft and stroking it as she smiled up at me prettily.

"You envisioned being fucked around a dying person?"

She undid my jeans, pulling my cock out to stroke the length of me as I hardened to a brick for her. "I told you a long time ago that I'd let you fuck me while someone took their last breath at my hands if they deserved it. And that cunt fucking deserved that."

"You know what you deserve?" I asked, spinning us around and lifting her by the neck up onto one of the stainless-steel tables, pushing all the tools off onto the ground. "You deserve to come, so many times you forget everything that woman put you through, once and for all. Because she's dead, and you won."

She purred, spreading her thighs and rubbing the head of my cock through her wetness. I wasn't even surprised she had not worn panties for our little date night out. "I deserve you." Arching her hips to take me deep, I thrust forward, giving her what she wanted as she dug her nails into the shaft of my cock until I was buried all the way in. "I love you, Psycho."

I growled, feeling the burn of the open wounds from her nails as I started fucking her deep and hard, surrounded by her own justice still burning in the corner. "I love you, Storm. And I love your darkness that matches mine."

Epilogue - Olivia

"I need to know what you had to wager against him to get him here." Peyton hissed at me as we walked down the dark street as she snickered. "Dressed like that."

"Meh," I shrugged, taking the silver pool noodle I carried and whacked Maddox with it for the hundredth time since we turned down the block. God, it was therapeutic. "He'll do anything for that little girl."

"Candy!" Maddox cheered in a singsong voice, echoed by Rory's cheery giggle as he tossed a handful of candy at kids walking by in their Halloween costumes.

The entire town was laughing at him. Including us.

And he didn't give a single shit, so long as Rory was having fun.

Sure, she was only seven months old and didn't understand that her dad was dressed head to toe in fabric streamers like a pinata, carrying her in a candy-bowl-decorated chest carrier as we walked through our new hometown while I hit him with a pool noodle. She was just living her best chubby cheek life and Maddox was more than happy to do whatever it took to keep her that way.

Hell, even Dane walked alongside them through the streets as we visited different Halloween booths at the town wide festival. He, of course, didn't go along with my plan to dress up like a second pinata and instead chose a black hoodie and a Ghostface mask. He could be such a killjoy sometimes.

Peyton sure did like the mask, though, pinching his ass every time he slowed down to check on her and ask if she was ready to go home yet.

She was walking on her own without braces, crutches or canes, finally, but she still got tired easily. Her rehab from the accident had been hard on her, but she never complained or gave up.

So, we were walking our way through the cute little town right outside of Hartington Estate, cruising slowly to allow Peyton's healing leg the chance to build up strength. Given that I was freshly into my second trimester of pregnancy again, I was okay with the relaxed pace.

Turns out Maddox was more intent on giving Rory a sibling than I understood.

Our son was due in five short months.

Giving us two under two. Fucking wild.

"Oh, look who it is, Rory!" Peyton cheered excitedly as the guys waited for us at a corner. "Uncle TeeTee!"

Maddox groaned and rolled his eyes as Rory flailed in her carrier, arms and legs swinging a mile a minute as Tamen walked up to us from the darkness.

I tried really hard to keep my past judgments of him to myself, but I still kept him mostly at arm's distance.

Rory, on the other hand, demanded every single time he was near, to be directly in his arms. And would scream bloody murder if she wasn't.

As if on cue, she wailed a loud screech of delight as he tossed his cancer stick to the ground and reached for her without so much as greeting Maddox as he took her out of the carrier. Uncle TeeTee only had eyes for one girl, and she was currently slobbering on the side of his face, giving him her newly discovered kisses.

"Where's your costume?" Dane asked, pushing his mask up on top of his head.

Tamen scoffed, "I'm wearing it."

"What are you supposed to be, exactly?" I asked, eyeing his completely typical black suit.

"Irresistible." He nodded to Rory as she giggled and kissed him again. "Duh."

I rolled my eyes so far; I thought they'd get stuck. "Oh, how could I have missed that?"

"I figured I'd come check out this small-town vibe before I get wrapped up in the city for the next few months. I'm going to be busy and won't make it out to as much of this stuff."

Peyton locked right in on his early avoidance of the holiday season and lit into him. "What exactly is so important that you will be MIA more often than you already are?"

We had a weird little family unit with the five of us and Rory, but it kind of worked. At some point along the way, some weird unspoken truce occurred between the boys and Tamen, leaving us all in each other's lives without a pivotal moment that started it.

Well, if you don't count the one where I was kidnapped and gave birth in an abandoned building surrounded by serial killers. Because apparently Tamen wasn't just a modern-day pimp, he was also dark and twisty with a knife and disappeared with the guys on hunts occasionally.

Like I said before, life was fucking wild.

Tamen shrugged and handed Rory back to Maddox when she let out a big fart, not wanting to be near her if she needed a diaper change as he avoided giving us any real information about his life. Another trait of his. "I bought a club. And the takeover of it is going to be extensive. Lots of things to change around."

"A club?" Dane asked, not buying it.

"Yeah." Tamen replied, looking out over the crowd as he put another cigarette between his lips. He wouldn't light it being so near to Rory, even if we were outside, but it gave away his anxiety hidden beneath his mysterious exterior.

"What kind of club?" Peyton pushed.

"A club." He repeated.

"A sex club." I deadpanned, already knowing a leopard never changes its spots.

The group all stared at Tamen and waited for him to either confirm or deny it, but we all knew I was right.

Eventually he groaned and faced me head on, "A legitimate place that respectable people pay a lot of money to go to where they can enjoy things with like-minded people."

"Is it legal?" I countered, and he waved me off.

"It's consensual." He replied. "That should be enough."

Maddox scoffed and hushed Rory, who was getting antsy with all of us just standing still. "It's not."

"Whatever." Tamen rolled his neck. "Good thing I didn't ask your bloody opinion on it then, huh *dad*?"

"We just want you to be safe." Peyton smoothed over for the group, but she was speaking for herself and maybe a little for Dane. Maddox and I couldn't care less about what happened to the guy other than Rory would miss him if he ended up in prison for prostitution. "And to be someone that we can be proud to call family."

"Oy," Tamen cringed at the word and shook it off, "I'm successful and I'm bloody rich." He smiled brightly at Peyton. "That should be enough."

Someone bumped into Tamen from behind, disturbing the vibe in the group and Tamen tensed, sliding his hand in pocket, no doubt grabbing for a weapon. At the same time, Maddox shifted toward me, shielding me and Rory with his body. But when the slight frame of an older woman came out around Tamen's dark shadow, they all relaxed a little.

"Oh, sorry Sunny, didn't see you there." The woman laughed, patting her hand against Tamen's arm.

Dane turned away from the woman, pulling the mask down over his face, crossing the group silently to stand directly in front of Peyton, ushering her out of our circle. My sister gasped and then giggled as he pushed her further from our circle and down the sidewalk without a word of conversation between the two of them. "Bye!" Peyton called to me. "Chat with you tomorrow!"

"No worries at all." Tamen's velvety smooth English accent echoed over the crowds around us as he smiled down at the old woman. The old woman seemed to melt into him as he spoke, and Tamen stiffened when she snuggled in against his arm.

"Ohh," She purred obnoxiously, "My, what a sturdy set of biceps you have, Sunny."

Maddox's eyes widened as he mouthed something to me across the space, but I didn't quite catch it.

"What?" I whispered back, and he took a step away from Tamen and the woman, who suspiciously looked like she was trying to wrap her arms around his waist.

"Feral Post Office lady!" Maddox hissed and my eyes rounded, remembering the way Dane and Peyton avoided the woman like the plague after an incident in a corn maze once.

I still didn't know exactly what happened in that corn maze, but there were hints that somehow Dane had ended up naked and the Feral Post Office Lady tried to take him for a ride.

"So, we've got to go." I called out, pulling Maddox away from Tamen, who locked eyes on me and his silent cry for help was obvious as the woman started rubbing her cheek against his peck. "See ya, bye!"

Maddox and I hightailed it away from the two lovebirds, cackling and wiping away tears from laughing as Tamen called out after us.

"I'll make you pay for this, Little Hacker!"

The feral woman's voice hushed him as it sounded like she pulled him away toward the festival, "Oh come on now Sunny, be a dear and help Dolly home."

The End

Sneak Peek Time

The Line Walkers

W ant more of The Line Walker Boys?

Here's a snippet of Tamen's story from Book 3, Bully.

Chapter 1 – Tamen

"Good evening, Mr. Duke." The front desk attendant purred as I walked through the doors. Her name was Cherry, or maybe one of the other berries. Fuck, the place needed an upgrade, starting with the girls' names.

She was a damn wonderful hostess; I should have known her name for as many times as I visited Vixen's Den the last few weeks. Even so, I was drawing blanks.

"Evening." I replied, glancing around the open lounge to see how busy it was for a Thursday night. Impressively, it was occupied, but it could have had far more customers if there was the right incentive to visit.

Something I would change right away as the new owner.

The best part about my frequent visits to the establishment was nobody had a bloody clue who I was. Everyone believed I was just a rich prick who showed up multiple times a week to get his jollies off. Even women I had hired through the Velvet Cage before it burned to the ground with Damon Kirst's messy death didn't catch me as they mingled with customers at their new place of employment.

Damon had it coming, really, I was a little upset that I wasn't the one to kill him though. He was a fucking pig who deserved everything he got, and if the situation had been different, I might have even begged Maddox to make it last longer or let me in on the fun. Oh well, either way, his death was dreadful for business because it left a void in the sex market that I intended to fill.

Enter the private sale of Boston's only exclusive sex club, turning it from Vixen's Den to—literally anything else. That name was terrible. The potential inside of the four walls of Vixen's was outstanding, but poor management and even worse ownership left it subpar, and desperately in need of a change.

And I was just the man to get the job done and make the club incredibly profitable. It would keep me in the states longer than I had ever desired to be, but there were other things around to keep me happy here once work slowed down.

"Which desires are you hoping to fulfill tonight, Mr. Duke?" Strawberry asked.

Maybe her name was Apple? Fuck.

"A massage." I replied, noting the way the next customer entered behind me, lurking and waiting for his turn to order his girl for the night like we were at a fast-food counter. Low-class procedure, and in desperate need of a change.

"Ooh, fantastic choice." Peach cheered excitedly, like she gave a damn about how I got my sexual satisfaction. It was almost believable, though, which made her perfect for the job. Peach wasn't right though, for the perky little blonde, maybe Plum? "On the screen is the list of available dates for the evening." She nodded to the tablet screen facing me and I scrolled through, contemplating who I was going to fuck for the night like I was choosing a meal, and settled on a blue-eyed blonde with tits bigger than my face. Those would be fun to play with for the night. "Perfect," Apricot smiled brightly, "You've been assigned to room forty." She leaned forward and stage whispered, "It's our most requested room." Before leaning back behind the counter, "Valentina will join you in a few minutes. Enjoy your evening Mr. Duke."

"I plan to." I nodded and moved away so the next chap could order his meal. As I stepped further into the bar area, I overhead the man behind me greet the hostess.

"Good evening, Honey." He said, and I rolled my eyes.

Fuck, I was *way* off.

Leaving the fruity hostess behind and moving through the lounge, I watched men and women interacting across the floor. Most of the customers were men, but I recognized a few women as buyers as they mingled and flirted with various available girls. Mingling in the lounge was one of the most common ways for customers to book girls in any club, but this one lacked something vital.

Order takers.

The working girls were responsible for hooking a customer in the lounge if they weren't booked for a private session already, but then they had to go handle the business part of the transaction personally at the front desk.

It took the high out of the hunt for the customer. Pushing pause on the event to pay killed the vibe.

Making it another item on the short list to change when I took over.

When Vixen's Den re-opened in a few weeks under its new owner, there would be hostesses walking around the floor with tablets in hand, ready to swipe a card or apply a charge to an account so the girls could take their customers back to handle the only business they had any interest in for the night without disruption.

Hardly any of the current customers mingling around this evening would be here when it reopened, though; they wouldn't be able to afford the girls when I was running things.

The only clients I was interested in hosting had deep pockets and strong connections across many platforms.

Random Johns off the street could hire a girl from the corner if they so pleased, but my club would be too elite for the same kind of transactions occurring tonight. This would be the last night that the Vixen's Den would be operating as it had been for the last decade.

The next time the open sign would flicker on, the women would be making triple what they did before.

As would I.

THE LINE WALKERS

Room number forty was underwhelming, to be honest. But compared to the other rooms I had rented; I could see why it was highly requested.

Champagne colored fabric covered the walls, and the lights were low and warm, creating the ambiance of elegance. In the center of the room lay a massage table, fit with matching champagne-colored sheets and an array of lotions and oils on a rolling stand.

My shoulders nearly screamed, just eyeing up the paraphernalia as I pulled my tie loose. I really hoped Valentina would be as good with her hands as she looked, because I had some tension to break through before I released it.

I tossed my jacket on the chair and stripped out of my shirt mindlessly as I stared at the fixtures and features of the room, when something caught my eye. The fabric on one wall was thicker and hung differently, drawing me into it as I pulled my belt free.

I slid my fingers through the thick drapery and pulled it aside where it split down the center, revealing a giant mirrored window behind it. The window looked out over a large open stage I'd been on multiple times before and I noted how other mirrors across from mine, matched, indicating they too were giant portals for guests above to watch what was happening below.

News to me.

Not that I cared any knowing that an unknown number of people had potentially watched me fuck prostitutes on the stage below.

It was an exhibition stage, after all. That's what it was for.

At the time, I just didn't know that there were more eyes watching than just the spectators seated around the raised platform below. What was more interesting, though, was the scene playing out on the stage. My earlier assessment of how busy Vixen's Den was this evening had been wrong.

A vast majority of clients had been hidden in the shadows of the private room when I arrived.

And I could see why.

On stage was a woman wearing a teal blue harness outfit and a pair of sky-high stilettos. With her rainbow-dyed hair cascading in soft waves down her curved back, she gracefully walked the stage, instructing couples locked in passionate embraces.

A sex teacher?

I'd seen instructions occurring before in various clubs, but never here at the den. The old owner, Tony, didn't like the attention the shows took away from paid girls. He was old school and didn't see the potential draw classes and exhibitions could hold for a club like his.

Or so I had thought.

I tracked the kaleidoscope of colors on the woman's head as she moved around the stage, altering positions and adjusting angles of the six couples around her. She moved with a grace I'd never seen.

Her legs moved like they were dancing on stage at a pristine ballet, not on a stage in a seedy sex club. Muscles flexed and rippled up the back of her claves and thighs as she turned on her toes and stood with that same graceful swoop to her spine right above her lush ass.

God, her ass was incredible. Over two handfuls and tight enough to know it was real, while supple enough to distract a man's thoughts from anything else of importance as it rippled with each step.

Bloody hell.

My dick stirred in my slacks as I stood at the window and watched.

She was standing with her back to me, and I scanned my eyes over her exposed skin around the blue leather harness lingerie, wishing there wasn't a stitch of fabric between us. When was the last time I physically ached to see a woman's nudity?

I had no fucking clue.

That was one downfall to being surrounded by sex and undress as often as I was, sometimes. The allure and the effect it had on me had diminished over the years, so much so that I usually didn't even get hard until my dick was deep inside of something wet.

But standing against the glass, simply observing the vixen on the stage below, I was rock solid and aching.

The door clicked open behind me and heels tapped across the polished floor as a soft feminine voice interrupted the silence surrounding me. "Hello, Mr. Duke."

I glanced away from the woman on the stage over to my purchase for the evening, already regretting the money spent on her. Not because there was anything wrong with the sweet blonde standing behind me in a baby pink nightgown and white heels with her massive fake tits plumped up over the top of her barely-there lace bra. There wasn't anything wrong with her at all.

She just wasn't the rainbow below.

The blonde was normal.

Expected.

Predictable.

However, the rainbow; mercy me. The vixen's hands were on the man's hips, and she was slowing down his thrusts, using her own body to roll against his, adjusting his thrusts until the woman beneath him started moaning and coming on his dick.

That man didn't understand how lucky he was as she helped him make his date orgasm for everyone to watch.

I had never wanted to be someone else so badly before.

The blonde I hired, Valentina, interrupted my thoughts again, "Would you like to get undressed the rest of the way for your massage, Mr. Duke?"

I didn't look back at her, unable to tear my eyes away from the scene below as I replied, "Who is that woman?" Valentina joined me at the window, pressing her body against my side as she peered down onto the stage. "The rainbow."

"Mmh," Valentina purred, as she smirked, rubbing her hands up my bare arm and back. "That's Ember." The woman touching me was a professional, and she knew what she was doing as she caught on to my body's desires. "She's fascinating, isn't she?"

Ember. Her bright eyes glowed in the lights shining down on her from beneath the row of windows, and they looked like liquid gold fanned out by thick black lashes.

"Why have I never seen her here before?" I asked, glancing at her out of the corner of my eye as she slid her hands over my bare abs from behind. "I've never seen her on the booking list."

Valentina pressed her lips against my back, moving to look around the other side of my body as her hands dipped down to the waistband of my slacks. I had never hired the blonde before, but I was going to request her exclusively if she was always going to be so damn good at getting down to business, even as I stared at another.

"She's booked out months in advance." Valentina replied, pulling the button of my slacks free and then dragged my zipper down against my erection like a teasing edge of pain on the most sensitive part of my body. "Ember only takes on our most exclusive clients here. And she rarely lets them fuck her. She's the owner's pet."

"How much?" I asked as she slid her hand down into my pants and dragged her nails over my shaft.

"She only books by the night."

"How much?" I repeated it firmly.

"I believe for a private client; she charges seven thousand."

Seven grand for a private evening with the rainbow. And you didn't even get a guaranteed fuck out of her.

She was worth twenty grand.

Even more.

"Change of plans, Valentina." I pulled her wrist until she circled around the front of my body and crowded her in against the glass. "No massage. Get on your knees."

She bit her plump lip and slowly sank to her knees like a goddess, instantly fisting my dick for me and stroking me before twirling her tongue around the head.

"You're going to suck me off while I watch her." I instructed as she opened her plump lips and sucked the head of my cock straight into her waiting mouth, already aware of my plans. But I wasn't going to be disrespectful about it. "I've booked you for two hours. And I'm going to come down your throat multiple times in that span. When those two hours are done, I'm going to tip you very," I groaned when she deep-throated me, and then continued, "very fucking well in cash for your efforts and I'll double your nightly profits if you introduce me to her."

She hummed and stroked my sack as she twisted her lips and fist around my shaft. "It would be my pleasure."

I chuckled sinisterly as she gagged when I pushed all the way down her throat as the rainbow enchanted me below. "No darling, it will be all mine." Laying one fist against the glass as I tightened the other in her blonde hair, I watched Ember below.

There was a man tied down on a bed like the woman had been, but his date was riding his dick as he laid there helplessly, being used like a toy for her pleasure. His date looked frazzled as perspiration beaded on her forehead as she hopped up and down on his dick like a bad porno.

Ember's rainbow hair flowed like a waterfall of melted metal as she gracefully climbed onto the bed and straddled the man's chest, facing the woman riding him. Ember's ass was right below the man's chin and my balls tightened as she took the cowgirl's hands, laid them flat on his abs and started rocking her own body against his chest, showing what she wanted the wild rider to do.

His date stopped her manic movement and clumsily started rolling her hips, mirroring Ember, changing the way she was taking his dick. I knew for a fact that her pleasure was the main focus with the new motions and, for some reason, knowing that Ember flipped the script to please the woman instead of the man, made me even harder.

"Is Ember a lesbian?" I asked Valentina, pulling her head back as she gasped for her breath even as she continued to stroke my shaft in her mouth's absence.

"We're all a little lesbian for the right amount of money, baby."

I grinned at her eager to please response and pushed back into her mouth.

"That woman is different," I mused out loud, though I didn't care if she agreed or not. "She does nothing she doesn't want to, strictly for someone else's pleasure. I can tell."

As if the rainbow below could hear my assessment of her character, her liquid gold eyes flicked up away from the woman she was teaching and glanced from window to window until they landed on the piece of mirrored glass I was staring through. I knew she couldn't see me.

She didn't know which room had clients and which didn't, but it didn't bloody matter.

It was all I needed.

Ember's lips curled up in a satisfied grin as the woman in front of her started orgasming with her head tipped back and I followed suit, filling Valentina's throat with come as I stared at the only pair of eyes to ever captivate me before.

"Ember." I growled, orgasming as she finally blinked away, releasing me from the trance I was stuck in on my side of the glass. "My pretty little Rainbow."

AUDIOBOOKS

THE LINE WALKERS

D id you know that the entire Line Walker Series is getting Audiobooks? EEK!!! I know, I'm so excited too!

Make sure to check out website- www.ammccoybooks.com, social media – Twisted After Dark: A.M. McCoy's Reader Group – on Facebook, and Audible for more details!

Also, did you know that my Beauty In The Ink Series got their very own audiobooks as well? Find those on Audible too!

Other Books

THE LINE WALKERS

Did you know Ally writes across so many other types of tropes and themes?

Check out some of her other books here.

Looking for Series and Duets?

The Line Walkers Series:
https://a.co/d/bx376wq
Beauty In the Ink Series:
https://a.co/d/6tc8M7M
Bailey Dunn & Co Duet:
https://a.co/d/i9gwqL2
Shadeport Crew Series:

https://a.co/d/dVzGcyo
Kings of Hawthorn Series:
https://a.co/d/h1AITKM

How about some spicy standalones?

Sinister Vows:
https://a.co/d/gbe35fF
Guilty For You:
https://a.co/d/1ef3UPU
Secrets Within Us:
https://a.co/d/cTZ04XQ

Stalk Me!

THE LINE WALKERS

Want to stay up to date with all of my shenanigans and upcoming news? Pretty Please?

Check out my website: www.ammccoybooks.com

How about TikTok, are you there? https://www.tiktok.com/@amm ccoy_author?is_from_webapp=1&sender_device=pc

Facebook? I've got a readers group there! Twisted After Dark: A.M. McCoy's Reader Group is mostly unhinged and full of exclusive news! https://www.facebook.com/share/g/b41rkBMkSurWz43i/

IG? https://www.instagram.com/ammccoy_author/

Amazon?
https://www.amazon.com/stores/A.-M.-McCoy/author/B07QNRJ

MLB?ref=ap_rdr&isDramIntegrated=true&shoppingPortalEnabled
=true

I think that's all for now!